SEAL TEAM BRAVO
BLACK OPS II

ERIC MEYER

First published in the United Kingdom in 2012 by Swordworks Books.

ISBN 978-1-909149-04-5

Typeset by Swordworks Books
Printed and bound in the UK & US
A catalogue record of this book is available from the British Library

Cover design by Swordworks Books
www.swordworks.co.uk

SEAL TEAM BRAVO
BLACK OPS II

ERIC MEYER

CHAPTER ONE

They stole through the night; thankful for the cool air and the light drizzle damping down the usual garbage stench that made the cramped side streets of the Mexican border city so noisome. A dog howled and was silenced with a whine. A light briefly showed, then a door slammed shut. In the background could be heard the hum of faint sounds, the strained heartbeat of this broken city. Far away, the sound of a truck engine receded into the distance as it continued its long journey south. A few miles to the north lay the broad sweep of the border that led to paradise, to North America. Norte Americano. But here was no paradise. This was the United Mexican States. Most people knew it as Mexico, a country of billionaires and paupers, and of hard working 'paisans', farmers, cooks, cleaners, truck drivers, and autoworkers. And a country of drug shippers, dealers, growers, enforcers, and the vast infrastructure that supported the most powerful, and most feared business in the country. Some economists estimated that illicit drugs constituted more than half of Mexico's GDP. The men who traveled through the tired streets this night were one tiny link in that industry, although Jaime Morales, a twenty-year veteran, would not see himself as a tiny link in anything. He'd entered the business at age five, when he ran ten peso bags for the older boys, avoiding the gaze of the local police. A brush with the cops meant a bribe, and that hit the profits hard. The Federales were even worse, as they'd want a regular part of the take. Young Jaime had avoided all of that; he was too young and too innocent to fall under suspicion.

He'd risen rapidly through the ranks, making his bones at the age of eleven by killing a rival supplier. Eight years later, he earned the respect and awe of his peers, killing a too-greedy cop. Jaime was tough, fearless and vastly experienced, so much so that he now owned a sizable chunk of the organization, both selling product locally and shipping it across the border. He was in process negotiating for a valuable shipment that had come up from Columbia, packed in innocent cartons of infant formula. Under his crumpled, sweat-stained shirt, he had the greenbacks tucked into a specially constructed vest, a half million dollars US. He looked at his companion, in fact his muscled bodyguard, Enrico, who had paused and was looking behind them. He looked concerned.

"What's wrong?"

"I don't know, Jefe. I thought I heard something, maybe someone following us."

They waited, but Morales heard nothing. He playfully punched his man on the arm.

"You're hearing things, my friend. There's nothing there. Let's get going. We don't want to be late."

They rounded a corner and stopped. A black Hummer

SUV was parked right across the road, so as to block it with its steel immensity. Eight men stood across the road in a line, dressed in a variety of civilian clothing, but alike in a single detail. They were all armed. Jaime started to move a hand toward the pistol in his belt, a Glock 17 he always carried, but stopped. Enrico was swinging his own weapon, an Ingram MAC 10 machine pistol from under his coat, but Jaime stopped him too.

"Wait, not now. There are too many of them. We'll go back."

They turned to go back the way they'd come, but four more men stood blocking their escape. Like the ones in front, they were all armed. They carried a variety of weapons, MAC 10s, TEC 9s, and even a futuristic Steyr semi-auto, the military model assault rifle. Jaime was already working out how to make up the loss of the cash, for this was clearly a stickup, plain and simple. He turned back to face the men stood before the Hummer. A man stood next to the heavy vehicle, hands on his hips, smiling, better dressed than the others. He didn't have a gun in his hands. This person had other men for that purpose, why would a man in his position of power and authority soil his expensive, cream linen pants with gun oil? The elegantly dressed man was the Boss, the Jefe, and the man whose word would determine life to Jaime and Enrico. Or death.

"What do you want?" Jaime shouted at him. He realized his voice was hoarse, and he made an effort to not sound as if he was afraid. Dogs like these people could scent fear. It was part of their stock in trade. "You've made your point! You know dammed well you've got us outgunned here. Tell us what you want, and we'll sort this out. We're all businessmen, after all. We don't want a war."

"That's very wise," the man grinned. He wore expensive, designer sunglasses, even though it was dark. "You and your man, put down your weapons."

"No!" Jaime shouted back. "We do that and you may as well kill us. You want a fight. You can have it! If you want to rob us, you know we can't stop you. But we're not putting down our guns." He spat on the ground. "Fucking hijo de puta, you think we're loco? Tell us what you want. We'll finish our business, and we can all go home to our families. Get it over with."

The man stared at him through eyes hidden by the dark lenses of his sunglasses. Then he shrugged.

"Okay, if that's what you want."

He nodded at the men who blocked their escape. Jaime and Enrico started to turn. They knew instantly how this would go down. They'd done it themselves plenty of times. They started to draw their weapons, simultaneously throwing themselves to one side into the dust to avoid the inevitable gunfire. But the men either side of them had seen it all before too, and they were just as savvy. While their Boss calmly looked on, they dispassionately emptied the clips of their weapons into the two men, shattering the peace of the night with explosions and flashes of gunfire.

Neither Jaime nor Enrico even managed to fully draw their weapons. They went tumbling to the ground to lie in bloody, bullet-torn heaps. The Jefe lifted up his hand, and instantly the firing stopped. He walked forward to inspect the bodies. Enrico was dead, his face unrecognizable from the bullets that had shattered his face. By some miracle, Jaime was still alive, although only just. He stared up at the man who had ordered his death. His chest moved up and down as he tried to suck in his final few breaths. His lips moved, but no sound came out. He waited. The Jefe took off his sunglasses, and Jaime looked into a pair of ice-blue eyes. Strange, he looked Mexican, Hispanic, except for those eyes.

"I guess before you die you'd like to know who is taking over your operation," he murmured quietly, almost reverently.

Jaime didn't move, except his eyes, and they trembled a fraction. The man smiled.

"I decided that you and your brother Emilio were an obstacle to my business plans, so you had to go. He will be dead too, before long. I am sorry, but you will understand we could not let him live. Oh, and your families too, wives and kids. All dead. It's bad business to leave behind someone who could take revenge. But you know that, don't you, my friend?"

Jaime's eyelids shivered again, his pupils were wide with agony, and the knowledge that his family was finished.

"I know, I know. It is sad when one's family members have to be destroyed. But I'm sure you'll understand. It's business, nothing more, just business. Oh, yes, my name. It is Alberto Salazar. I'm sure you've heard it before."

The eyes moved slightly. The eyelids closed and then reopened.

"I thought so. My brother, Victor, he sends his regards and his condolences. We will take good care of your business, and it will become a useful part of our empire. You have built a strong organization, too strong. We thank you for that. But, of course, we could not ignore it. We had to take it over. This territory belongs to us."

He nodded at the man who stood nearby; his gun

pointed at Jaime's head. Alberto Salazar stepped back quickly as the bullet took Jaime Morales between the eyes. He was careful not to splash his expensive linen pants with Morales' blood, which was slowly soaking into the dust of the unpaved street. He looked around the street, the buildings, the vehicles, checking that everything was as it should be. A curtain moved slightly, and he smiled. These people would see nothing, not if they wanted to avoid the fate of these two men lying in the dust. Alberto Salazar looked around again. He was a careful man. The streets were clear. He nodded to the shooter, and they strode to the Hummer and climbed into the wide rear seats. Two of his men tumbled into the front. One started the engine, and the other held his gun ready in case Jaime had other men in the locality. Protecting the Jefe was a serious business. The rest boarded a pair of Chevrolet Suburbans, and the convoy drove off, leaving the bloody corpses for the local cops to dispose of when they finally decided to come out and 'investigate' the murder scene. They would not hurry, and the investigation would be perfunctory. The Salazar brothers paid well for the services of the Ciudad Juarez police.

* * *

David Lopez felt sick. He'd done well, very well, to infiltrate the Morales brothers' drug empire. He'd done so well, he was a trusted business associate of Emilio Morales so that he traded for product on a regular basis. Morales shipped it over the border, or under the border, in one of his tunnels, and Lopez took delivery in some anonymous El Paso motel. It was a good arrangement, and the brothers had done well out of him. He'd done well out of them, or his organization had. Lopez was DEA, the United States Drug Enforcement Administration, and one of their more successful agents. The intelligence he'd forwarded to Washington on suppliers, shippers and dealers had made an impact on the US drug trade. Now everything was about to end, and he knew that he had only minutes left to live. He'd been meeting Emilio in the office inside their Ciudad Juarez warehouse, actually an autoparts business that fronted for their dealings. A heavy, yellow dump truck had rammed the doors, and before they recovered from the shock, armed men jumped down and covered them with automatic weapons. At first, he'd thought it was a drug bust and wasn't unduly worried. Now he knew different. He glanced at Emilio Morales, who lay on the floor after a rifle butt had clubbed him down. A man stood over him, dressed almost like a Mariachi singer, minus the sombrero. But the clothes were only a nod towards the Mexican culture. These had clearly been hand sewn by a designer house a long way from Ciudad Juarez, black jacket and pants, with silver trims that were heavy and ornate. A heavy, pure white silk shirt, with a red silk scarf tied casually at the throat. Hand tooled leather boots and vastly expensive. The man was almost mocking his own culture, as if to say, 'Hey, I'm a Mexican, just like you. But don't try and copy the look, it'd take you a lifetime to pay the tailor's bill. You're down there, and I'm up here.' He was a big man, well muscled, shining, coiffed hair, slicked down with expensive pomade. His strong face was hard, cruel and expressionless, and his dark eyes were almost like slits, with uncharacteristic blue eyes. Just like his brother, Alberto. He stood in a relaxed posture, as relaxed as a puma before it makes the final leap to take its prey. His voice was low and cultured.

"You must accept your fate, Emilio. Arguing with me is a waste of time. You're going to die, and so is every one of your family and associates. Accept it, and die well, like a man." He gave an icy chuckle, almost like water tumbling down a drain. "Although I guess I don't really care how you die. Dead is dead, eh, Emilio?"

Morales lifted his head. "Victor, my family, you do not need to kill them. Let them go."

Victor Salazar smiled with amusement. "Let them go? Are you serious?"

He looked at the others who stood in a group, along with David Lopez, two women, the wives of Emilio and Jaime Morales, and five children.

"I am sorry, real sorry. But I cannot let any of you live. That would be bad business, plain loco. If you want to say a prayer before you die, go ahead, but make it quick."

"You fucking piece of filth," one of the women shouted, and she ran towards Salazar, her fingers hooked ready to claw his face. One of his men raised his pistol. There was a flash and a loud explosion, and she fell dead at his feet. He shrugged.

"Stupid to show yourself up in front of your kids," he nodded to his men. "Kill them, all of them."

They raised their weapons, and David Lopez made one, last desperate effort to head off the inevitable.

"Stop, don't do this. I'm an agent of the DEA! They'll come after you with everything they've got if you kill me."

Salazar looked bored. "DEA, I eat the fucking DEA for breakfast." He looked at the man nearest to Lopez. "You can kill Mr. DEA agent first."

"No….."

The last sounds Lopez heard were the reports of the three bullets that slammed into his body. He felt a terrible pain, then numbness. There was a roaring in his ears, and his vision began to go fuzzy and fade. Then everything went black.

* * *

Chief Petty Officer Kyle Nolan waited while the physician checked through pages of printouts and graphs. A Navy Seal feared very little; their training kept them at the very peak of physical fitness. As for military skills, the Seals had few peers in the world. They had enemies, plenty of enemies, enemies they'd gone up against and decisively beaten. Enemies who'd learned to fear them. But there were others too, ones you couldn't see and couldn't fight, like the enemy within. That was a different matter. How could you fight something you couldn't take down with a burst of gunfire? Cancers, tumors, leukemia, they couldn't be fought using the Seals' fearsome array of martial skills. Instead, it was necessary to rely on people like this short, bespectacled, plump doctor, a man with his own special range of skills, and who was taking his time to give a final verdict. Finally, he looked up at the man in front of him. He saw a tall man, six-one, according to his chart. He was lean, with the kind of features some people called chiseled. The doctor guessed most women would find him handsome, and he felt a twinge of envy. His face was average, yet there was something about him. Something that was anything but average. Maybe it was the strong, determined chin and calm, clear eyes that seemed to focus in the distance, yet remained aware of what lay immediately in front of them. They were the color of a clear blue sky. It was hard to pin it down, but a stranger meeting this man would know that he was anything but normal. His thick, dark brown hair was cut short at the front, so there was no danger of it falling over his eyes while he was shooting, although he had no way of knowing why his patient adopted such an unusual style.

"Mr. Nolan, how long is it since you last experienced one of these blackouts?"

They'd started after his wife was killed, and more than once had struck him down during a mission. As a result, he'd paid to consult this civilian doctor. If there were a chance of something that could affect his military career, he'd deal with it himself. That was his way. Besides, it was no business for a Navy physician, who could bench him. Or even put him on the beach, permanently. Service docs were good, but everything they wrote down would stay in his service jacket forever. He'd keep it private for as long as possible.

"About four months, Doc."

The doc nodded, hummed and muttered. "Four months, yes, I see. Well, this chart doesn't look too bad."

"So am I in the clear?"

The doc looked into space, thinking to himself. Then he looked at Nolan who was watching the medic's small, careful eyes hidden behind thick lenses, waiting for the verdict. He blinked and instinctively looked away. "What kind of work do you do, Mr. Nolan?"

"I'm a businessman, Doc. I travel around, sorting out my company's problems, that sort of thing."

"Hmm, I have to say for a businessman, you have

astonishingly good health. In fact, you're probably the fittest patient I've ever had in this office. Do you work out?"

"Oh, yeah, all the time."

"That explains it, I guess." He drummed his fingers on the table. "Yes, I'd say you're in the clear. There's nothing showing on the printouts, so I'd guess your problems were due to a recent emotional trauma. Did anything happen?"

"My wife, she..." He had to work hard to get the words out. "She was killed."

"Ah!" His expression brightened. "In that case, I'd say it was definitely temporary, a stress reaction. But if you feel it coming on again, you'll need to come back, and we'll look into it further. In the meantime, here're some pills for you to take, just a mild sedative to calm things down in your life. Try and stay away from anything too physical or challenging."

"Okay, Doc. Thanks."

He took the small, brown bottle of pills and left the office. Outside, he found a rusting dumpster overflowing with garbage, and pushed the little bottle well down inside. There was only one solution he'd ever found to most of life's problems, and it wasn't to be found in any bottle. It was to be found in one place. Action.

He checked his military wristwatch and hurried to his red Camaro; he was running late. He'd promised to pick the kids up from school. His in-laws, Grace's parents, John and Violet Robson, looked after his two children when he was away, but when he had any time, he spent every possible minute of it with them. It would take them more than a few months to get over the loss of their mother, and as good as John and Violet were, they needed their father.

He hit the gas pedal hard and weaved his way through the bustling San Diego traffic, enjoying the adrenaline rush of threading the big, powerful car through the dawdling traffic. Horns spat out their protest, and fists waved at someone who would dare to upset the normal, stately but chaotic procession of rush hour traffic, but he ignored them all. On this afternoon, he felt good to be alive.

He screeched to a halt with a stink that was a mix of tarmac and hot rubber, parking his Camaro outside the school. He was surprised when the Principal, Madeleine Packer, came out of the main door and waved for him to go inside the school. He opened the car door, climbed out and walked inside to find her office.

Oh, shit, what've the kids done now? Had one of them been involved in a fight? Or was their work falling behind, God only knows they had enough on their young plates.

He knocked and went in, feeling more like a truant schoolboy than a US Navy Chief Petty Officer and member of one of the world's elite military units.

"How can I help you, Ma'am?" he asked the stern looking woman, after she'd indicated a chair, and he'd sat down.

Did anyone ever refuse the order of a school principal?

He looked around at the office; the usual mix of bookshelves packed with an eclectic range of books, box files bulging with documents, photographs and certificates on the walls, and heavy dark wooden furniture placed on a slightly worn carpet.

Persian probably. I've seen similar rugs in that country. At least this one isn't stained with the blood of an enemy.

"It's more how I can help you," she replied, peering at him over the rims of her half-moon spectacles. She had a thin face, dark brown hair and eyes, and a trim, disciplined body clad in a smart business suit, over which she'd draped a string of heavy pearls. Her hair was presented like the rest of her, neat and trim. She was a picture of efficiency and no-nonsense authority, and he surprised himself by admitting that she awed and unnerved him. He laughed inside at his own hangover from his schooldays.

"Do your children, Daniel and Mary, have any relations who are of Mediterranean descent, possibly Hispanic, maybe even Arab?"

He was puzzled by the question, but instantly on alert. What the hell is this? Racial profiling?

"No, nothing, my own ancestry is Irish, going back several generations, and their mother was Caucasian American, as far back as anyone can remember. What's this all about? Have the kids been saying something they shouldn't?"

"No, they haven't. It's nothing like that. But we were concerned that someone of that ethnicity seemed to be watching them earlier. I guess we're all much more careful about the security of our schools these days, and we look out for anything strange or out of place. These people, it was two men, have been seen outside the school on a few occasions just lately. At first, we didn't know who or what they were interested in, but when we saw them looking especially at Daniel and Mary, I thought I'd best ask you about any relatives that may be looking out for them. Or anything else, any reason they might be watching."

"You did the right thing. You know what I do for a living?"

"You're in the Navy, Mr. Nolan?"

"That's right, Ma'am, a special part of the Navy, the

17

Seals. Our work tends to be very sensitive. Sometimes we deal with matters of National Security."

"I see. You think this may be connected with your employment?"

"I can't see how it couldn't be, but it's possible. It could be that they're planning some kind of an operation. Possibly revenge for something I've been involved with in the past. Yeah, it could be they're planning a kidnap, or maybe even worse."

There was only one crime worse than kidnap. Murder. Their eyes met. He gave her a challenging stare.

"Does that worry you, Ma'am?"

She stared right back at him. "Of course it worries me, Mr. Nolan. I run a school, and I have the safety of my children to consider. But I'm also an American, and if these people are enemies of America, we need to deal with them, not run from them. One thing I can promise you, I personally will not run scared from anyone, terrorist or otherwise. Tell me what can I do?"

He smiled his thanks. Plenty of principals would have politely asked him to take Daniel and Mary out of school until the threat was over.

"Nothing at the moment, but I'll talk to our people, and see what measures they can take to look into this and counter any problems, if there are any. There could be an innocent explanation, although I doubt it. In the meantime, let me know if you see these people hanging around again. I'd like to have a word with them. A photograph would be useful, if you ever saw them and had the chance to take a snapshot without endangering anyone."

She smiled. "I'll do my best. But I suspect you'd want to do more than have a word with them. I seem to recall that the Navy Seals are not known for polite conversation with their enemies."

"That's right, Ma'am, we're not. I'll take the kids home now, and let you know later what our people decide to do to about this problem. Can I call you at home?"

"Sure." She gave him a card with her cellphone number on it. "Call me anytime. And if there's anything we can do, we'll be glad to help."

He thanked her and went outside in time to catch his kids who'd just emerged into the schoolyard. Mary ran into his arms and gave him a huge hug. Daniel stood politely to one side, too much of a man to demean himself with such sloppy behavior. Nolan drove them home in the Camaro, looking around carefully as they went into his Craftsman house, the home he'd shared with Grace. It still made him think of her. Every time he set foot inside it, he thought of her. There were no strangers lurking, no obvious watchers. Their kid's gray haired grandparents, John and Violet Robson, were waiting at the door to greet them. Despite their obvious age, they were both fit and active, if a little podgy. He grinned at the thought; they were entitled to relax at their age. He nodded a greeting, went in and allowed Daniel and Mary to finish telling him in stark detail about the highlights of their day. Then he sent them to do their homework on the laptop computers in their bedrooms. He smiled ruefully as they made their feelings plain.

"But, Dad, we never do our homework straight after school. Mom always used to let us play for a time."

"I know that, Daniel." The mention of Grace stabbed him like a knife, but he went on. "It's just for now, kids, only the once. I need to talk to your grandparents for a short time. I'll call you both back down when we're done."

After they'd left, John and Violet Robson waited for an explanation.

"What's wrong, Kyle? What's happened? Are you ill?"

He shook his head.

Thankfully, that shouldn't be a problem, not now.

He explained about the people who they thought had been watching the kids at the school. John Robson shook his head in disbelief.

"Are you sure about that? I haven't seen anyone suspicious, and I've taken and picked up the kids from school a number of times."

"I think I saw something!" They looked at Violet. "It was only yesterday when I collected them after school. I noticed two men in a gray Toyota Compact. I hadn't seen them before. I wondered who they were at the time, as they seemed so out of place. You know, with all of this worry over pedophiles and so on. They were Middle Eastern too. At least I thought they were. It seemed strange at the time. I hadn't seen any Arab kids in the school. But then I thought they might be maintenance men, and I didn't think about it again until just now."

"They weren't Hispanic?"

"I don't think so, no. There was something about them, but no, they were definitely Arabs. But I didn't realize they were watching Daniel and Mary." She looked fearful. "I guess I wasn't looking for it."

They sat in silence for a few moments.

"I'm going talk to our people about it," Nolan said. "They can check it all out for us. It may be something, and it may be nothing."

After another silence, John Robson put his hand on

Nolan's arm. "Kyle, we should take them away for a short time. It may not be safe here, you know that."

"Christ, John, they're all I've got," he replied angrily. "After Grace was killed, I, well, you know." He was quiet for a few moments, but his mind was working furiously.

Why am I thinking of myself? It's the kids' welfare at stake here, not mine.

He nodded. "You're right. Daniel and Mary need to be somewhere safe while we track down these people and deal with them. Can you take them somewhere safe?"

John nodded. "We have our vacation place up near Santa Barbara. We can take a break for a few days, a couple of weeks, or however long it takes. We're retired, so it doesn't matter much to us either way. But the kids will miss you a lot. Why don't you come up with us?"

Nolan was tempted, very tempted. They were all he had left, except for the Seals, his other family. And he could extend his leave. They'd understand.

"No, I have to stay and take care of this problem. I can't let these people drive my family away from their home, without find a way to put a stop to them."

"Will the Navy help you out?"

"Sure, of course they will. And I'll talk to that detective in the San Diego PD, Carol Summers. She'll look into it."

They both looked up sharply when he mentioned her name.

"What?"

"She seems very nice," Violet murmured. Her face was expressionless.

"Yeah, sure, she is, but I don't have time for that sort of thing," he replied. "Grace was my life. I can't just forget her. She was very nice too," he added drily.

"Of course, but don't you leave it too long," Violet continued. "Grace was our daughter, but there are the children she left behind for us all to consider. They could do with someone, you know. It's not disloyal to Grace to think along those lines."

"Yeah, sure," he muttered, embarrassed and angry. It was his life, and the kids', not theirs.

"I'll make a call and ask Carol to look into this business. Then I'm going to the base, and I'll talk to the guys about it. But first off, I'll go up and say goodnight to the kids and tell them about their unexpected vacation."

Kids always seemed to know more than you thought they did. He'd found that out very quickly. It was called 'being a father'.

"A vacation! Is that because of those camel jockeys hanging around the school? Are you going to kill them, Dad?"

He kept down a smile. "You mean Arabs. No, Daniel, they may be just innocent people going about their business, but I need to check them out. Your grandparents will take you first thing in the morning, and I'll be up to Santa Barbara to see you when I can get away."

"You kick their asses, Dad," Mary exclaimed. "Give 'em hell. Nuke 'em!"

He nodded at her, unsurprised by her choice of words. Kids nowadays learned their language and culture from computers and the Internet.

"Believe me, Mary, if their asses need kicking, I'll do it."

When he climbed into his Camaro, he didn't drive away immediately. He used his cell to call Detective Carol Summers of the San Diego PD. He'd spent all his spare time lately with the kids. And despite their previous close friendship, he'd had little time for her recently, so she was understandably a mite cool.

"I'm busy right now, Kyle. What was it you wanted?"

"How'd you know I wanted something?"

"Because it's the only time you ever call me, lately."

He winced. That was a blow below the belt, but he knew he deserved it.

"I've been busy, with work and the kids. You know how it is."

How could I sound so lame? She's a great girl, and she deserves better.

"Yeah, I know how it is. I rate a poor third," she responded bitterly.

"Dammit, that's not fair, Carol. It's been pretty hectic just lately, what with work and the family," he snapped. More sharply than he'd intended.

Christ, I've had enough problems on my plate.

"Whatever." Now she sounded pissed. "Tell me what you want."

He rapidly gave her the lowdown on the mysterious middle-easterners who'd been maintaining some kind of surveillance on the kids. Her attitude changed instantly.

"That sounds like it could be a serious problem. I'll check it out myself. What about NCIS, have you talked to them?"

"I'm on my way into the base now, but I'm not hopeful. They weren't any use when Grace was killed."

"It's not easy for them, Kyle. They have their own jurisdictions and rules, just like we do in the SDPD."

"That won't help my kids."

"No, of course not. I'll do what I can. Call me tomorrow,

and I'll tell you what I've come up with. I really am on a case now. It's a murder, very nasty I'm afraid, and it can't wait."

"Yeah, I get it, jurisdictions and rules. I'll call you tomorrow, so long."

He hung up, angry with both her and himself.

Dammit! She was investigating a murder. He should have cut her more slack.

He didn't bother with NCIS, not yet. His first stop was to find his buddies, his platoon, Bravo Platoon. A few of them would be in Popeye's, the local bar frequented by Frogs and Squids, Seals and Navy guys.

He took out his anger with himself on the car, stamping down on the gas pedal and cutting a across a passing cab threading its way through the traffic. The driver hooted angrily, leaned out, glared, and gave him the finger. He let it go and went straight to the waterfront, to Popeye's. At least some things never changed; Art in his usual place behind the bar, the stink of stale beer, and trophy mementos tacked to the wall. Lieutenant Talley was there, the platoon leader. As ever, when he was off duty, he wore tinted aviator glasses and a lightweight, beige Italian-cut suit. He rarely smiled. He was a serious man, who took the job of getting his men into and out of their missions with minimal casualties. He was tall, narrow, and long-limbed, with curling, dark brown hair over a long, pale face. When he spoke, he chose his words carefully. Talley was always meticulous, always made sure he said what he meant, and his men understood he meant what he said. His record was second to none within the Seal platoons, and he was a popular choice for the most difficult missions. He was with Vince Merano, Kyle Nolan's opposite number.

He was of Italian extraction, short, dark, and built like a wrestler. Vince was the second unit sniper and worked in parallel with Nolan. Will Bryce, the big, tough, black PO2 sat nearby with Carl Winters, the ace demolition man who just lived for blowing things up. Carl was a lean, hard, tough fighter, and a veritable wizard with explosives. He often claimed with a grin that blowing things up was his sole passion.

"Hi, Chief," Talley greeted Nolan. "Come and join us for a beer."

"Yeah, I will, but I need to have a word with you guys."

Art Winkelmann, the retired Navy Master Chief who ran the bar, poured him a beer, and the Seals moved to a quiet corner table. Nolan explained their suspicions about the characters the kids' school.

"If these guys are targeting our families, Seals or Navy families, it could be the start of a new terrorist attack. On the other hand, it may be a revenge hit against me personally, for something in the past. Either way it needs to be dealt with, and fast. I told Detective Carol Summers, and she'll be taking a look into it. But I figure it may need more than that, something more direct, and I'm not talking NCIS. Those guys were no help before."

"So the kids will be away on vacation until this is resolved, until it blows over?" Talley asked, his face grave with concern.

"Yeah, that's right."

"Good. Listen, Chief, whatever needs to be done, we'll get it done, you know that. But we're due to ship out in a couple of days, so right now, it will have to be handed over to NCIS. I'll talk to 'em myself, and make sure they do a job of it this time." He looked at the others, who were staring at him in surprise.

"Where're we going?" asked Will Bryce. "This is news to us."

Talley looked around the bar, but there was no one within earshot.

"You'll know soon enough, so I guess there's no reason in keeping it secret. A senior jarhead, Major General Allan Hicks, USMC, his nephew was murdered down in Ciudad Juarez. There's a new gang in town, Colombians, the Salazar family. They're trying to take over the opposition. And that means killing them off."

The men grimaced at the name of the infamous murder capital of Mexico. Ciudad Juarez.

"That shithole," Carl murmured.

"Yeah, tell me about it. The poor guy was undercover with DEA. He got caught up in the crossfire between rival drug gangs, and they executed him."

"And the good General wants revenge," Bryce nodded.

Talley shrugged. "I believe the brass would call it justice, but yeah, something like that. I think they've got a point. If these criminal gangs think they can go around bumping off US government officials, well, we need to disabuse them of that notion. But that's not my decision. We go where they say, do or die."

"Theirs not to reason why, theirs but to do and die," Will Bryce intoned.

A line from Tennyson's poem about the ill-fated Charge of the Light Brigade, Talley grinned.

"Yeah, well, I expect we'll do better than those poor bastard cavalry. We leave in forty-eight hours, and the mission is to find these people, these Salazar brothers who're responsible for killing this General's kid. They want 'em out of business, permanently."

"So it's another kill mission?" Kyle asked quietly.

Talley nodded. "It's vital that we entirely destroy their infrastructure, and that means their equipment, transport and personnel. Everything and everyone that's connected to their operation is toast. We go in, hit them hard, and get out."

"Ciudad Juarez is a major battleground," Nolan pointed out. "The drug gangs have whole armies of soldiers, and they're well armed and equipped." He looked thoughtful. "We'll need to keep the mission objective real tight, get in hard, and get out fast. A protracted battle would hurt us badly."

They all nodded as Talley continued. "I agree, and that's exactly what I told the brass. They're giving us plenty of support. The General made it clear. He wants their people taken down, so anything we want; it's ours. But this operation in Ciudad Juarez will hit only a small part of the wider drug empire. It'll hit the tip of the iceberg. If this one goes well, and the brass decides on follow-up operations, it's something we'll likely be involved in later."

" What about the Mexican government, do they know we're going in?" Nolan asked.

Talley shook his head. "Not this time. If we tell anyone over there what we're planning, especially the local cops or Federales, we may as well tell the Salazar brothers direct. No, this one is under the radar."

Nolan was thankful his kids would be away while he was working. There were dangers across the border and possible dangers here in California. He wondered who the hell was targeting his family. During his long service, he'd taken out a number of America's enemies, so it could be any of them. Terrorists, drug dealers, or even a pedophile gang, although the latter would fall inside the province of the San Diego PD. And that meant Carol Summers. So if it were pedophiles, he'd have to rely on her people. He shuddered. It would be better for those particular undesirables if he never got his hands on them. He looked up as he realized the men were talking quietly about the coming mission.

"We'll be taking the new guy, Roscoe Bremmer. It'll be his first live mission with the Seals, so keep an eye on him," Talley was saying.

"Are you sure he's ready?" Will asked him. "The kid's got a lot to learn. I'm not totally convinced."

Like Will Bryce, Roscoe Bremmer was black. But unlike Bryce, he was from wealthy middle-class parents; his father was a successful dentist. And also unlike Bryce, he had a chip on his shoulder a mile wide, which he used to constantly needle and irritate those around him. Talley knew exactly what Will meant.

"Let's give him a break, I think he's ready."

The Lieutenant looked at Nolan, who shrugged. "It's your call, Boss."

"But you're not comfortable with taking him along?"

"I didn't say that, no. He's been well trained, and he has to start somewhere. I guess he'll learn." He looked at Bryce. "Will, you need to cut him some slack."

"If you say so," Will mumbled. "I guess he'd go screaming to the ACLU if we didn't take him along."

"Okay, that's settled," said Talley, quickly ending the discussion. "Chief, I'll talk to the NCIS guys in the morning. We'll get them looking into this business with your kids. I think that takes care of everything. We'll have a detailed briefing in the morning. I suggest we don't waste any more of our drinking time."

Nolan was thoughtful as he drove home afterwards. He hated being separated from the kids when their security was threatened. But he had a job to do. He resolved to talk to Carol again in the morning. But in the event, he didn't have to wait quite so long. In the early hours, he was awoken from a restless sleep by the ring of his cell.

"Yeah, who is it?"

"Kyle, it's Carol. I've been looking at this business of these characters hanging around the school."

He looked at the clock on his bedside; the expensive alarm clock that Grace had bought him when he joined the Seals because it was so reliable. It had a small motif on the front, a smiling dolphin. It was an insider joke. He noted her voice sounded weary.

"Christ, Carol, it's three thirty. Are you still at work?"

"Yeah, that murder case took some time to sort out, but we've got the guy safely locked away now. I pulled everything we've got on reports of middle-east type strangers in the area. Traffic stops and violations, petty crime, that sort of stuff, anything that links to an Arab name or ethnicity. The thing is, one of our officers did stop a Toyota compact night before last, a Corolla. He took details of the driver and passenger, and he called them in. They were fake."

"Did he arrest them?"

"He tried, but they waved a gun in his face and drove off. This officer said they were possibly Afghans, but he couldn't be sure. We had another report they looked like South Americans, Colombians. We're looking for them now, and there's an APB out, but so far no luck."

So they could have been anyone, Afghans or Colombians, or maybe someone else entirely.

The only thing he was sure of was that it was revenge for some mission he'd carried out. He'd done a good few operations in Afghanistan and South America, including Colombia, so there were more than a few people with reason to be pissed. He heard Carol's voice as she continued.

"I will keep working on it, Kyle. Are you planning on calling round my place?"

"I can't." He told her about shipping out and felt a wave of disappointment down the phone line. "Can I take a rain check?"

"Okay." Her voice was cool, expressionless. "I'll send you a text if I get anywhere with it. What about the kids?"

"Their grandparents are taking them on vacation, Santa Barbara."

"Yeah, that makes sense. It's a good distance from San Diego. Listen, Kyle, if I do find out anything more, how do you want to play it? I mean do you want me to tip you the wink first, or get my people onto it straight away? I know it's sensitive, with you being a Navy Seal."

Christ, they're trying to harm my kids! I want to kill them!

"I'll handle it, Carol, don't worry. When I find these characters, they go down, and personally, I don't give a shit about jurisdiction. I won't need warrants, lawyers or any of that crap. There's nothing in my life more important than the kids, nothing. Not even the Seals. Nothing."

There was a silence on the line, and he realized he'd been less than generous to her.

Why didn't I include her? After all, she means a lot

to me. I've lost too many people who were close to me. Maybe that's it. I can't lose any more.

Even so he should have reassured her, but it was too late, he'd dropped the ball.

"Yeah, right, I'll keep in touch, Kyle." Her voice had cooled even more, if that was possible. "Good luck on your mission, wherever it is."

"Yeah, thanks."

When he hung up the phone, he had a lot to think about. How could he return any warmth and affection, godammit! He'd told her it was too soon, on more than one occasion. He'd lost so much! And now there was a threat to his kids he had to take care of! They weren't just his son and daughter; they were the only real link back to his wife Grace, their mother who'd been killed in a drive-by shooting during a drug war. When he looked at them, he saw Grace. He knew that for her memory, even if for no other reason, he'd do anything to keep them safe.

And my career in the Seals; am I being selfish? Should I be thinking of giving up to spend more time with Daniel and Mary?

No, he didn't even need to think about that. The Navy Seals existed to keep Americans safe from outside threats, all Americans, so his work directly contributed towards Daniel and Mary's safety. If it came to it, he would resign from the service, but he knew he could do more for them by staying in. Without access to the immense resources of the Seals, his family could be rendered almost defenseless against these anonymous threats. And that was all that mattered to him, Daniel and Mary. All that was left of Grace, all he had to come home to. He'd give his life for them if necessary. Yet Kyle Nolan was no fool. He understood that while he was on the Ciudad Juarez mission, the people who'd been watching the kids may have something planned, something he would be unable to stop if he was a long way away. He mentally shrugged. He'd do everything in his power to prevent it happening, whatever it was. And they were up in Santa Barbara, well away from any threat. He couldn't do any more.

CHAPTER TWO

The slaughter in Ciudad Juarez had made the newspapers, but there'd been no mention of any DEA involvement. That would send up a flag that the US might retaliate. Bravo Platoon assembled in an abandoned truck depot they'd 'borrowed' in El Paso, Texas. It was stripped almost bare, just an empty, dusty space, with a pile of old truck tires stacked in one corner. The air was stale, and stank of dust, oil and rubber. Lieutenant Abe Talley, platoon commander, called the men to listen as he went over their final mission briefing.

"Here's the deal. It's just as I told you last night. Our mission brief is to disrupt and destroy this Salazar operation. That means if anyone gets in our way, they go down. These guys have got to pay."

Vince nodded. "They kill our guys, there's only one way for 'em to go, and that's down." He was holding his rifle as if it was a baby, which in a sense it was, A Mk11 SWS, a sniper weapon system with a twenty-round box magazine and a Leupold Vari-X Mil-dot riflescope. As he was listening to Talley, he screwed on the QD sound suppressor so that the weapon was ready for its primary purpose; a bringer of silent death, or to use the sniper slang, 'a weapon to reach out and touch someone'.

"When do we go over?" Nolan asked. "Our jump off time has been changed twice already."

Like Merano, Nolan carried an identical SWS fitted with the QD suppressor. Each Seal was a specialist, and as well as being Talley's number two, Nolan was a sniper. Some said the best there was, and in a service where top snipers were thick on the ground, it was some compliment.

Talley checked his watch. Like them all, he was dressed in night camo with a flak vest over his CGF Gallet half helmet, and NVS night vision goggles in position ready to swing down for instant use.

"We have a definite go. The Border Patrol will ignore their surveillance returns in exactly one hour from now. We have fifteen minutes to get over, and then all bets are off. Their agents have directed us to a break in the fence. We'll go through there, and they'll seal it up after we're through."

He pointed out the route to the fence, then the narrow path that wound through the Ciudad Juarez backstreets to their objective.

"This is where we're headed. It's the Salazar warehouse. Intel suggests they'll be in there, so we go straight in and take 'em down. Will, you're the breach man, that okay?"

Will Bryce looked back at him from deep, almost black, piercing eyes under thick, bushy eyebrows topped by wiry black hair. Bryce was a man with tremendous physical strength, but he carried authority too.

"Suits me, Boss."

None of them knew what they'd find when they got to the objective. Breachers were highly skilled, and the man responsible for forcing their way into closed buildings. Will Bryce was skilled in the use of a range of specialized explosives, called breaching charges. They were shape charges designed to be surgical in the application of force to send the preponderance of their blast forward into the room, and not back at the assault team. Breachers were also expert in using the lockpicking kit they carried if stealth was needed, and a heavy sledgehammer for operations where blunt force was required. As was expected to be the case now, Will had a sledgehammer on the floor beside him. Just in case.

"I'll need a pair of shooters in the assault team, so..."

"I'll go in with Will."

Talley stared at the man who'd interrupted, a new man in the platoon, and a replacement for casualties in the last mission, Roscoe Bremmer, son of a Los Angeles dentist. He was black, like Will, but there the resemblance ended. Will was tall, whereas Roscoe was short, although he was formidably strong, like a miniature Joe Frazier. And Will was confident, calm and totally self possessed; he dealt equally with everyone, white and black. Bremmer, despite his wealthy upbringing, still viewed the world as 'us and them', black and white. For all that, he was a good man, and his training scores were impressive. Talley gave him his chance.

"Okay, you're good to go, Roscoe. Zeke, you're first in too, with Will and Roscoe.

Zeke Murray nodded. A trim six-footer with curly black hair and shiny teeth, his mother was first generation Mexican; a factor they'd used before on missions south of the border. Talley looked at the waiting men.

"Chief, you and Vince cover us as usual. Find a good stand and if anything looks out of order, shoot first, and ask questions afterwards. I'll follow the first team in with Dan, Carl and Dave." Dave Eisner, Carl Winters and Dan Moseley. All three were veterans of countless missions, and they nodded quietly. Carl was the demolitions specialist, and his job would be to prepare the building for destruction after they'd secured it. Talley looked at the last man in the squad, Brad Rose. "Brad, you'll stay back with the Chief and Vince. I want you on the commo, in case anything changes."

"Hey, Boss, I'm okay, really. I'd sooner go in with the assault team."

Talley smiled at the unit dandy. Long hair tied with a bandana to keep it off his face, he was as handsome as he was tough, and expert at every aspect of Seal operations.

"No way, I want you out in the bleachers for this one. Next time maybe, but you were hit hard out in Afghanistan, and you need more time to get over it."

"That's a load of crap, Boss. I'm as good as ever, you know..."

"End of discussion, Brad. If Salazar's people come a running when the shooting starts, you'll have plenty to occupy your mind, so do your job. Are you carrying Beowulf rounds?"

Rose nodded. "Yep, locked and loaded. Carl's carrying the same."

"Good, we don't know what they'll throw against us, so be ready to use them."

The Beowulf round was a rifle cartridge developed for use in a modified AR-15 or M-16 family rifle. The cartridge was a variant of the .50 caliber Action Express, a cartridge originally developed for the Israeli Eagle pistol. But the Beowulf had significant modifications to improve its firepower. The result was a round with massive stopping power. Against a vehicle body or engine block, it had no equal in the arsenal of portable, lightweight weapons carried by Special Forces. If the Mexicans pursued them with heavy vehicles, even the armored vehicles they were known to possess, the Beowulf would sure slow them down.

"That's it, carry out your final weapons checks and be ready to move out," Talley ended the brief.

They walked through the El Paso night, careful to follow a pre-prepared route that would keep them away from prying eyes. They came to the border fence, just off the wide, well-lit Cesar E Chavez Border Highway. The fence was built of layers of reinforced steel planks laid edge on edge and supported by steel girders. Either side was a wide, open space to make it difficult for folks to cross without being seen, at least, being seen in the day; or at night when the night vision devices and infra red scanners were being monitored. Talley led them to a place between two posts, each marked with seemingly random graffiti. It wasn't random; they were territorial markings for local gangs. And they marked the place where the fence had been breached. The Seals moved aside a section of the steel planks that had been pre-cut at some earlier time by smugglers to allow access into the US, climbed through, and replaced them. They were in Mexico.

Talley checked the men as they assembled, ready for the last part of their journey. Each man, apart from the snipers, carried a Heckler and Koch 416, the modern assault rifle chosen by many Special Forces units to replace the M-16 variants that had been its mainstay for so long. Lightweight and immensely reliable, the gun fired a NATO standard 5.56 millimeter round that would hit anything the user was aiming at, with unerring accuracy. Four of the men carried rifles fitted with the AG-C/EGLM single shot 40 mm grenade launcher. In addition, each man carried a sidearm, the Sig Sauer P226, fitted with a sound suppressor. Some carried combat knives and spare grenades for the launchers. Each was in communication with the others by means of their tactical headsets, and Brad Rose carried the small, portable, encrypted satcom which kept them in contact with their headquarters, or anywhere in the world, if necessary; including the office of their Commander in Chief, at a pinch. They'd stopped a mere hundred yards from their objective, the Salazar warehouse, identified by the sign on the front of the building, 'Salazar Brothers, Foodstuffs. Import/Export'.

"Communications check," Talley murmured into his headset.

The replies came back, five by five. He nodded.

"Bravo Three, call in. You snipers all set."

"Affirmative, Bravo One."

He made a final visual check. The area was dark, so they'd switched to night vision equipment. When they went in, they'd have to remove immediately after the breach; they expected the inside of the building to be lit up. Salazar's was not a nine to five business. He looked at the assault team, invisible without night vision in their dark, mottled gray camouflage and gray stripe-painted faces.

"Bravo Two, go."

Will Bryce ran lightly and silently forward, a miracle for

a man of his size. His rifle was slung on his back, and in his hands, he carried the sledgehammer. Roscoe Bremmer and Zeke Murray were right behind him, HKs held ready. Talley's group fanned out and walked slowly and warily towards the objective. If anyone turned up now, they had to be taken out, quickly and silently. Bryce reached the door and stood for a second, the hammer poised. Bremmer and Murray gave him the nod, and he swung it back, hitting the top door hinge with enough force to stop an M1 Abrams battle tank. The noise was appalling, a crash that resonated through the whole neighborhood. But the door had sagged. He hit the lower hinge, and it crashed open. He threw the hammer to the ground and stepped aside, unslinging his assault rifle as the two shooters ran past him. It was a wide-open space, stacked on either side with wooden crates and sacks of foodstuff. In the center was a huge, square worktable, of about twenty feet to a side. It was piled with electronic scales, smaller boxes, and plastic bags. Ten men were working at the table, and they looked up in astonishment and froze like a tableau. There were four armed guards at the sides of the warehouse, and they recovered quicker.

"Gringos!"

The first man lifted his rifle, an M4 A1 carbine and went down under a hail of bullets from Roscoe Bremmer's HK. Zeke Murray fired a series of short, three burst taps that took down two more of the guards. He ran over to check them out while Will came up behind, ready now with his HK and looking for the fourth man. He saw a movement out of his right peripheral vision and swiveled fast. The guard had circled back behind a pile of wooden crates and had almost reached the door. He fired a snapshot that missed. The guy had reached a position where Roscoe stood between him and a clear shot.

"Roscoe, duck!"

Bremmer ducked fast, but it was too late. The guard went out the entrance like a hare and ran out into the dark night. The man saw Talley's group approaching, jerked to a stop and leveled his gun.

Nolan and Merano watched the warehouse. They'd stayed with their night vision equipment, watching Talley's group walk across towards the warehouse. The man came running out with his M4 A1, and both snipers drew a bead on him. As he leveled his gun, both fired. The force of the heavy bullets threw the man back. He went down a bloody, bleeding corpse.

"Good shooting, Chief," Talley's voice came over the headset. "We're going in. Watch our six."

"Roger that."

They entered the warehouse and dived for cover as the sound of heavy gunfire erupted. Then the lights went out, and the interior of the building was plunged into darkness.

"Talk to me," Talley spoke urgently on the commo.

Will's voice came back to him, calm and clear.

"Salazar's men, they were sorting the drugs on a big workbench. When they thought we weren't looking, they pulled weapons from under the table and started shooting. One of 'em shot out the lights."

"Copy that. Let's all switch to night vision. Do we have any casualties?"

"We're good. Six of the hostiles are down, but four are still active. We're looking for them now."

"Copy that. Go to the rear, and we'll come in slowly from the front and drive 'em towards you."

"Hear you, moving now."

Talley glanced around to make sure they were ready. Then he started forward. "Let's do it."

They went fast through the doorway and spread out inside the near wall of the room. Through the goggles they could see Will, Roscoe and Zeke at the far end. They were kneeling down behind the cover of wooden crates but were distinguishable by their goggles that showed clearly.

Flashes almost overrode the goggles; flares of light that blinded them for brief seconds. Then the firing stopped, but they'd identified the hostiles' location. They were close to Will's group; too close to fire in a grenade, sheltering behind a huge, rusting heap of steel machinery. Before he could decide on a plan, more trouble announced itself.

"Bravo One, this is Three."

"Go ahead, Chief."

"We've got people out here, Boss. They came out of the woodwork when the shooting started. There's about twenty of them, but more turning up. They're all armed, assume hostile. I'd guess they're local soldiers of the Salazar brothers. Yeah, and something else, a cop car just arrived. Four cops got out and linked up with these people. They're armed with riot guns, heading towards your twenty."

Talley thought for barely a second. "I'll send Eisner out to cover the doorway. Carl is busy preparing the charges. We've still got some hombres on the loose, so we can't help out. You'll have to take 'em, Chief. If they're on Salazar's payroll, they know their chances. Once you start on them, most of 'em will run."

"And the cops?"

"Yeah, I know, but take 'em first. They're the ones who allow this to happen."

"Copy that."

Talley stared forward. He caught sight of Carl Winters a few yards away, working on plating his charges.

"Carl, you are carrying the Beowulfs?"

Winters looked up. "That's an affirmative."

"You see that big, ugly old machine, three quarters of the way down the room."

"I see it."

"Okay. The hostiles are sheltering behind it. They're much too comfortable behind there, so put ten rounds through it, that should bring 'em out. We'll do the rest."

"Copy that."

Outside, Nolan and Merano watched the big group of men moving toward the warehouse. They were pushing the cops to the front, patting them on the back; these were their heroes. They'd make short work of these Gringos who came south to ruin their livelihoods. The cops smiled back, basking in the glow of unexpected praise. They held their riot guns ready and marched on, until the two snipers fired; four bullets, four kills. The cops went rolling in the dirt, one of them screaming in pain from the bullet that had just missed a vital organ. Vince fired again and finished the job. Then they went to work on the ringleaders, who were shouting at the increasingly nervous crowd to keep going and kill the foreigners. Two men went down, then three, two more, and the crowed was running. On the open ground in front of the warehouse, all that remained were bodies.

"Bravo One, this is Bravo Two. Hostiles have dispersed, you're clear."

"Copy that, Bravo Two."

Brad watched the snipers at work, furious that he wasn't an active part of the operation, until he heard the sound of an engine in the distance, a big, powerful, noisy engine. He tapped Nolan on the shoulder.

"Truck coming."

The Chief looked around. A massive semi tractor-trailer was bearing down on the warehouse. The vehicle looked old and battered, the bright red paint mixed with patches of rust and dented steel to almost look like some kind of weird camouflage.

"What's your assessment?" he asked Brad. "He doesn't look innocent. I reckon he's aiming at us?"

The Seal shrugged. "It ain't nothing good. That's for sure. He's coming at us like a bat out of hell."

"Use the Beowulfs, Brad, and see if you can hit the engine or something important. Vince, try and take out the driver. We want to stop that mother before he gets here. That trailer could be carrying anything, but my guess it would be soldiers. Stop 'em now before they get any nearer."

He called up Talley on the commo. "Boss, trouble coming in. Big tractor-trailer. Could be loaded with reinforcements, even heavy weapons, probably both. We could do with some help from another Beowulf out here."

"Copy that, Chief. I'll send Carl out."

"Make it quick. We want to stop him before he gets any nearer. He could drive straight into the warehouse and cause a lot of misery."

"He's on the way."

Vince was shooting at the cab of the semi, trying to get a hit on the driver, while Brad sent bullet after bullet hammer into the charging vehicle. Nothing seemed to stop the behemoth in its mad charge toward them, and to the warehouse. Then Carl rushed out, kneeled in the road, and put his rifle to his shoulder. He started shooting, and more of the big, heavy Beowulfs smashed into the truck. Then there was an explosion as at last, the bullets found a vital part of the mechanics. The truck slewed across the road, tilted on two wheels, and slammed back on the road. It was less than fifty yards away, and Vince Merano was able to use his sniper skills on a target that was not jinking across the street. The driver was flung back as the heavy 7.62mm slugs smashed into his head and body, and the semi driven by a bullet-riddled corpse for the last few yards of its journey. The rear end snaked around as it jack-knifed, and the rig slid along several store fronts, destroying them but bringing the truck to a stop. For a few moments, there was silence. Then Nolan heard more shooting as Talley's squad poured on fire to the remaining hostiles inside the warehouse. The firing increased in intensity, and the interior of the building was lit up with muzzle flashes. Simultaneously, the rear door of the trailer clanged open and men started to drop out. Nolan, Merano and Rose sniped at them, and a score of bodies were flung into the dust and dirt of the roadway. But another group, maybe twenty more, hurried around to shelter behind the truck. It was their turn to come under fire as the new arrivals started shooting, and they came under fire from a score of automatic and semi-automatic rifles and pistols.

"Boss, we've got more trouble. Twenty hostiles arrived in that semi."

"Copy that. We'll finish up here and join you. Carl is

about done."

Less than a minute later, Nolan saw Talley's squad hurry out of the warehouse and watched them as they darted over to join his group.

"What's the situation?" Talley asked.

Nolan nodded towards the semi. "We whittled them down apiece, but there's still twenty behind that truck."

"Okay. You men with launchers, get ready to hit that truck with everything you've got. As soon as the last grenade has gone, we're getting out. The Federals will come a running before much longer. I guess the local cops will be pissed as well, losing four of their own people."

He made a last sweep of the street and then nodded at the four Seals with M203 launchers. "Fire! Everything you've got."

The four launchers went to work, and grenades flew through the air whilst the rest of them poured on gunfire to add to the misery of the Mexicans. Carl and Brad fired round after round; the Beowulfs smashed through the thickest steel of the semi-trailer, and some of them found targets in the men who were sheltering behind. A few tried to run and were picked off by Nolan and Merano, shooting coolly and methodically with their Mk 11 SWS rifles. The street was a blazing hell of hot steel as the intense fire ripped apart the hostiles. A few threw up their hands and tried to surrender.

"Boss?"

"Finish 'em."

During a lull in the firing, they heard the sound of police sirens heading towards them, and the 'whump, whump' of a Federales Bell 412 helo.

"Time to get out of Dodge," Talley shouted. "Cease

fire, let's go."

As they retreated through the dark streets, they could sense that eyes were watching them from behind shuttered windows. But no one was on the street, not a soul stirred. They weren't certain who had arrived to bring a welter of death and destruction to the streets, where it was almost an everyday occurrence. But they were certain that this was something new, and something they hadn't experienced before. A force that was almost elemental in its raw power to destroy and kill. Carl Winters almost casually thumbed the button on his remote detonator, and the warehouse behind them exploded with a deafening roar; flames shot into the sky lighting up almost half the town. The Federales Bell helo had almost reached the site, and they grinned as the Mexican pilot veered away in a panic-stricken maneuver to avoid the massive explosion that sent a jet of smoke and flame two hundred feet into the air. He tipped his craft almost on its side and swerved violently to avoid ramming into a church spire.

They slipped through the streets, finding their way along little used alleyways and back-doubles until they reached the border fence. Five minutes later, they were on American soil, staring at the neutral face of a uniformed Border Patrol officer who'd come to check them back in. It was a courtesy from the local law enforcement people, except one man didn't see it that way.

"What the fuck's this? Ain't you got anything better to do than hassle our tails?"

Roscoe Bremmer stared angrily at the uniformed officer, who held up his hands.

"Hey, whoa there, buddy. I'm not asking to see any ID. I'm here to help."

"What the fuck do we want your help for? Haven't you seen what we did across there? We've taken care of business, and we sure aced those mothers. That means you can go on back to your nice comfortable desk and leave the serious business to the experts. Fucking amateurs."

As he spoke, Roscoe placed his hand on the man's chest and pushed him out of the way, and then he strode past. The man opened his mouth to shout an angry retort, but Nolan stopped him.

"I'm sorry about him, officer, he's new and something of an asshole. We'll deal with him later. I just want to let you know that most of us appreciate the courtesy just fine."

The man nodded reluctantly. "Yeah, okay. But that black boy will get himself into trouble if he goes around shooting off that big mouth of his."

"I hear you. I'll tell him he's not in Kansas now."

"I guess you mean Detroit," the officer fired back.

Nolan nodded. "Yeah, maybe you're right."

The Blackhawks were waiting to take them back to Coronado. After the debrief Nolan climbed into his Camaro and drove home. He was only a couple of blocks away when he smelled smoke. Some poor bastard's house was on fire. He drove nearer, and then with a sinking feeling in his guts, knew that it was his house. There were three appliances drawn across the street outside, and firemen were playing hoses on the burning remains of his home. He thanked God the kids had gone away with their grandparents. Then a familiar figure came across to him.

"I'm so sorry, Kyle. I heard about it on the scanner, so I came out to take a look."

Nolan gave Carol Summers a nod. "Do they know how

it started?"

She paused for a moment and looked back at the house, or what was left of it.

"It was arson."

"Jesus Christ, Carol. Of course it was fucking arson! I asked how." He almost choked as he spoke.

Why do I always get off on the wrong foot with this girl?

She was dressed as usual in jeans, a blouse and a tailored jacket to hide her gun. She was so petite that the gun always looked incongruous on her. Carol's short brown hair was slightly awry, and she hadn't touched in her makeup in a while. Her freckles were more pronounced than ever, as was the tiny scar on her face that seemed redder in the reflection of the fire.

She was annoyed by his anger. "There's no need to take it out on me. I came out to see if there was anything I could do."

He realized his behavior was as bad as Roscoe Bremmer's had been to the Border Guard. She didn't deserve it. But neither did he deserve having his family home burned down. "I'm sorry, Carol. It's just, you know, a shock."

She nodded. "Yeah, it's terrible. A couple of guys were seen running away as the blaze started. The Fire Chief just gave us his initial findings. It was probably a fire bomb of some kind, and likely thrown through the living room window."

Nolan felt an icy chill course through him. "They thought they were going to kill me and the kids."

"That's sure the way it looks, yeah."

A man in a suit came up to them and nodded at Carol. "This is the house owner?"

"Yes, Chief Kyle Nolan, he's Navy. Kyle. This is our Chief of Police, Max Weller."

The man shook his hand. "I'm sorry about this, Mr. Nolan. We'll do our best to find who are responsible. Believe me, we'll haul their asses down to my jail as soon as we have a name."

Kyle stared at him. The consummate politician, even in the early hours at a house fire, he was ready for the arrival of the media. He was tall, fit looking, and tanned. On his feet he wore expensive, tooled handmade boots.

"I appreciate that, but you'll need to find them before I do."

The man's smile slid off his face. "If you're thinking of some kind of vigilante action, you can forget it. I'm the law in this town, and we'll deal with this by the book."

"Yeah?" Kyle stood only inches away from him. "Where the fuck was your book when these bastards firebombed my house?"

He flushed but didn't reply. In that moment, Kyle Nolan knew that he had a new priority. Despite the Police Chief's warning, he had to find the firebombers, presumably the same guys who'd staked out the kid's school, and finish them. There was no other way, whatever it took and no matter how long. His life had changed, and until they were dead, his family would never know any peace or security.

CHAPTER THREE

Carol took Nolan by the sleeve and tried to lead him away from the confrontation, but he shook her off roughly. She stared at him, obviously hurt, and shrugged.

"I guess you'd better take care of things. The Fire Department will need to discuss what you want done to secure the house." She turned and smiled at her Chief of Police. "I'll give Mr. Nolan some help with the details, Chief. There's no need to trouble you with it."

He gave her an angry glance. "Yeah, well you tell him to keep out of trouble. This is police business, so make sure he knows that."

"I will, Chief, sure, he'll be okay. Kyle, let's go find the Fire Chief and let him know how you him to handle sealing up the house."

Nolan allowed himself to be led away.

"Kyle, try and keep it under control," she muttered to him. "The Chief is a total asshole. He'll be more than happy to put you in a cell if he thinks you're breaking the law."

"Instead of investigating the crime?" Nolan replied bitterly. "Some police department you work for."

She looked tired. "Now you understand we're not all perfect. Hey, where will you stay tonight?" She looked up at the dawn sky, threaded with pink fingers of dawn's early light forcing their way through the blackness. "My mistake, I guess it's not night anymore. You look like hell, and you need somewhere to sleep."

"I'll check into a motel, or one of the guys will put me up."

"You can stay at my place. There are even some clean clothes that'll fit you. I mean, for now."

Her husband had been Navy and had died on active service in Iraq. He looked at her expression, but it was devoid of any meaning. He nodded.

"Yeah, okay, that'd be good. Thanks."

"Okay. You can use the spare room if you want."

He looked at her, but her expression was neutral. He spent a few minutes talking to the Fire Chief, and they agreed to call a company to board up the house once the fire was doused. Carol Summers drove him to her home and made coffee. She sat opposite him, declining the space on the couch that he'd assumed she'd occupy, next to him.

"I'll make up the bed in the spare room while you finish your coffee. You can stay here for as long as you like. There's a shower next to the room. I guess you'll want to use it first. You stink of smoke."

"Yeah, okay, I'll do that. It's been something of a night."

"Anything you can talk about?"

"The mission? No, but I have to contact the base. I need to tell them where I'm staying, the address and telephone number."

"Sure, that's fine, use the phone while I go and make up your bed."

She left him, and he called the Seal base. He finally got through to a petty officer at Coronado and gave him the address. "The Platoon isn't here at this time of the night, Chief. Oh, yeah, of course, you know that. By the way, well done last night. I hear it was a good one."

"Yeah, thanks. It went okay. Tell 'em I'll call in later."

He put the phone down and looked up as Carol came down the stairs.

"It's all ready for you. Do you want any breakfast?"

"Are you sure? I don't want to impose."

She smiled gently. "You're not imposing. I'm happy to do anything I can. Besides, I've been on duty all night, so I'm pretty famished. Take a seat, and I'll whistle up something to eat, eggs, hash browns, ham, that sort of thing okay?"

"That'd be great, yeah."

She was as good as her word, and shortly they were eating and talking about the arrangements for securing the house. And the work that needed to be done.

"Can it be repaired?" Carol asked. "It looks pretty bad."

"I guess so, yeah, it should be okay. I'll call a builder later today and the insurance company as well. They should cover it all. I just thank Christ the kids weren't in there or..."

He stopped. They both knew he was about to say Grace. But Grace was dead.

"I understand," she said quietly.

"Yeah, but that's not the real problem."

"I know that. You're worried they'll go looking for the kids. You intend to find them and deal with them. I know that."

"Yes. I have to."

He slept through the morning after a long, hot shower. He heard the doorbell and was about to get up to answer it, but he heard the door open and someone speaking, so Carol was still at home. A few minutes later, she came up the stairs and knocked on the door of his room, but he was already half dressed.

"It's someone from the base, Kyle. They're waiting downstairs."

"Yeah, okay, tell him I'll be down soon. Is it one of the guys from the Platoon?"

He wasn't too surprised. They were bound to call around and check that everything was okay.

"I don't think so, no. Not from the Platoon, but he's from the base. I'll make some coffee."

"Thanks, Carol, tell him I'll be there in a few minutes."

He took his time shaving, wondering who'd come calling.

Talley, maybe, no, it was probably Vince Merano. Yeah, it had to be Vince.

He selected clean underwear and a t-shirt and jeans she'd left for him. Thankfully they fitted. He pulled on his lightweight combat boots. They still stank of smoke.

From the mission, or my burning house? Maybe both, but Vince won't mind.

He checked himself in the mirror and grinned. He looked like shit, hair still askew, and eyes bleary after the events of the night before. But what the hell, he wasn't standing on ceremony. He sauntered down the stairs and gazed in astonishment at the visitor sitting on Carol's couch, sipping coffee; Seal Commander Rear Admiral

Drew Jacks, the man who ran the entire Seal operation at Coronado. Jacks was in his forties, short and bow-legged, but broad shouldered and rock-solid and with close cropped blonde hair. He walked around the base with a hint of a bantam swagger, but it was the swagger of pride in his men, not of boastfulness. His razor-creased working uniform was devoid of unnecessary embellishment, just the name patch, Jacks, and the insignia of a Rear Admiral on the collar, the single star and gold stripe. Despite the crisp lines of his uniform, Jacks was not known for false vanity. His uniform was a perfect fit to a hard and trim physique that was the result of constant training and long workouts.

"Sir, I'd no idea you were here. I'd have been down sooner." He realized that absurdly he was almost standing at attention.

"Relax, Chief, your charming friend had kept me entertained. How are you today?"

If that didn't beat all, the Admiral coming here to ask after him, it was almost unheard of.

"I'm fine, Sir, yeah. Good."

The Admiral looked at Carol. "He looks as if he could do with some of your coffee, Ma'am."

She nodded. "Of course, I'll refill yours as well."

She took his cup and went into the kitchen.

"I gather it went well last night. You stirred our friends up a fair bit."

"We did, yes, Sir."

"Sad about the house, Chief, but at least your kids were away."

"Yes, they were, and I'm keeping them out of the area for now. I'll get the house rebuilt."

How the hell did the Admiral find out about my house burning down? Still, I guess anything on the wires concerning the Seals finds its way to his desk.

"I'm sure you will. The Chief of Police contacted me this morning, something about not allowing vigilantes in his town."

"He didn't say anything about catching the guys responsible, I guess?"

"No, he didn't. I got the impression he's not trying too hard, either. He wouldn't be my first choice for Police Chief."

Nolan stayed silent.

"Listen, Son. I know what's going through your mind..."

He stopped as Carol came in with two cups of coffee. She smiled at them.

"You guys carry on. I have to get on with some chores upstairs. Call me if you need anything."

They watched her walk up the staircase.

"She's a sensible lady," Jacks said appreciatively.

"Her husband was Navy," Nolan replied, "killed in Iraq, suicide bomber."

Jacks nodded, that explained everything. They'd all lost those they loved. This was a military town.

"So what're you planning to do? I mean about the characters that torched your place. I've looked at the files, talked to a few people, and I gather the guys that attacked your house have been nosing around for some time. Was it some sort of a revenge hit?"

"I guess so, Admiral. As for what I'm going to do, they have to be stopped. Someone's got to do it."

Jacks fixed him with a hard stare. "We're talking about

legal measures, yeah? Don't give me any crap about breaking the law, Chief Nolan. You know I can't condone that."

"Legal measures, yes, Sir!" He almost shouted the response.

Jacks gave him a small smile. "Of course, I never thought anything different. But it'll have to take a back seat. There's a mission on the board that has a triple A priority. I know it's too soon, but Bravo Platoon is slated to take it. It's a personal request, rather than an order, but it's one I happen to agree with."

Nolan was puzzled. "Asked by who, Sir?"

"By Major General Allan Hicks, USMC, the man whose nephew, the undercover DEA man, was murdered by the Salazars. He was impressed by the way you dealt with their operation over the border, but now he wants to see this Salazar drug empire finished for good. Period. And he wants Bravo to handle it."

"But Sir, it's..."

"Listen, Chief. This scum is responsible for countless American lives lost, not just our DEA officers. Every addict who overdoses, every cop killed in the line."

"But..."

"Your wife, even."

That stopped Nolan; Grace, his wife. Murdered during a drive-by shooting, in the wrong place at the wrong time.

"Exactly why are you here, Sir? Shouldn't you talk to Lieutenant Talley? He's the platoon leader."

"I'll talk to Talley later. But when I was putting all the threads together, I decided to come see you first. You're the senior petty officer, so the Platoon hangs around you. You're the glue that keeps it together, Chief. That's the way the Navy works. And when I heard of this new problem with the attack on your home, I thought I'd speak to you personally. I came to ask if you're able to give it your best shot, even though it's so soon after the last operation, and with your house burning down and all. I want Bravo to go down to Columbia…"

"Columbia!"

"Columbia, that's right, and to finish what you started in Ciudad Juarez. Personally, I'm in agreement. Although, I wouldn't normally tolerate interference in the way the Seals are run. There's a good argument for using one of the other platoons, but General Hicks is right. You've shown you can hit them hard and come out with the unit intact. You know your enemy, and that counts for a lot. I don't need to remind you of the fallout when we take casualties, and we have to avoid that wherever possible. If you can do it, Chief, I want you to go. In which case, I'd want you to give me a promise to carry out this mission to the very limits of your abilities."

"But, Admiral, I always give it one hundred…"

"No, you don't get it, Chief. This is not a normal situation. I'm asking you to put aside your own problems for the time being and get this done. And afterwards, I'll give you help to take down these people that pose a threat to your family. It can't be done before then. I need you one hundred percent committed to this mission. And when you're one hundred percent committed, that means Bravo is too. I have to know that. And you'll have us behind you one hundred percent when you go after the scum who torched your home."

Nolan's mind chewed over the permutations of what the Admiral was saying. First and foremost he was a Navy

Seal. And it was fortunate that the kids were well away from San Diego and out of the firing line.

But are they safe, really safe, even up in Santa Barbara?

"I just don't know how serious the threat is, Admiral. If they find out where they've gone, well…"

Jacks nodded thoughtfully.

"I'm sympathetic to your concerns. I can have NCIS keep an eye on things, and they can liaise with the local cops in Santa Barbara. We do it all the time, so it won't raise any eyebrows. They'll be safe, Chief Nolan, you have my word on it."

He felt a deep sense of relief. The Admiral's personal intervention would be an added layer of protection for the kids.

"Thank you, Sir, and I'll sure give it everything I have. You can count on that."

"Good. Don't forget, I've got a Marine Corps General staking out my office, itching like a dog with fleas to launch this mission to finish off these Salazar brothers. So I can reassure him, tell him you're totally behind this operation?"

"You can, Sir. We'll nail those bastards. If it can be done, Bravo will do it."

Admiral Jacks gave him a satisfied nod. "I'll pass that on, and we'll get things underway. Bravo is due to be at operational readiness again tomorrow at 0800, and we'll go through the briefing then. What about that cop, Detective Summers?"

"What about her, Sir?"

"Does she know anything?"

"No, Sir, definitely not. You know that's not the way we work."

"No. She's a nice looking girl."

Nolan returned the speculative look. "She's all of that, Sir. And there're lots of nice looking girls in Southern California. I know. My wife was one of them. But it's too soon after her murder to look at anyone else."

"Yeah, I guess you're right, but a word of advice, Chief."

"Sir?"

"Don't leave it too long. I'll talk to you in the morning."

He saw the Admiral out of the house, and when he turned around, Carol was stood in the living room.

"He seems a nice enough guy."

"Admiral Jacks?" Nolan was surprised. Some people found him intimidating and aggressive, mainly aggressive. He'd been one of the mainstays of Operation Anaconda, which took place in Afghanistan during 2002. The United States military, including elements of the Navy Seals, worked with the Afghans in an action to destroy large numbers of al-Qaeda and Taliban forces. The operation took place in the Shahi-Kot Valley and Arma Mountains southeast of Zormat. It was the first large-scale battle in Afghanistan since the Battle of Tora Bora in 2001 when the US tried to capture Osama bin Laden. The operation combined conventional and Special Forces for the first time in a major action, and at the end, more than five hundred hostiles were reported killed, in return for eight US servicemen. It was a success for JSOC, Joint Special Operations Command, as it was for all the units involved. It was a success for the Navy Seals units involved, and for Jacks, then a Captain. His brand of aggressive fighting won him a great deal of admiration and a step on the road to his Admiral's flag.

"Yeah, he's a straight shooter, but you wouldn't want

him on the opposite side. He's as tenacious as a bulldog, a good fighter. Knows what he wants, and always gets it." Nolan grinned. "He's said to subscribe to General Patton's three maxims of warfare."

"Yeah, what are they?"

"Audacity, audacity, and audacity."

Carol nodded. "I guess that means he's no shrinking violet."

"Not so as you'd notice."

They stared at each other for a few moments. She took a step towards him. "You're going back into the field soon, aren't you? That's why he was here."

He felt cold, but something more, too. "Carol, you know I…"

"Dammit, Kyle, I know you can't talk about it. Are you going or not?"

"Yes, we're being briefed tomorrow morning. It's a continuation of, well, something we started and needs to be finished."

"You mean a lot to me, Kyle Nolan. I don't want you to get hurt."

The perennial problem of servicemen on the battlefront the world over, the women they left behind. But she wasn't his woman.

"I won't get hurt. Besides, you're a cop, and your job takes you into danger some of the time. I wouldn't want you hurt either."

"You mean that?"

Their faces were only inches apart. He smelled her perfume, the faint, spicy musk of her body. Saw the freckles, and the half-hidden scar.

God, she's pretty.

Of course he didn't want her hurt. She'd done a lot for him, and she'd stepped forward when no one else was interested. His mind dissolved into a numbed confusion. They swayed towards each other, their lips met, and they were kissing; a passionate embrace, and like the unexpected onset of a violent storm, it took them both by surprise with the strength of its sheer, elemental power. He held her to him and felt her arms holding him tight to her. He pulled away, but only for breath.

"Carol, I…"

"Schh, save it. Just take me to bed, Kyle. I want you to fuck my brains out."

It was the moment of decision, and it was so soon after Grace's death. But how long should he wait? And tomorrow they'd be briefing for a new mission that would take them into harm's way, where all bets were off. But still…

"Yeah, okay."

Afterwards, they lay in bed. Warm and content after the sex that had been, well, earthshaking. He tried to close his mind off and just concentrate on the moment, on what she'd given to him.

"Damn, it's been so long, Carol. I think I saw stars. You're quite something, you know."

"You're not bad yourself, Kyle. It's been a while for me too."

Then they were silent. He couldn't discuss any future plans. There was too much in his life to be resolved, too much baggage, and the problem of the unidentified Arabs who were still around. He had to take care of the kids. And not forget that they'd have problems too. It wasn't just that he'd lost his wife. They'd lost their mother. And then there was Columbia.

"This new mission, is it dangerous?" she asked him. "I mean, really dangerous."

He thought about Columbia, the drug lords, the FARC rebels, the corrupt and maybe a few not so corrupt government forces that may help or hinder them. It was true; the whole country was an armed camp with an economy that relied predominantly on the drug business. They'd have support, sure, but mostly it would be at arm's length, UAVs, drones, satellite intelligence, overflights, and a few agents on the ground, maybe.

"Yeah, it's a tough one. But we'll be okay. We always are."

"Just be more okay that usual, Kyle."

"Sure." But he wasn't sure about anything.

* * *

The following morning they assembled for the briefing. Admiral Drew Jacks stood on the platform with a Marine Corps General, wearing the Marine Corps MARPAT camo uniform. Jacks introduced Major General Allan Hicks and then began the briefing.

"Men, you should know that the single factor that kicked off this mission was the murder of General Hicks' nephew by the Salazar brothers. But even so, that doesn't make it purely personal. Any US citizen, duly authorized by a sovereign government, should be free to walk on foreign soil without fear of murder by criminal gangs. That is not the reality, and you know it. But sometimes, a number of factors come together that enable us to make it a reality. It is so here. The Salazar organization undermines the government of the United States with its pernicious trade in illegal drugs. Our ally, the Columbian government, is equally concerned to put a stop to them. They murdered General Hicks' nephew, so of course he wants justice. Even the Mexican government is severely threatened by these Salazar brothers' activities, and I think we all know that the Mexicans have bitten off more than they can chew with the drug gangs."

There was a rumble of laughter. In December 2006, President Felipe Calderon sent 6,500 federal troops to the state of Michoacán to end drug violence there. It was regarded as the first major operation against organized crime inside Mexico, and was generally viewed as the starting point of the war between the government and the drug cartels. Calderon continued to escalate his anti-drug campaign, and there were now 45,000 troops involved, as well as state and federal police forces. In 2010, President Calderon said that the cartels were looking to replace the government, and were trying to impose a monopoly of their trade by force of arms. In some cases, they were even trying to impose their own laws.

"Lastly," he continued, "we most of us live and work in San Diego and the surrounding area, and many of us have felt the impact of the drug gangs."

He looked directly at Nolan, whose mind flashed to a picture of Grace the year before, when he'd never thought that anything could shatter his happiness.

"So this time, we're going in to finish the job. The Salazar brothers are toast."

"Hooyah!"

They shouted in unison. Admiral Jacks nodded, satisfied that there was no lack of commitment. General Hicks also nodded, and his grim face relaxed into a faint smile. His nephew, David Lopez, would be avenged. Jacks held up his hand.

"I'll hand over to Lieutenant Talley who will complete the briefing. Thank you, men. And good luck."

Talley climbed up to the platform. "Thank you, Admiral. Men, here is the objective. The Salazar brothers' operation is centered on Medellin. I don't believe that city needs any introduction."

Someone groaned. It was going to be tough, even tougher than they'd expected. Talley ignored it.

"Their operation has its headquarters to the west of the city, in an area known as La Castellana. They used to operate out in the countryside, but they were too vulnerable to government sweeps and intelligence from our satellites, so they moved into the 'burbs. We'll have support from Creech Air Force Base, and they'll be putting up a permanent umbrella of UAVs, Reapers, and the MQ-9s. These babies will be armed with Hellfire missiles and 500 lb laser-guided bombs. We'll be in contact with them the whole time, from infiltration to exfiltration, so any air support necessary can be called in right away."

Vince Merano put up his hand. "What about infiltration and exfiltration, how're we getting in there?"

"HALO drop, we don't want anyone knowing we're on the way. There's a…"

"Does that include the Columbian government?" Nolan interrupted.

"I'd guess the answer to that one is yes. It'd be better if they were kept out of the loop. We do have a legal basis for going in, as part of our signed agreement to assist them to fight the drug barons. On the other hand, the less they know of our operations, the better. But this time there is an exception. We'll be teaming up with one of their Special Forces units, the Agrupación de Fuerzas Especiales Antiterroristas Urbanas. That's the Urban Counter-Terrorism Special Forces Group, for those of you who don't speak any Spanish. They're an elite unit of the Colombian Army, and their primary mission is counter-terrorist operations and hostage rescue. They're pretty good, and it's important we work in cooperation with them. So there's no room for any fights over territory or jurisdiction."

"Yeah, that'll be a first, fucking Dagoes! I'd trust 'em about as far as I could throw 'em," someone murmured loudly. Nolan looked around and sighed. Roscoe Bremmer, his eyes bright with anger at the prospect of working with the Columbians, was mouthing off.

"That'll do, Roscoe. If we're ordered to work with them, that's the way it'll be."

Bremmer turned his angry eyes on Nolan. He held the gaze for a few seconds and looked away, muttering something inaudible. The men around him shuffled their feet and gave him some space, embarrassed. The Navy Seals was no place for big mouths. Talley went on.

"As I was saying, it'll be a HALO drop, to our first lay up point ten miles outside of Medellin. Our intel guys, I guess that means CIA, have set up a building for us to use as an FOB, a forward operating base. It's an old engineering shop, and it's been abandoned for some time. When we meet up, the password is Flame of Freedom. We'll carry most of our equipment in with us, but they'll be able to help with anything more we need. Communications will be the usual commo, and we'll be constantly uplinked via satellite to Creech and here. We'll be equipped with cameras that will uplink to HQ, and Chief Nolan and myself will be using e-tablets to receive any updates they consider necessary. We'll have the use of the RQ-11B Ravens. They'll be waiting for us in the FOB, so local recon shouldn't present any problems."

The Raven was a hand-launched reconnaissance UAV, an upgraded model aircraft, really. The RQ-11 Raven was developed in 2002. Powered by an electric motor, the aircraft could fly at six miles mph at altitudes of up to 15,000 feet, at a speed of up to sixty mph. For troops operating behind the lines in unfamiliar territory, they would put an eye in the sky to locate and pinpoint enemy strongholds. Nolan realized that Bremmer was still mouthing off, and this time that 'model airplanes were for kids'. He turned around.

"Bremmer, can it! Any problems, you take it up later, not at the briefing."

This time, the black Seal didn't back down. "Why's that, Chief? You got some problem with a black guy saying what he thinks? This briefing is just for you and the Lieutenant to say what you think, is that it?"

"I'll answer that," Talley called over. "PO3 Bremmer, you're new to this outfit, so I'll say it only once. Wise guy remarks will get you beached, as quick as poor performance in the field. Black, white or any other color, I don't give a shit. If you've got something to say that's worth hearing, say it. Otherwise, button it. Clear?"

Bremmer nodded, but the men around him could see it was anything but clear. Talley cleared his throat. "We'll need to carry some heavy firepower. I would remind you that these characters are very heavily armed. They're frequently known to outshoot the military when they come into contact. I'm splitting into three teams, and each team will carry an M240. The weapons will be available in the FOB when we get there, and with as much ammunition as we're likely to need. You'll carry your regular HK416s, with the exception of Vince and Kyle, who obviously will carry the MK11 SWS. I want every HK assault rifle fitted with a grenade launcher. I'll instruct them to put a few cases of grenades in the FOB too. That covers the hardware, and now for the mission objectives. First and foremost, we take out the Salazar brothers, that's a given. Next, we destroy their personnel and infrastructure. Carl, your explosives will be shipped in, so there'll be plenty for you to work with. When we leave, I want the Salazar operation to be history, staff, stock, equipment, vehicles, and buildings. That's it. Oh yeah, exfiltration. Five miles west of La Castellana, there's a wide landing ground, good for helos. They're sending in a pair of Boeing V-22s, the Ospreys, to collect us. That's all."

"Boss."

He looked across at Will Bryce. "Yes, Will, what is it?"

"What's our jump-off time?"

Talley nodded, and smiled. "Yeah, I missed that one, wheels up tonight, Gentlemen, at 2200 hours. Sorry it's such short notice, but the Brass is worried about any leaks on this one. As from this moment, you are all confined to base. Mission duration is twenty-four to thirty hours. We lay up during the day in the FOB and begin operations as soon as the light starts to fade. We'll be using our standard night vision equipment, both for the jump and for the operation."

Nolan was heartily pleased his kids were out of

harm's way, although he was sad he wouldn't be able to say goodbye. You never knew. He could see on the other men's faces the mixed expressions. Concern that like him, there would be no farewells, but the adrenaline rush had its effect, and already there was an air of calm determination to locate the enemy and mete out the kind of punishment that the Navy Seals did best. The Salazar organization only had hours left to continue its operations. Then Nolan had a sobering thought.

The Columbian Special Forces, can they be trusted? If not, this operation will get a whole lot harder.

CHAPTER FOUR

The ramp of the C-130 had opened to acclimatize them to the external environment, the night sky outside the aircraft. There was little breathable air at that height, and they'd long since switched to the portable oxygen supplies they'd need for the jump. They were ten minutes out, fifty miles from the drop zone, and so far everything was a go. They'd checked their gear, and Talley had gone to the cockpit to signal their contact in Medellin. He came back a few minutes later and nodded to Nolan.

"We're good to go, and intel says there's some kind of a fiesta down there in the town, lots of smoke, noise, fireworks, and hombres firing into the air. It couldn't be better. How's everything at home, are the kids okay?"

He remembered that he hadn't called them.

Jesus, what kind of a person am I turning into?

He'd noticed Carol's sharp and questioning look as he'd left the house. He knew he was cold towards her, but he just couldn't help it. He felt cold. But the kids, he'd have to make it up, somehow. He realized Talley was waiting for him to answer.

"Yeah, er fine. Maybe it'll be a tad easier if they're carousing. We need all the luck we can get on this one. Medellin's not going to be a bed of roses. It's full of soldiers, and they carry pretty heavy ordnance."

"Maybe so, but there's no reason why we shouldn't be in and out before they even wake up to us being there. It's gonna be a good one, Chief. I can feel it in my bones. Maybe we won't even need to do so much shooting this time out. We can leave it to Carl and his C4."

Nolan smiled at the Lieutenant's enthusiastic grin. Just as an explosion out on the starboard wing caused the aircraft to buck and lurch, and the port wing started to tip her over into a skewed, nose-down attitude.

"Buckle up, men, hang on," he shouted along the fuselage at two of the men who were looking around wildly, close to panic. One of them was Roscoe Bremmer. The others were calmer and like him, they were appraising the situation before taking any action. "Boss, we need to know what the hell happened."

Talley nodded. "Yeah, I'll go forward and see."

But as he spoke, the cockpit door crashed open, and the jumpmaster staggered through, grabbing at handholds to stop him from being flung along the cabin by the wild gyrations of the aircraft.

"We've taken damage to the starboard outer engine and the control surfaces. The skipper says she won't make it to the jump off point. We need to lighten up if we're going to get this baby home."

"Any ideas what caused it?" Talley asked.

The man shook his head. "Nothing yet, could be anything. It wasn't a missile. We'd have seen it coming in on the radar. Could have been a fuel leak or maybe something else."

"A bomb?"

"Christ knows! It could have been anything. Maybe just a faulty component, some kind of fuel leak that exploded. You guys need to bale out here if you're going, otherwise come back with us and abort the mission. Skipper says he's turning around in one minute." He checked his watch. "Make that half a minute, what're you going to do?"

Talley looked at Nolan. "Chief, what'd you think?"

He calculated like lightning. They'd be thirty miles further out from the drop zone by the time they landed, and the drop zone was ten miles from the first LUP, the lay up point outside of Medellin. So they'd be forty miles out. He thought of Admiral Jacks; he'd told him he'd give it one hundred and ten percent.

"Let's go now."

Talley looked at the jumpmaster. "Tell the pilot to hold it for another few seconds, then you can give us the green light."

The man nodded and staggered back to the cockpit. Nolan began final preparations.

"Okay, you've got thirty seconds max. The mission is a go. Make fast checks on your gear, now! Make the LZ exactly thirty miles due north of the previous marker."

He and Talley checked each other's gear, in as fast a way as time allowed. They almost ran to the ramp. The aircraft had steadied and was flying more or less straight and level. The jumpmaster came back and shouted at them. "Pilot says he can't wait any longer, so it's now or never."

Simultaneously, the green light came on, and the mass of Seals stepped off the ramp out into the South American night.

They were using night vision gear and wrist mounted navigational systems to plot their descent. Nolan watched the Columbian landscape approach below him as he held the skydiving position and glided into the LZ. He checked his navigation and looked around for the other platoon members. None were visible. All were swallowed up by the dark night, the swirling clouds, and multitude of shapes and patterns that made up the night sky over Columbian. He checked his altitude, 5,000 feet, time to wait before opening. A parachute was a huge sign that said 'look at me' to anyone in the area. Even at night, a chance sighting was possible. He checked again, 3,000 feet. It was time. He pulled the cord and felt the sharp tug as the 'chute opened and slowed his descent. The jungle canopy came towards him, and he pulled on the cords, steering towards a small, open patch of ground. At the last moment, he relaxed his body and bent his legs at the knees. The landing was gentle, no worse than hundreds he'd done in the past, even though this one was a last minute scratch operation. But he knew that he'd been lucky, finding the clearing, and others may not be so fortunate. He unhitched the shroud lines and stowed away the 'chute in a small pit that some small animal had dug underneath a fallen tree. All around him he could hear the small sounds of the jungle, insects calling, birds screeching, and here and there the soft footfalls as an animal prowled around, looking for prey.

He keyed the mic. "This is Nolan. I'm exactly on the coordinates for the LZ. Is anyone in trouble?"

There was a silence for a few seconds. Then Vince Merano came down only feet away from him, twisting at the last moment to bring his 'chute to one side, so he could rapidly stow it away. Then Talley was down, Bremmer, and Winters. They'd used their NVS like him to locate the clearing, even Bremmer, the new boy. More men dropped in beside him, and he counted them off in his head. Brad Rose, Dan Moseley, Dave Eisner.

"Where's Zeke?"

Zeke Murray, the handsome Latino electronics and communications expert.

"I ain't seen him."

"Nor me."

"Okay, let's see what happened to him," Talley ordered. "We'll start a grid search. He can't have come down far away. Chief, split the men into squads to cover the four quadrants. Let's make this quick, we've got a fair ways to travel."

They split up, and Nolan led a team that went south. He recalled Zeke leaving behind him, and that meant he should have glided slightly further, all things being equal. They found him in a tree less than fifty yards from the LZ. He'd been stunned into unconsciousness by a thick tree branch when he landed badly. Dave Eisner shinned up the trunk and cut away his lines, then lowered him gently to the ground, using the remains of the parachute shrouds. Nolan kneeled down to look at him.

"Zeke, how're you doing?"

The Seal opened his eyes slowly. Then he grinned, showing a row of white teeth that glowed with a greenish tinge in the NVS, and contrasting with the dull, mottled shades of the surrounding jungle.

"I guess I screwed up."

"Whatever. Is anything broken?"

Zeke groaned as he tried to move. At first it was hard,

but he managed to sit up and start to explore his limbs.

"I reckon not, Chief. I'm good to go."

"Yeah, but you'll need to take it easy at first. We'll split your gear between us. Roscoe, take his backpack. Dan, carry his rifle. When he's feeling better, he can have 'em back."

"Chief, I'm okay, I don't need no nursemaid."

"You're still recovering from a blow to the head, so just take some time to get over it."

Roscoe picked up the backpack with ill grace, and Dan the HK416. Nolan heard him muttering something about 'black servants', but he ignored it. Bremmer was going to need a thorough talking to when they got back; his branding himself a racial victim got on everyone's nerves. It could cause even more trouble if it took men's minds off their job. He helped Zeke to his feet and formed the men up to march. Talley assigned the point to Will Bryce with Dan Moseley at the rear. Nolan and Merano, the unit snipers, were assigned the flanks wherever possible. In the thick jungle, the going was tough, and often they had to follow tracks only wide enough for a single man. They marched fast in the knowledge that they had a lot of miles and time to make up for. By 0400, it was obvious that they weren't going to make it. Nolan and Talley conferred. They'd have to find somewhere to lay up for the day and head on in after dark. It was not optimal, as there was always the chance of being discovered when hiding out for the day. It also meant the advantage of going in undercover of the fiesta was lost.

"Unless they're still hungover," Talley said reflectively.

"I wouldn't count on it, Boss."

He smiled at Nolan. "I guess you're right, that was

wishful thinking. How's Zeke holding up?"

"He's good. I've got two of the men carrying his gear. I'm not sure he's fully over it, as that was some bang to the head. Maybe the layup through the day will do him a power of good."

"I think so, too."

They'd reached the top of a ridge and were looking down into a shallow valley.

"We'll make camp on the far side of the crest, fifty yards below. Let's make sure we can keep the whole valley under observation," Tally looked all around. "That should give us warning of any approach from the front. Ask Vince to set up an OP to cover our six. We'll relieve the position every two hours, so we can all get some rest." Talley looked at Nolan and spoke quietly. "It's a tough one, Chief, but we've done them before. I'll get through to headquarters on the secure commo and give them a heads up. They'll need to reschedule the UAVs, and let the undercover guys in Medellin know the score."

"Right, I'll go talk to Vince, and give him a hand to establish an OP over the ridge.

As Nolan walked over to speak to Vince, he thought about what lay ahead. It was true they'd been in bad situations before, but this mission had started bad, too bad. Small units of lightly armed Special Forces relied on silent infiltration to reach their objective, hit hard, and get out before the enemy realized that they were even there. The C-130 explosion must have been like a signal flare in the sky. Instead of an ordinary radar signature, Colombian air traffic control would have reported an aircraft that behaved in a peculiar fashion. The information would flash around the wires, and the only question was, how they'd interpret it and who would they tell? The Platoon had to assume the worst. Then there was Zeke, who despite everything would slow them down, even if it were a little. And losing the day, there would be people who'd prepared for their arrival. Could they do the same again the next night? Who knew whom they'd bribed, and who they'd threatened or killed? There was no point in deluding themselves. They were in the shit.

The men were mostly sleeping through the heat of the day, sheltered beneath the camouflage of leaves and branches cut down from the jungle canopy. Nolan was dozing, thinking about the kids, Mary and Daniel.

What will they be doing, right now? Settling into a new school, I guess. That could be a problem when they came back to San Diego, if they come back.

"Chief."

He looked up. Will Bryce had been on sentry, and he was leaning over him, speaking in a whisper.

"What is it?"

"Movement, down in the valley."

"Copy that. Wake the others, and I'll take a look. Who's out back?"

"Roscoe."

"'Okay."

He scanned the valley below with his binoculars, careful to make certain they weren't in a position to reflect the sun's rays. It was hot, very hot, and very humid. Sweat trickled down his back inside his shirt and down his forehead, making it difficult to see. But he could see enough; armed men, scores of them, about a mile away.

"What do you make of it?"

He looked aside as Talley lay down next to him and

used his own binoculars to sweep the scene.

"They're guerrillas of some kind, so I'd guess that makes them FARC. About a hundred of them, that'd be my best estimate."

"FARC! Shit, that's all we need." Talley shook his head worriedly, and with good reason. The Revolutionary Armed Forces of Colombia was a guerrilla organization with an anti-imperialist cause. They claimed to represent the rural poor against Colombia's wealthier classes and bitterly opposed any United States influence in Colombia. They were funded principally through ransom kidnappings, gold mining, and the production and distribution of illegal drugs. As an organization, they were well funded, well organized, and highly motivated.

The Lieutenant finished his sweep of the valley and then used the encrypted satellite commo to talk to headquarters, which meant Rear Admiral Drew Jacks. He outlined the problem.

Jacks' response was one word. "Shit!" Then he went on to question Talley. "We wouldn't have checked out the area as we didn't expect you to go anywhere near it. They told me about the problem with the aircraft, and they're looking into that now. How do you plan to play this? Can you get around them?"

"We'll have to try, I guess. We could use an overflight, and downlink an image of the whole valley and the outlying areas. But if it means a detour, it'll slow us down even more."

"I'll get onto it. We can have something for you in a couple of hours. In the meantime, I'll get onto our intel people and find out what FARC are doing there. They generally operate in the south east of the country, not up in your area. I'll get back to you as soon as I know anything. Just hang in there, we'll find a way around this, any more problems?"

"Nothing we can't handle."

"I hear you. Out."

Talley said nothing. He just looked out across the valley as if he could see the size and scale of the FARC encampment. Finally, he glanced at Nolan.

"This operation could be a bust. It'll be hard to trek to Medellin without attracting some attention from those characters. They're not so dumb."

"Maybe, we've sure had our share of problems. I'm wondering what the hell they're doing, so near to Medellin. Are they with the cocaine gangs, or against them?"

"The FARC is a communist outfit, and the cocaine gangs are known to hate the commies. I guess that means they're against them."

"What, you reckon they're planning their own attack on Medellin? That'd be interesting."

Talley nodded. "Yeah, I guess it would."

They waited for three hours, and then the secure satcom activated. Talley answered.

"Bravo."

"Yeah, Bravo, this is Base. We have new intel on the FARC presence in your valley. We're sending in a FARC expert to join you. There've been some developments, and we need someone with knowledge of how they operate. For now, hold your position."

Talley was puzzled. It was an unfamiliar voice, and the order was stranger still. "When's this expert due to arrive?"

"He'll make a HALO drop straight after dark. He'll drop onto your coordinates. As soon as he arrives, your platoon is to be ready to pull out."

"Pull out? What's the deal, where are we going?"

There was a hesitation. "Going? Medellin, of course. Out."

They waited through the day, speculating on what faced them when this so-called 'expert' arrived.

"The last thing we need is a passenger, some academic or diplomat who wants a feather in his cap for going into the field," Talley grumbled. "Like I said, this mission looks like a bust. What the hell can this guy do? Fight his way through a hundred guerillas?"

"Unless he's planning to do a deal," Nolan pointed out.

"A deal with the FARC? Jesus, those guys are a bunch of commies. The only time we talk to those guys is when they're the wrong end of our gun barrels. Damn, it's hot out here!"

Nolan nodded. The heat of the afternoon was like a heavy shroud that clamped down over them, making every movement difficult. The humidity was high, very high, and it made everything worse. Finally, the light started to fade. Vince crawled over to where Talley and Nolan waited.

"The guerrillas in the valley, they're moving."

"Which way?" Talley asked, his eyes lighting up with interest.

"South, toward Medellin."

He grimaced. "And we sit here on our fannies waiting for fucking Captain America to drop in. Jesus! This mission is fucked."

Nolan and Merano grinned at each other. It wasn't often the Boss was downbeat during a mission.

"Maybe this new guy won't be so bad," he pointed out. "He may know something that'll put us back on course."

"He'll need to know a shitload of stuff if he's going to do that, and bring an army with him to get through those guerillas."

The message arrived just as the light was fading to twilight, and the time when visibility is at its worst. Zeke Murray had recovered enough to take over the satcom, and he called quietly to Talley and Nolan.

"Signal just came through, the guy just jumped. He'll be with us in five minutes, maybe less."

"Copy that."

Talley got to his feet. "Men, our visitor is due, so keep your safeties on, we don't want to give him a fright before he even gets here."

They smiled but checked their weapons as they watched the night sky.

"I see him," Vince said softly. He'd been using night vision equipment. "He's at about five hundred feet, just over to the north west. It looks as if he'll come down plum in the center of us."

"Maybe he's done a jump before," Talley grumbled. "At least we may not wind up with a total amateur."

There was a silent rustle, and a man dropped neatly into the center of the Platoon. He stripped of his 'chute and expertly stowed it into a bundle while they watched. It was hard work to keep a straight face and to hide their astonishment. He was dressed exactly like them, in dark jungle camouflage uniform, the MARPAT woodland digital pattern. Like them he carried an assault rifle, an HK416, as well as a pistol in his belt holster, the Sig Sauer P226. He stripped off his half helmet and grinned at them. He was short, bow-legged, with cropped blonde hair. Despite being trim, hard and fit, he was also old. The men snapped to attention as they stared at Rear Admiral Drew Jacks, commander of Seal Team Seven, Naval Base Coronado, San Diego.

"At ease, men. I guess you didn't expect me."

"Well, no, Sir," Talley replied.

"Yeah, well I'm not completely off active duty, not yet, anyway. This is one mission where I may be able to help out in the field. Call your men together, Lieutenant, we're wasting time. This show needs to get on the road. And the mission brief has changed. I'll spell it all out for you."

He scanned the valley ahead through night vision equipment as he waited for the men to settle, turning to get their attention.

"Men, I'm aware that things haven't gone well up to now, and I'm the last person you expected to see on a live mission. I can tell you now that things are going to get a whole lot worse."

They stared at him. A few faces fell, and there were a couple of groans.

"Quiet," Talley murmured.

"That's okay," the Admiral said. "Okay, here's the deal. Our radio and cellphone intercepts suggest that these FARC guerillas are about to attack a couple of the major players in Medellin. It sounds like a great idea, yeah, save the US government a deal of time and trouble, not to mention a few bucks?"

They nodded.

"Right, but it isn't. We've discovered that FARC is short of funds, and they like to use drug money to buy weapons and equipment, that's their style. That's why they're going into Medellin, to set up their own operation by taking down two of the major players."

"So why don't we leave those boys to it?" Roscoe Bremmer interrupted. "What's the point of me risking my black ass if they're doing our work for us?"

"Pipe down, Roscoe," Nolan said quickly.

"PO3 Bremmer asks why we don't just leave them to it?" Jacks continued. "It's because there's a third major player inside Medellin, the Salazar brothers. If we let this happen, instead of three squabbling organizations, there'll be one formidable combination, FARC and the Salazars, for us to deal with, and that, Gentlemen, is not acceptable."

"You're here, Sir, so that means there's some kind of a plan," Talley said.

"Yeah, that's right. I've fought the FARC on a number of occasions, and we've come up with a plan. Essentially, it's much the same as you came here to do. Destroy the Salazars. But we're going to do it undercover of the FARC attack on the other guys, the Barreras and the Olveras. So we let these bastards destroy each other. And while these guerrillas are hitting the Barreras and the Olveras, we hit the Salazars. With any luck, we'll cut out a running sore that's been hurting America for more than a few years."

There was a silence after he'd finished speaking. The prospect of involvement in a massive urban conflict was enough to make the bravest man think seriously. Yet it made sense, to deal the drug industry a huge blow at one stroke, if they could get away with it.

"That's it then," Jacks filled the silence, "any questions? If not, we'll move out. The guerillas have already moved out, and we have a UAV on permanent station over this area for the duration of the mission. They've checked the whole valley and reported the hostiles' movement. So we've got a clear run at it. Let's go and..."

"Admiral, Sir," Talley interrupted him.

"What is it?"

"Chain of command, Sir. I imagine you're in charge, now that you're the senior officer."

"Then you imagine wrong, Son. I'm here as an advisor, period. You're in command of the platoon, and the mission is yours. Clear?"

"Yes, Sir." Talley sounded relieved.

"However," Jacks went on, a sly expression on his face, "I'd appreciate you taking notice if I did have any advice to offer. Just think about."

"Of course, Sir."

Talley grinned. The meaning was clear; he was in command, but Admiral Jacks would have the final say. That was fine, Jacks was a warrior, no question, a legend even to many Seals.

"Yeah, well, as I said, I've fought against these FARC people. I also speak fluent Spanish, as do a couple of the guys in the Platoon, so that may be useful. One more thing, Lieutenant, and this is for all of you."

They fell silent.

"You're not alone on this mission. We have an open line to the Colombian government, although they don't know any of the details of this mission, only that we're operating somewhere inside Colombia. As a result, we have a range of air support, UAVs, Reapers, Predators; you name it. The Air Force has put a pair of AC-130 gunships at our disposal, and they're maintaining station off the coast, courtesy of a fleet of tankers keeping them topped up. The second they're needed, and they'll point their nose inland and come straight in. The President of the United States had taken an interest in this mission and was in the Situation Room for a briefing as I left. The Colombian Special Forces, the Agrupación de Fuerzas Especiales Antiterroristas Urbanas, are holding position a few miles due east of the town, close to the Parque Arvi. They have the strength of about fifty men, and they're well armed and equipped. We're meeting up with them outside the town before we go in. Intel estimates the FARC attack will begin at 0500. We'll be position by then, and as soon as they've created enough confusion, we go in and deal with the Salazars. We have a lot of ground to cover, so I suggest we move out. Lieutenant, we'll need someone to scout ahead and link up with the Colombian Special Forces. I don't want any surprises on the way, not when the two forces meet."

Talley nodded. "Chief, would you go on ahead and make contact. You have the coordinates, and take Roscoe with you. Keep your eyes peeled for those FARC guerillas. We don't know if they've left any back markers in place. Now we're splitting up, you're designated Bravo Two."

Nolan nodded and picked up his pack and sniper rifle. "Copy that. Roscoe, let's move out."

CHAPTER FIVE

The FARC had cut a path through the jungle. It was the only factor in their favor, and it meant they could make up for much of the lost time. Nolan took point and Bremmer brought up the rear, ten paces back. They were only ten miles from Medellin, and Bremmer was doing what he did best.

"Motherfuckers, sending us out like this. We've got aerial surveillance for this shit. Ain't one of the guys got a Raven RV-11 in his pack?"

The Raven was a small, hand-launched remote-controlled unmanned aerial vehicle, a UAV. Developed for the US military, they gave small units in the field the capacity to launch short range, short duration surveillance flights that downlinked to their tactical electronic tablets.

"We're carrying one Raven, and that's for battlefield emergencies, Roscoe. You get into a firefight, and you may be glad we kept a rain check on that baby."

"Shit, Chief, didn't you hear? They've got a round-the-clock air cover with those damned Reapers. Jeez, they send in those babies and they'll do the work for us. If we…"

"Quiet!" Nolan hissed.

Roscoe mumbled quietly beneath his breath, but he went still, and they both dropped to the ground.

"What the fuck is it?" Bremmer whispered. "What's going…"

Nolan signaled for silence. Then he crawled forward to check what had alerted him, a sound, a tiny, almost inaudible sound in the center of the jungle's confusion of animal noises, insects, birds, and foliage that moved and shifted; and a single, metallic 'clink'. But there was nothing metallic in the jungle, unless it belonged to man. And if there was someone up ahead, it meant nothing good.

"Stay here and keep your head down. I'll go see what's up there," he whispered to Roscoe.

"I'll come with you, Chief, I can…"

"Stay here."

He didn't wait to hear any argument. Nolan crawled forward, and only ten yards further along the track and just around a sharp bend, there was a FARC blocking position. Using night vision, he could see two men dug into a foxhole, just off the track. They were good. If he hadn't heard the noise, which he could see had been made by one of the sentries removing his clip and checking the load, they could have walked into trouble. The 'clink' sounded again, and this time he saw the man push the clip back into his assault rifle. The other man was sat behind a light machine gun. It was a Soviet RPD mounted on a bipod, with the iconic drum magazine making it instantly recognizable. Simple to operate, and firing seven hundred rounds per minute of 7.62-millimeter military grade ammunition, made it a formidable weapon. Both men were hunkered down behind thick tree trunks that they'd used as a natural barricade. They were going to be difficult to kill. He crawled back to Roscoe and explained the hostile position.

"They're well positioned, and we need to get them out of that foxhole to finish them."

"What about a grenade? I've got the launcher. I can pop one in there, no sweat."

"And if the main force is near enough to hear the explosion?"

"Yeah, I see what you mean."

"Right, I'd take them with the sniper rifle but getting into a good stand to take the shot is going to be slow and difficult, and we just don't have the time. I want you to sucker them out of there."

"Me? What the fuck do you want me to do?"

"I speak Spanish, so they won't realize we're not FARC until we get close. You'll pretend to be wounded, so you can lean on me. I'll talk to them and call for help. Make sure you stagger as we get there."

"What about my rifle?"

"Sling it behind you. They won't see it. Keep your Sig in your hand, but make sure it's out of sight. That's it, make it convincing."

"You sure this is going to work, Chief?"

"Sure, why shouldn't it?"

Roscoe shook his head. "I don't know. It sounds like some fool white man's shit to me."

"Can the racial comments, Roscoe. Let's get the job done. You're wounded and in agony, so moan or something."

"Fuck this."

Nolan slung his SWS behind him and grabbed Roscoe under his arms to support him. Then he started walking forward.

"Shout, you're in agony, remember," he hissed at the PO3.

Roscoe gave out an unconvincing moan, but it was enough to alert the sentries.

"Quién va?" Who is it?

"Ayúdame! Rápidamente, es uno de nuestros hombres! Él está mal herido!" Help! One of our men is badly hurt.

He heard them talking urgently amongst themselves. They hesitated, and as he watched, the barrel of the machine gun swiveled towards them.

"Rápidamente, Él está mal herido. Se está muriendo."

They muttered quickly between themselves, and it sounded like an argument. Then they started to climb out of the foxhole. Nolan breathed a sigh of relief and whispered to Roscoe, who he was almost dragging along, his head hanging down. He had to hand it to him; it was a good performance.

"You took the safety off your Sig?"

"Yeah."

"Okay, wait for me to shoot first. Nearly there."

They were almost abreast of the two men who were now running toward them, concern written on their faces, until they saw the unfamiliar uniforms.

"Qué es esto? Dios mío!"

"Yeah, bad call," Nolan muttered as he swung up the Sig Sauer and fired twice, then twice again. Both men were hit, and Roscoe was firing his suppressed Sig to make sure. Both men fell to the ground, dead.

"Let's get 'em off the track and into the jungle. If any

of their people come back, we don't want to advertise our presence," the Chief said quickly to Roscoe. "One at a time, these guys weren't on starvation rations."

It was true. They were both a good few pounds overweight, as if they'd spent too much time in camp, eating too many rations. Clearly, jungle warfare was not as arduous as it used to be. When the bodies were hidden, Nolan stripped the ammunition out of the guns and scattered it into the jungle, then smashed the barrels.

"If we come back this way," he explained to Roscoe, "we don't want them using these things against us."

Before they pushed on, he called it in. "Bravo One, this is Two."

"Go ahead, Two."

"Two hostiles taken out. Just a rearguard, no complications."

He gave them his position.

"Copy that."

He signed off and turned to Roscoe. "Let's go, we're running out of time. We're nearly four miles short of our objective, and we need to get there in no more than an hour."

"What happens in an hour?"

"The FARC begin their attack. All hell will let loose in Medellin, and if anyone sees a pair of Gringos in camouflage kit, they're gonna shoot first and ask questions afterwards."

Roscoe's eyes widened. "The fuck they are, what are we waiting for?"

Nolan suppressed a smile as he led the way forward. There was no time left for caution. They had to be in position before the attack started, to hold a secure base for the Platoon from which to prepare their own attack. They crested a rise on the path and looked down on the town of Medellin, or rather the city.

"Motherfucker, that place is huge," Roscoe breathed.

"Yeah, it's a city of over two million people, and all of them ruled by three families, the Barreras, the Olveras, and the Salazars. Most of them probably earn their living from one of the families, so they're not going to like any kind of action that destroys their livelihood."

"There's only sixteen of us, what can we do?"

"Seventeen with Admiral Jacks, and remember, we're not invading Medellin. This action is to destroy the Salazars. We watch the FARC move in and hammer the Olveras and the Barreras. Then we hit the main target. We kill the personnel and destroy their infrastructure."

Roscoe nodded. "Yeah, that sounds easy enough."

"It won't be if the FARC get's an idea of what we're up to, so keep it tight. Let's move in."

They reached the highway and almost ran through the suburbs of Medellin, only stopping to drop out of sight when vehicles appeared on the move. Nolan checked his watch, and they were still a half-mile short of the FOB when a flare shot up into the sky, followed by the sound of automatic fire. The FARC had attacked.

"Make it snappy," he called behind him to Roscoe. "They'll be looking out of their windows now for anyone carrying a gun. We don't want them to get a fix on us."

Roscoe nodded. They hurried on past a sign that read 'Parque Arvi', and at last Nolan saw what he was looking for, the old engineering works that bordered the main fence of the park. He veered into a narrow lane running along the side of the building and started to relax. They were out of sight of the street. He put a hand out to slow Roscoe down; it was the last stage.

"Let's check this place out before we call it in, you ..."

A flashlight pierced the darkness. "Manos arriba!" Hands up.

Neither of them moved their hands. Nolan sensed rather than saw Roscoe's hand slip down to his side, to his holstered Sig. He had to take a chance before anyone did anything stupid.

"We're Americans."

The light didn't waver. "I said put up your hands."

Nolan stared at the dim figure behind the flashlight, and at the gun barrel that was illuminated in the beam.

"I said we're Americans. Flame of Freedom. You're Agrupación de Fuerzas Especiales Antiterroristas Urbanas?"

The beam snapped off, and the man walked forward. "We had to be careful. Come inside, and you can meet the men. Are there only two of you?"

"The others are coming up behind. We came in first to check the place over."

"Very wise."

They went through a small side door. The man pushed aside a canvas curtain, and they walked into a dimly lit workshop. The man turned and held up his hand.

"My name is Raoul Castro. Captain Raoul Castro, of the Agrupación de Fuerzas Especiales Antiterroristas Urbanas. These are my men."

They looked with interest at the impressive looking force of men gathered in the space that had once contained rows of machinery. Now it was empty of any machines, except for the machines of war, four SUVs fitted with machine guns mounted on the truck beds, and the men. They were all in civilian clothes and looked more like a street gang than an elite para-military unit. Raoul Castro was an exotic looking man, short and powerfully built. He wore a sweat-soaked brown shirt with cut off sleeves that showed every muscle. His khaki pants were grease stained and worn over work boots coated with grime. His hair was thick and shaggy. It hung to his shoulders and was held in place by a thonged leather headband. He had fine, almost delicate features that he'd tried to camouflage by growing a mustache and beard. The mustache was black and luxuriant, and it dropped over his lips, glistening like fur. He looked like almost like a kid playing a role in a play about gangsters; except for the assault rifle he held casually, a Heckler & Koch G36 5.56 millimeter with spare clips in their black leather cases festooned over his canvas webbing. He grinned at Nolan.

"It's deliberate. Our war is against the soldiers of the drug gangs, and this is the way they dress. By the time they realize we are not part of them, it is too late."

"I guess it would be," Nolan agreed. "But I reckon this time the war has already started."

The town was alive with the sound of gunfire, single shots, and automatic weapons firing in short and long bursts. In the distance, the odd scream of pain as someone was hit, and the sound of racing engines as people ran to reinforce their hard-pressed comrades, or to escape.

Castro shrugged. "It will cover our operation, which is as our masters planned it, no?"

"Yeah, I guess so." He keyed his mic. "Bravo One, this is Bravo Two. Have contacted friendlies. You're clear to bring the Platoon to the rendezvous point. I'd make it fast.

There's a war breaking out here."

"Copy that, Bravo Two. We'll be with you in ten."

"Mr. Nolan, your equipment is over there, explosives, body armor, and some replacement ammunition," Castro said.

"Yeah, thanks. We'll need all the help we can get taking on the Salazars."

"What? What is this about the Salazars?"

The man who'd spoken was a tall, heavily muscled member of Castro's team. Nolan eyed him carefully. There was something about him that screamed 'danger'. His face was heavily pockmarked, the result of untreated childhood illness, no doubt. Columbia was a poor country. But he wore two knife scars, slashes that ran down on the left side of his face; slashes that proclaimed a checkered past. Castro hastened to introduce him.

"This is my sergeant, Sancho Vidal."

Nolan nodded. "Does it make a difference? We're here to hit the main organizations, all of them. What does it matter who we hit first?"

"I know nothing of this," the Sergeant replied sulkily.

Nolan shrugged. He ignored the man and continued speaking with Castro. "Did they brief you on our mission?"

"Sure, you're here to carry out a strike on some of the Medellin drug gangs and interdict shipments to the US."

"They didn't mention the Salazars?"

"The Salazars? No, of course not."

Nolan was aghast. It was the fundamental and most important part of the operation. They could attack the drug gangs as much as they liked, but until they'd destroyed the Salazar operation, the whole thing was a bust. Castro looked confused.

"They said nothing of the Salazars," he said again. "You're talking of the Salazar gang here in Medellin? That is outside of our brief. I was specifically told to target the Olveras and the Barreras, and not to worry about the Salazars this time. I understood they'd be taken care of at a later date."

"Yeah, Jesus Christ, we hoped you'd help us fight our way into their operation. Are you totally sure those were your orders?"

Castro looked worried. "Of course I am sure. Our orders were to meet your men here and offer you such assistance as would be required against those two gangs, the Olveras and Barreras. We are also ordered to make certain that no Colombian laws are broken. Your American operations have a certain, shall I say, reputation? We are happy to see the power of the drug barons squashed, but it must not be by way of breaking the law or killing innocent civilians. As for the Salazars, they are the most powerful group in the city, and they will not be easy to destroy. We must leave them for today."

"That's not gonna happen, Captain. And as for them being difficult to destroy, I guess they wouldn't have sent us if they were so easy to kill. As soon as the rest of the Platoon arrives, we'll head on out to their compound. And by the way, how you gonna stop the FARC from breaking the law, amigo?"

Castro flushed. "We will fight them as necessary. So you will not fight the Olveras and Barreras?"

"We're going to the Salazars first. We'll worry about the others afterwards. Do you have any intelligence on their strength, the layout of their place?"

"No, I have had nothing concerning them."

"Then we'll go to their main warehouse. If there's a war breaking out on the streets, I guess they'll head in to protect their product."

"In that case we will offer our support," Castro replied. "Believe me, you will need it."

"Because of the FARC?"

The Colombian smiled. "The FARC? No, Senor, the FARC are a problem. But the Salazars, they are a nightmare. They will fight like maniacs to protect what is theirs."

"You should listen to the Captain, what he says is true. Leave the Salazars and concentrate on the Olveras and the Barreras."

Nolan glanced at Sergeant Vidal. "It's not happening, pal. We have our orders, and we'll carry them out."

* * *

Talley arrived with the Platoon inside of the ten minutes he'd promised, and the men started donning the body armor and helping themselves to ammunition and ordnance. Rear Admiral Drew Jacks looked around at the ragtag collection of Colombian Special Forces, and then shook hands with Castro, who'd been talking in rapid Spanish on a radio inside the cab of one of the SUVs.

"Pleased to meet you, Captain. It sounds like all hell is breaking loose out there. Have you fixed up a plan with Chief Nolan to get this show on the road?"

Castro was astonished to see a real live US Navy Admiral with the Platoon.

"Admiral Jacks, your Mr. Nolan wants us to do direct to the Salazars' warehouse. Is that what you wish?"

"I'm along for the ride, Son. You need to speak to

Lieutenant Talley here. He's the man in charge."

Talley frowned. "If the Chief says that's the objective, then that's the way it is. Are you telling me there's some kind of a problem?"

"I have been talking to some of my people. I have observers at key points inside the city. The man I was just speaking to informs me that the Salazars have put up roadblocks all around their warehouse to protect it. It will be impossible to get through. We should choose a different target."

Talley nodded. "Is that so? Give me a few minutes, and let's see what we can do about that. Any FARC activity in the area?"

Castro shook his head. "Not so far, no."

"Okay, let's check this out."

He used the satcom to contact the forward controller who patched him through to Creech Air Force Base.

"Creech, this is Bravo. How's our surveillance looking?"

"We're circling the city right now, Bravo. What can we do for you?"

"I want you to send live images of the following coordinates to my tablet. It looks as if we may have some business for you."

"Always happy to help, Bravo. If you want us to deliver some cookies, it'd be a pleasure. We hate to go home with the larder full."

Talley took out his tactical tablet and powered up. Seconds later, the image began to appear on his screen. It was like a scene from hell. Or maybe Beirut, in the bad old days of the faction fights when Muslim groups like Hezbollah tore the city apart to impose their own iron discipline on the terrified residents. Central to the image was a warehouse in the center of a compound. The compound was surrounded by a high wall, and clearly visible on the crystal clear color video image. The UAV had locked the camera on the center of the coordinates and was maintaining a low, lazy spiral over the city, unnoticed by the residents below. Outside, in the streets that approached the Salazar compound, four roadblocks could be seen. In each case, they consisted of a pair of trucks parked across the street, with as many as thirty or forty armed men sheltering behind them. Talley nodded, satisfied.

"Creech, this is Bravo. Confirm ordnance on the overhead Reaper."

"Bravo, that bird's carrying four Hellfire missiles and two five hundred pound GBU-12 Paveway II laser-guided bombs. Do you have a fire mission for us?"

"That's affirmative, Creech, and it'll need those four Hellfires. I'll be back in just a few seconds, standby."

He placed the cursor over each roadblock and clicked the button that forwarded the coordinates to the UAV, by way of Creech US Air Force Base in the Nevada Desert.

"This is Bravo, confirm receipt of four separate coordinates."

"This is Creech, confirmed. Targets locked in, one Hellfire missile assigned to each target. Waiting for your go ahead."

"Lieutenant!" Captain Castro shouted as he walked towards Talley. Sergeant Vidal was behind him clutching his assault rifle. The meaning was clear. "You are not planning to launch an unprovoked attack on this city? This is outrageous and illegal. You must not do it."

Admiral Jacks intercepted him. "Now hold on there,

Son. You and I both know we're here for the same thing, to take out those drug lords."

"Yes, but, Admiral, I have my orders. I must protest!"

"You protest all you like, Son, and I'll make sure our Lords and Masters get to hear of it." He looked across at Talley. "What're you waiting for, Lieutenant?"

Talley keyed the mic. "This is Bravo. Confirmed four targets are go. Fire at will."

"Four targets are go, understood."

The AGM-114 Hellfire was an air-to-surface missile developed for anti-armor use. These particular missiles were the AGM-114M Hellfire IIs, designed to hit bunkers, light vehicles and urban targets. A one hundred pound precision guided weapon, the Hellfire was a combat-proven tactical missile system.

As Raoul Castro raved and shouted, and Admiral Jacks worked to calm him, the four missiles burned into their targets. Talley and Nolan watched in real-time, the UAV images downlinked to the tactical electronic tablet display. It was quick, 'blink and you'll miss it' quick. Four roadblocks manned by heavily armed men, conscious of their unassailable power, posturing to deter anyone who might dare to venture near; then an almost invisible streak of movement, and the roadblocks erupted into smoke and flame. When the smoke cleared, they could see the remains, broken vehicle parts, bodies and a few survivors running away. Talley shouted at the Platoon.

"They're gone. Let's go pay the Salazars a visit." He turned to Castro. "Captain, we could use some transport." He waved at the vehicles parked nearby. Castro nodded.

"Sure, yes." He looked dazed and indecisive. Whatever

Jacks had threatened or promised him, it had done the job. "My superiors provided two of the trucks for your use. That should be sufficient for you and your men."

"Sure. And you, Captain? Aren't you coming with us with your men? I understood you were here to offer us support."

"I, I need to get further instructions from my commander. We will follow you shortly."

"Suit yourself. Men, let's go. Admiral, would you care to ride in the lead truck with me?"

"I wouldn't miss it for anything," Jacks smiled. No longer the deskbound senior officer, he looked ready for war in his dark Seal camouflage, half helmet, and lightweight body armor. Like the men, he carried an HK416 as if he knew how to use it. "Let's go."

They squeezed into two of the Colombian trucks. Each had a heavy machine gun mounted on the truck bed, and Dave Eisner manned the lead truck's gun with Brad Rose to act as crew, feeding the heavy belts of ammunition. Will Bryce took the rear, using Zeke Murray for his crew. Carl Winters and Dan Moseley took the wheel of the front and rear trucks respectively, and they roared out of the building and out onto the road that led into the city, and the Salazars' compound. In the cab of the rear vehicle, Nolan heard Talley's voice.

"Chief, we'll stop just past the roadblocks and make ready our assault. I'm thinking of using one of those five hundred pound Paveways to knock on the door. It's not exactly a stealth approach, but I don't think there's any chance of catching anyone unawares right now."

Nolan smiled to himself. It was good thinking.

"Copy that, Boss. I guess they'll hear the knock first

time round."

They reached one of the roadblocks, smoke and flames were still pouring out of the wreckage. Talley was already sending the coordinates of the next target to the control center, and while they watched and waited, the men went around checking for any threats in the vicinity of the roadblock. But there were none, and the only presence was dead bodies, lying in and around the wreckage. A massive explosion made them look to the front, but Talley shouted across. "That's the gate, let's go."

They scrambled back into the trucks and held on grimly as Winters and Moseley stamped on the gas, and they surged forwards. The compound was only a couple of hundred yards away, the main gate and surrounding machine gun bunkers a smoking ruin after the hit from the Paveway. The two trucks drove straight through and into a wide, open yard. There were a half a dozen vehicles parked in front of the main warehouse; a modern, well constructed building, like the headquarters operation of any normal business. At either end of the flat roof was a barricaded machine gun position, which immediately started pouring fire down onto them. It was wild and inaccurate, but when enough bullets are in the air, sooner or later they're going to hit something, or someone important. Except that in this case, Will Bryce and Dave Eisner were manning the M60s mounted on the trucks, and their shooting was anything but wild and inaccurate. Both Seals fired a continuous burst of heavy, 7.62-millimeter lead at the machine gun positions, which were mounted behind a flimsy screen of sheet metal. The bullets ripped through the screens and decimated the gunners and their crews. The gunfire stopped. Ahead of them was a roller shutter door, the entrance to the warehouse.

"Keep your foot on the gas and go straight though it," Talley ordered. "Hold tight, there's going to be a bump."

Carl Winters rammed his foot down on the gas, and the truck surged forward and smashed through the roller shutter almost as if it was paper. The torn metal was thrown to one side, and Carl brought the truck to a halt inside the building. A group of men with assault rifles gaped at them and started to raise their weapons to shoot, but Dave Eisner opened up on them with the M60. The other Seals joined in, and the Colombians went down under a hail of fire that was impossible to resist. The second truck drew alongside them only seconds later, and already the fight for the warehouse space was almost over.

"Fan out, check the building. We have to find the Salazars," Talley shouted.

The Seals jumped down and rushed through the doors that would lead to the office area. Nolan went right with half a dozen Seals in support. He kicked open a door and dodged aside as a pistol fired straight at him. The man behind wasn't so lucky, and he took a bullet in the chest, a hit to his flak vest. It would hurt like hell, but at least he was alive and still fighting. Nolan shot the man with a single round from his SWS, checked the rest of the room, and ran out to check the others. On the other side of the warehouse, in the adjacent office spaces and storerooms, he could hear the sound of firing. He led the men across to join the other group, Talley's, and was in time to hear the sound of an engine starting. A black Hummer raced across the open warehouse space. They scattered aside as the vehicle sped through the warehouse, almost running down to Seals who were slow to jump. The windows were blacked out, but there was no doubt that inside was at least one of their primary targets. Nolan's men started to squeeze the triggers to prevent the escape but stopped when Talley shouted across to them.

"Don't shoot! Leave the Hummer, leave it."

Nolan glared angrily at his Lieutenant. "What's the deal, Boss? There has to be at least one of the Salazars in there, maybe both of the brothers."

"You're probably right, Chief, but they had a prisoner with them, one of ours."

"Jesus Christ, who was it got taken?"

Talley looked downcast. "He separated from my group and went to check inside what he thought was a storeroom. It turned out to be a secret garage for the Hummer, some sort of last-ditch escape plan. They grabbed him and took off. They didn't even try to fight. It's as if they sacrificed their own men to distract our attention so they could escape."

"Yeah, I hear you, but who?"

"Admiral Jacks."

"Oh, fuck!"

CHAPTER SIX

They stood in the smoking ruins of the Salazar warehouse, surrounded by wreckage, broken-open wooden crates, burning sacks of cocaine and dead bodies. They took stock of the enormity of what they faced. The mission was a bust, despite the huge amount of grief and damage they'd caused to the Salazars' empire, because they'd missed the main players. The men all had a photo of the two brothers, and they'd quickly established that they weren't amongst the casualties. So wherever they'd gone, they had the freedom of their enormous resources in money and men to regroup and rebuild. And they had a senior US Navy admiral, Rear Admiral Drew Jacks. No, it wasn't a bust, Nolan realized. Talley echoed his thoughts.

"It's a disaster, a total, one hundred percent disaster. They'll crucify me for this one."

"It wasn't your fault, Lt. There's something fishy about this whole operation. We were supposed to have support from the Colombian Special Forces. Where they hell were they?"

"It won't make a scrap of difference. I'm the man leading the charge, and it'll be on my head."

"The fuck you say," Will Bryce snorted ominously. "We ain't finished yet. We haven't taken any casualties, and we've got an awesome heap of firepower and surveillance overhead." He grinned. "In fact, I'd say we're just getting started. What we need it to…"

He was interrupted by the sound of engines entering the compound. The unit of the Agrupación de Fuerzas Especiales Antiterroristas Urbanas had arrived. They traveled in the remaining two SUVs with mounted machine guns, one in the lead and the other bringing up the rear. In the center, the bulk of the men were loaded into two larger open backed trucks.

"Don't they just look so fucking warlike," Vince Merano commented sourly.

It was true. They bristled with assault rifles and machine guns. The two M60s on the SUVs were traversing from side to side, as if they were traveling though a warzone, which they would have been, ten minutes earlier. Castro jumped down with his scarfaced sergeant. He walked up to Talley, looking around wide-eyed at the damage.

"What exactly happened here, Lieutenant?"

Talley waited long enough to make a point before he replied.

"We did our job, Captain. The job you were ordered to do."

Castro sighed. "We were not ordered to attack the Salazars. I told you that."

"Why not? What's so special about the Salazars that you wouldn't attack them?"

Castro looked uncomfortable. "I don't know what you

mean."

"Dammit, you know exactly what I mean. Our orders were to interdict the narco trafficking industry here in Medellin, and that included the Salazars. So why were you so worried about helping us out?"

Castro looked nervously at the Sergeant. "It is not that simple," he said softly to Talley. "There are politics involved. You do not live here, so you cannot know."

Talley had both seen the look. "Captain, I'd like a word with you, just you. Would you come over to this office where we can talk without being overheard. Chief, I want you there too."

The Sergeant looked angry. "This is wrong. You cannot order my Captain to..."

"It is okay," Castro said to him. "I will speak to them and see what they have to say."

They walked into the empty office. Castro grimaced at the pool of blood that lay on the floor.

"What is it, Lieutenant Talley? What do you need to talk to me about that you cannot say in front of my men?"

"You know what it is, Castro. The Salazars had protection. They must have known we were coming, and they sacrificed their men to make their escape. If they thought they were fighting local cops or army, they'd have stayed to fight it out. So tell me, what's going on?"

The Captain sighed. "It is difficult to talk of these things. All I can say is that yes, the Salazars do have protection in high places. We were ordered to stay clear of their operation. My sergeant, Vidal, he is not my regular man. He was assigned to me to look after the interests of the Salazars by the Colombian Ministry of Defense. That is how high their protection goes. If I attack the Salazars, and he reports it back to the Ministry, I will be dismissed. It is possible that I could be killed, along with members of my family." He had a sudden thought. "Why is the Admiral not here listening to this? Where is he?"

"Taken, by your friends the Salazars," Nolan replied.

"My, God, an American admiral, how could that be?"

"Because the fucking Colombian Special Forces that were supposed to watch our backs were all on the take," Nolan hammered back at him.

"So you want them to kill my family?" Castro flared at him. "Is that the price you would pay to fight these people, to have your family killed? Would you want to see your wife and son gunned down in cold blood?"

Nolan lost it. He stepped lightly forward and swung, connected with the Captain's chin, and saw him go down to the floor.

"You don't know a thing, Motherfucker!"

Talley grabbed his arm and pulled him off, helping Castro to his feet. "It's not what you think," he reassured the man. "Are you okay?"

"Your man hit me. I could have him shot!"

"Yeah, a lot of people have tried to shoot Chief Nolan, but he's still standing, and they're pushing up daisies. You couldn't have known, but his wife was shot by drug traffickers."

Castro rubbed his chin. "I wish you'd told me that before. He hits hard."

"Yeah, he does. You're not going to hold this against him, Captain?"

Castro looked weary. "No. As I said, I wish I'd known before. These bastards, these drug traffickers, they threaten every decent thing we stand for. What are you going to do about your Admiral Jacks?"

"We're going to get him back and finish the job, my friend. That's what we do."

They sat down on the office chairs. "We really need your help, your local knowledge," Talley continued. "We have to know where they may have taken him."

"None of this must get out to my sergeant," he said. "What I told you is true. They will kill my wife and son if the Salazars find out I have helped the Gringos."

"Surely the government can offer protection?" Talley asked him.

Castro smiled bitterly. "Protection? It is too late. When they found out who was to lead this operation to aid the Americans against the Medellin traffickers, the Salazars kidnapped my wife and son. They are holding them in a hideout known only to a few of their people. It is in a small town outside the city, Copacabana. If I go with you, or am seen to help you in any way, they will kill them."

Talley nodded. "I'd like to help you, Raoul, but I have mission priorities. Where would the Salazars be, and where would they hold Admiral Jacks?"

The Captain nodded. "Yes, you must do your duty, I understand, and my commiserations for your wife, Mr. Nolan."

"It's Chief Nolan, Captain." Castro nodded his understanding. "And thanks. Maybe we can help each other. Where would these traffickers hold the Admiral? Assuming he isn't dead," Nolan replied.

"No, he will not be dead," Castro said quickly. "Someone of that rank will be very valuable to them as a hostage. But I doubt he will be at Copacabana. They have a processing laboratory out in the jungle. It is very remote, and you understand that this is only their storage and distribution facility. The laboratory is the most likely location. When we were on our way in here, we heard a helicopter take off nearby. We watched it head to the west, away from Copacabana, and in the direction of their jungle laboratory."

"Could you lead us there?" Talley asked him, staring at him intently.

But Castro shook his head. "Not while my wife and son are being held, no. I am sorry, but it is too much to risk."

They heard the sound of renewed firing outside, and Will Bryce ran in.

"We just came under attack. The men are setting up a defensive perimeter, Boss. We need to decide how we're going to play this. Do we fight them here, or move out and hit them somewhere else?"

"Maintain the perimeter. Chief, you'd better get out there and set up a sniper stand with Vince." Nolan nodded and ran out. "Captain Castro, are you on our side with this one?"

The Colombian nodded reluctantly. "We will have to deal with this attack, or none of us will come out alive. In any case, these traffickers are like vultures, so it is probably one of the other families. If they think the Salazars have run, they'll be trying to make a play for their stock of cocaine. Yes, we'll fight, but afterwards, I cannot help you against the Salazars."

"Until your family is safe?"

"Until they are safe, yes."

"Then we'll see what we can do. But for now, let's go knock down some of these narcos."

They ran into the main warehouse that had emptied of

almost all of the men. The Seals had deployed their trucks outside the building to act as defensive machine gun posts. Castro noticed that his two trucks were stationary with their crews sheltering behind them from any incoming gunfire. He ran over to them.

"You, get these vehicles moving. Get out there and start shooting!"

One of the men was Sergeant Vidal. "But Captain, the Salazars…"

"It is not the Salazars," Castro snapped. "It will be one of the other families trying to steal their product. I don't care who it is, just get out there and stop them."

"Yes, Sir!"

The Sergeant started barking orders, and the trucks started up and drove outside, the gunners already swinging their machine guns into position and ready to fire. Seconds later, they were in action, and all four SUV mounted M60s were firing at the attackers.

"Boss, up here!" Talley looked up to see Brad Rose at the foot of an iron staircase. "We've set up a command post on the roof. There's a good observation point up there."

Talley ran up the stairs, through a narrow doorway, and out onto the flat roof. He immediately dropped to the floor as bullets whined overhead, but there was a low wall of about eighteen inches high that would protect a man, as long as he didn't stand. He crawled across to a sandbagged position the traffickers had prepared in the center of the roof where there was a good view of any attack to the front of the building. Brad followed him inside.

"What's happening?" the Lieutenant asked Will Bryce who was in command.

"I detailed some of the men to take over the SUVs and M60s. Chief Nolan and Vince Merano are at opposite ends of the building, and they've established a sniper stand apiece. Zeke Murray is at the back of the roof, making sure they don't make an approach from that way, but so far they're coming in from the front."

Talley nodded and peered over the side. The scene was one of utter chaos. The Seals' two SUVs were busily firing their M60s at a determined group of attackers who'd arrived in a series of heavy trucks and slewed them across the road. They made a barricade to protect their men and stop what they thought were the survivors from the attack on the Salazars' warehouse removing their stocks of hoarded cocaine. Castro's men were firing back, and a hail of bullets buzzed and whined through the air from both sides, turning the whole area into a hurricane of death. At either end of the roof, Nolan and Merano fired accurate, single shots. They took a higher toll of the enemy than all of Castro's massed fire from his men's assault rifles. While he watched, man after man cried and went down as the 7.62-millimeter bullets struck their bodies and killed them.

"Any estimate on numbers?" Talley asked over his shoulder.

"I reckon there's a hundred of them out there, or there was before we started shooting. Now, I'd guess we've whittled them down to about sixty."

"That's still a lot of firepower," Talley muttered, as much to himself as to Will. "That Reaper up there had a Paveway five hundred pound bomb left on the racks, as I recall. I'm calling it in. Tell Captain Castro to pull his men back inside. There'll be a hell of a blast when it arrives."

"Copy that."

Will crawled off to speak to the Colombians while Talley booted his tactical pad and zeroed in on the scene in front of him. It was strange looking down on the scene of carnage. He could see the attackers blazing away; they were all civilians, wearing colorful shirts. They gestured and shouted, and he could even see their lips move. He centered the cursor on the barricade and called Creech on the satcom.

"Go ahead, Bravo."

"I have a fire mission for your remaining Paveway, Creech, sending you the coordinates now."

"We copy that, Bravo. Confirm your clearance to launch the bomb."

"That's confirmed Creech. Affirmative, go for it."

"On the way."

Talley saw Castro's men falling back in small groups, each covering the other. The two SUVs overtook them and rolled inside the warehouse. He looked around and checked. It was too late anyway, but as far as he could tell, the good guys were under one sort of cover or another. The attackers, realizing that the defenders had pulled back, made the fatal error of assuming that they were winning. They scrambled to their feet and bunched up ready to make a final attack on the warehouse; just as the Paveway struck, and their world was blasted to small pieces almost in the blink of an eye. The Seals closed their eyes to prevent temporary blindness from the explosion. Forewarned, they'd tracked the missile exhaust just before it hit. When they heard the roar, they waited a couple of seconds and opened their lids to survey the effect of the five hundred pound Paveway. Where the barricade had been was just a twisted junkyard of scrap metal, mixed with bloody, broken bodies of the dead. By the mysterious physics of blast radii, half a dozen of the Colombians had survived and were staggering around like zombies in some ghastly post-apocalyptic scenario. But they differed from the TV and film image of zombies as most still carried assault rifles, and therefore were possibly able to recover their wits.

"Finish 'em," Talley shouted into his mic. "Don't leave any of them alive. If they start blazing away with those assault rifles, we'll have it all to do again. Besides, we don't want them calling for reinforcements."

The Seals needed no further encouragement. Merano and Nolan started their deadly killing rhythm, and almost before the others could pull the trigger, four of the survivors were down. The rest were quickly dispatched. The Colombian Special Forces hadn't even opened fire.

Talley climbed to his feet. "Regroup down in the warehouse, men. We'll be leaving soon. Brad, there's no need to watch the back. I think we got them all."

"Copy that."

They ran down the iron staircase and onto the warehouse floor. Talley spoke quietly to Nolan and then called his platoon around him to listen to the next phase of the operation. The Colombian Special Forces watched from the sidelines.

"The next phase of the operation is to go after the next narco trafficking gangs, the Olveras or the Barreras. We'll be pulling out in a few minutes, just as soon as I call in our mission progress."

"Boss, what about this warehouse," Nolan shouted on cue. "If we leave it empty, they'll come back for the coke."

Talley nodded. "Yeah, you're right. Captain Castro, we

need you and your men for the next part of our operation. Taking on two families, the Olveras and the Barreras, will be too much for our platoon. Could you accompany us and leave a small guard force here. Say, a sergeant and three men?"

Castro looked mystified. "You think that's necessary? We have a lot of work still to do."

"I do think it's necessary, yes. It'll need someone you can rely on. Sergeant Vidal looks a good man."

The Sergeant nodded his scarred face enthusiastically. "Sure, I can do that, Captain. It is important that we guard the Salazars' cocaine."

He gave Castro a meaningful look; a look that said 'your family will be endangered if anything happens to it'. The Captain nodded his agreement.

"Very well, Vidal. Take three men you can trust and set up a perimeter. No one is to come in here, no one. Is that clear?"

Vidal smiled. "Of course, Captain. I will see that the cocaine is looked after."

Castro looked at Talley. "In that case, my men are at your disposal."

"Good." Talley looked around. "I'll call in while we're on the way. Let's go. Captain, you can ride with me."

They started heading out of town to the west. Castro turned to the driver, Carl Winters. "No, no, this is the wrong way. Their operations are centered to the north and north east of the town."

"We're not going to attack the other two families, Raoul," Talley said quietly.

"No? But where are we going?"

"To Copacabana, and we're going to get your family

out."

The Colombian started abruptly, swiveling around to stare at him. "You are not serious? You'll get them all killed."

"No, Raoul, we won't. If they stay with the traffickers, they're likely to get killed. We're going to get them away."

"But, what you say is impossible. They are in a part of town that is entirely under the control of the traffickers. If we even go near, they'll kill them."

Talley noted the 'we'. It was promising. "In that case, we'd better make sure they don't see us going near."

Castro scowled, but made no reply, and the truck coasted along the road between Medellin and Copacabana in silence. But Talley could see the Colombian Captain was unhappy, and finally Raoul turned to look at him.

"Lieutenant Talley, you know nothing of the drugs trade in Colombia, do you?"

The Lieutenant thought about that. "I've taken in a lot of intel about the drug infrastructure, so I guess I'd know a fair bit," he objected.

Raoul shook his head. "But when your work is done, you can go home. Do you have your home town ringed with hundreds of men paid by criminals, and carrying AK-47 assault rifles?"

"No, I'd have to say that San Diego isn't like that," he grinned. "We get the odd problem, mostly Saturday night specials, and the odd crazy with a semi-auto."

"No, I guessed that was the case. Let me tell you about life in Colombia, my friend."

As Carl kept the wheels turning, Castro gave Talley and him a quick lowdown on life in the world capital of the cocaine trade.

"Many of our problems exist because of the Central American countries. You know of course that the US is the biggest customer for Colombian cocaine?"

"Yeah, but what's that got to do with Central America?"

"Wait, I will explain. During the Cold War between America and the Soviet Union, Russia shipped tens of thousands, maybe hundreds of thousands of weapons to Central America, in the hopes of supporting a communist revolution. As a result, there are warehouses in those countries stacked with brand new, unused weapons. Machine guns, pistols, assault rifles, RPGs, and grenades, the list is endless. Take Honduras, it lies directly on the route between Colombia and the US. They have enormous stocks of the AK-47, and the exchange rate for these guns is between three and eight kilos of cocaine."

"For each gun?"

Talley was astonished. It sounded like a lot of coke.

"For each gun, yes, and for an assault rifle worth maybe five hundred dollars, they exchange twenty thousand dollars of cocaine. Why not? Cocaine is plentiful, and there is no risk. It means that the cartels are equipped with massive amounts of heavy weaponry, often far more than our own military. It is the same in Mexico, is it not? The traffickers are heavily armed?"

Talley thought about Ciudad Juarez on the Texas border, the murder capital of Mexico and therefore continental America. He nodded.

"Yeah, I guess it is."

"Yes. The town I live in, Bello lies between Copacabana and Medelli My family has a bungalow in the military barracks, so they are safe when they are at home. But they have to go out, to school, shopping, visiting friends and

117

family. When they do, they are at risk."

"Is that when they took them?"

"Yes, my wife was taking our son home from school when they were taken, and even now the town is patrolled by soldiers of the narco traffickers. Our own troops are unable to go where they wish inside the town for fear of being shot by the gangs. You have to understand that when you go home, I still have to live here. They will come for me again, no matter what happens to the Salazars."

"Raoul, listen." Talley stared intently at the Colombian. "I can't solve all of your problems. If it's as bad as you say, you'll need to consider witness protection or something like that. It must exist in this country."

Castro nodded. "Yes, it exists, as a last resort."

"It's better than dying, buddy. And it's also better than living the life of a frightened man under the cosh of the arrogant scum who threaten you. Is that what you want for your son, an existence as a terrified slave of these people?"

For several minutes Castro didn't answer as he thought about what Talley had said. Then he leaned across to Carl Winters. "Take the next turning on the left, Senor. I will direct you from there."

Carl glanced at him. "We just passed a sign that says Copacabana is to the right. What gives?"

"If we are to do this job properly, these vehicles will not be enough. There is a man in my town, Bello, who has something that may help us."

"In what way?" Talley asked him.

"Wait and see, Lieutenant. Believe me, this is important."

Carl looked at Talley for instructions.

"It's okay, Carl. Go where he says, and let's see what

this is all about."

They drove along the crowded, dirty streets of Bello. It was early in the day and few people were around. Outside a crumbling apartment block, a man looked up and stared at their convoy. He didn't carry an AK-47, but they clearly saw the large automatic pistol tucked into his waistband. He took a cellphone out of his pocket and made a call.

"They know we are here," Castro said to the men in the cab. "Now we have to get off the streets as quickly as we can. The presence of so many armed men in the town will alert them that something is happening. Fortunately, we are nearly there. Senor," he turned to Carl. "Take the next turning on the right, yes, yes, that's it. Now drive through that arch."

They stopped inside a large, enclosed courtyard with room enough for their vehicles. Castro jumped down from the truck and shouted for his men to close the gates. They ran to obey him just as a man in greasy mechanic's overalls came out of a workshop just off the courtyard. He was short, muscular, very dark, and with crew cut dark hair and a flashing smile. He walked up to Castro, smiling.

"Raoul, my friend. What's all this? Are you planning on starting a war?"

"It's already begun, Jorge."

The man nodded solemnly. "Yes, we all heard the gunfire and explosions from Medellin. What's it all about?"

Castro explained the problem, the presence of the American Navy Seals, and his family held by the soldiers of the Salazar cartel in Copacabana. Jorge nodded, taking it all in. Nolan came up with Talley to listen, and Castro introduced them.

"Jorge, this is Lieutenant Talley and Chief Nolan.

Gentlemen, Jorge Montenegro."

They shook hands, and Castro explained why they were there. What astonished the Americans was the matter of fact way they discussed the local affairs. Talk of murders, kidnappings, and the huge, private armies of the traffickers was so matter of fact. Jorge nodded as the story came to an end.

"So you're going to get your family back? And then what, a new identity?"

"It is the only way, Jorge. These people cannot be allowed to win."

"It is a terrible way, for you to have to go permanently into hiding."

"It's the only way to fight them. Otherwise, they will win. Is that we want?"

"No, I guess not. But you will make sure that Juanita is safe? And Jaime."

Talley had been listening. "Is that your wife and son, Juanita and Jaime?"

"Yes, that is correct," Castro replied. "Jorge here, he is Juanita's brother. He is my brother-in-law."

"Right, so how can he help us?"

The Captain looked at Jorge. "Do you still have that vehicle?"

"The one I salvaged from the Army when they were forced out after that firefight?"

"Salvaged? That's one way of putting it."

Jorge smiled. "Whatever. Yes, I have it. You think it could be useful?"

"Yes. May I borrow it?"

He grinned even wider. "I guess it belonged to your army in the first place, so how can I refuse? I've repaired it, and it's all running well."

"What vehicle is this?" Talley enquired, curious.

"Show the Americans what you have, Jorge."

The greasy little man led them over to a pair of double doors that led off the courtyard. They were locked with a huge, high security padlock and chain. He unlocked the padlock and dragged open the doors. They stood looking dumbfounded at the vehicle that was inside.

The BTR-70 was an eight-wheeled armored personnel carrier developed during the 1960s. Powered by two V8 gas engines, the vehicles were exported all over the world by a Soviet Union desperate to help revolutionary regimes succeed. The vehicle was heavily armor plated, fully amphibious, and capable of carrying ten men over any surface, land or water. It was also served by a heavy machine gun, the KPV 14.5 millimeter. In addition, it mounted a coaxial 7.62 light machine gun. With a top speed of almost fifty mph over land, and five mph over water, it was a go anywhere fighting vehicle capable of inflicting a great deal of damage whilst offering the men inside the maximum protection from external threats.

"What the hell is this?"Nolan asked. "Surely it's not still functional?"

Jorge grinned. "I have kept it in working order. When the Colombian Army abandoned it, one of the engines didn't function properly, and there was a leak in the hull. They tried crossing a river, and when it started to sink, left it abandoned in the shallows. I towed it out and brought it here. It's one hundred percent ready to go. If you need it to get Juanita and Jaime back, it's yours."

Talley nodded at Nolan. "Check it out, Chief. I'll start preparing a plan for the assault, along with Raoul. We're going to need as much local knowledge as we can get for this one. I'll assign Carl to help look it over. He knows more than any of us about mechanical and electrical systems."

Nolan nodded and climbed through the access door into the iron monster. Carl followed him. Inside, they were in the dark womb of the cold war relic, steel green paint and the unmistakable firing handles of the 14.5 mm machine gun. The interior of the hull was painted in a dull gray, and it all looked like something of a throwback to a bygone age, which in effect it was, despite it having been restored to full fighting condition. The gunner position was inside the turret where he could direct fire from both machine guns. There was a driver's position, a commander's seat, and several dark gray vinyl seats for the soldiers who fought from the vehicle. It was dark, almost claustrophobic, and forbidding.

"Like something out of a science fiction film," Carl shuddered. "Boy, I'd hate to have to spend much time in one of these. And that hatch, bailing out on the move could put you under the wheels."

He started the engines. They rumbled into life with a mighty roar and throbbed with a deep, menacing note as he reduced the revs to tick over.

"It all seems okay, but I'd like to know how it'll run when it goes out on the road."

Talley popped his head through the hatch. "That'll have to wait, Carl. We've put together the makings of a plan to get these hostages out, but we can't show this vehicle until it's in motion. It's our ace in the hole. I want both of you out here, and we'll go through the way we're going to play this."

Outside in the courtyard, the men were lounging in a circle, gulping down iced water brought out in pitchers by a very pretty Latino girl. She struck a chord with Nolan that puzzled him for a few moments. Then he realized why it was. She reminded him of Detective Carol Summers, and therefore of his deceased wife, Grace. Slim and pretty, dark hair, dark skin, perhaps a little darker than the San Diego detective, but she was built just the same, short; what most folks would describe as petite. And she had that same demeanor, serious, yet he could see she was the kind of person who had a boundless appetite for life, for having fun; for doing things and going places. Like Carol Summers, and Grace. She came over to him and fixed him with a pretty smile.

"Iced water, Senor?"

Raoul Castro came up to them. "This is Gracia Montez. She is one of my relations. Gracia, this is Chief Nolan."

He nodded a greeting. "The name is Kyle, Ma'am."

She grinned. "And I'm Gracia, not Ma'am. It makes me sound so old. Gracia, is like Grace in English, yes?"

He worked hard to keep his emotions under control. "Yes, it is the same."

She gave him a tumbler of iced water. It was flavored with a slice of fresh lemon and tasted delicious. He mumbled his thanks, and she smiled again.

"Anytime, Chief Nolan."

"It's Kyle."

"Yes, I know. But I prefer Chief, especially as we are to work together. It makes me feel more like one of your men."

"Say that again?"

But she smiled and went away to dispense more cool

drinks. He heard Talley calling him over and walked to the group of Seals and Colombian Special Forces.

"We're planning to make the assault and hostage rescue tonight, undercover of dark, men. The first part of the plan is that no one leaves this compound for any reason until we pull out. There are too many prying eyes in this area. Clear?"

They all nodded. A couple of Colombians looked unhappy. Did they want to find a bar, maybe a hooker, or something else, perhaps? The traffickers had too many friends in the military and the police as a result of their massive profits.

"For the same reason, operational security, no one is to use their cell phones."

Now there was a very audible groan.

"No, it is essential for our security. We have no way of knowing whether the cartels can listen in to our cell phone conversations. We will spend the day preparing our weapons and equipment. During the evening, we'll drift into Copacabana. The Colombians are already in civilian clothes, so Jorge will arrange for us Seals to have some civilian clothes to change into. We will infiltrate the town in small groups, twos, fours, and several men on the local bus service. Weapons and equipment will be carried in bags, suitcases, or hidden inside your clothes. The building where the hostages are being held is here, on the outside of the town."

Castro rapidly drew a map in the dirt of the courtyard. He looked up at the men.

"The main road into town is here. Bello is here. And on the outskirts of the town, this is the house they are being held in."

Talley nodded. "We'll go over it in more detail later, but that's the rough outline. Chief, you won't be going in with the main assault. Nor will you, Carl. The operation should go well, up until we assault the building. At that point, the shit will hit the fan. Almost every inhabitant in Copacabana can be considered sympathetic to the traffickers, either willingly or by force. The second they know something is up; they'll flood the place with their people. And they're well armed, as we know. That's where you two come in. You are to wait here with the BTR-70 and come a-running when we call. It'll be your job to get us out of there, that's the hard part. We reckon that an armored vehicle mounting a heavy machine gun will make all the difference. Any questions?"

Carl stepped forward. "That BTR, Lt. It's designed for a crew of three. Have you got anyone in mind to come with me and the Chief?"

"Yes, good point, Carl. Gracia has volunteered to go with you in the APC. She knows the country well, and she's no stranger to action."

The Seals swiveled to look at the girl.

"What kinda action, Boss?"

"She was an officer in the military, Carl."

"Which military?"

"The FARC."

CHAPTER SEVEN

It was early evening, and the light was fading. Nolan, Carl and Gracia had spent the past hours checking and rechecking the mechanical workings of the Soviet APC. They came to the gun, the big, heavy 14.5-millimeter KPV. It was mounted in a narrow turret, which allowed the gunner enough room to poke his head inside and use a variety of day and night vision devices to locate targets and shoot the gun. Aligned to the same firing mechanisms was the 7.62-millimeter PK machine gun, with the ammunition fed through a belt into the breach.

"If you wish, I will handle the machine guns," Gracia said quietly. "I have had experience with both weapons. If there is a problem, it will be best for me to deal with it."

"You used both these types in the FARC?" Nolan asked, interested. "The KPV seems heavy for a guerrilla unit."

"We were equipped with a wide range of weaponry, including heavy machine guns. We used them mainly for anti-aircraft operations. The Colombian Air Force made frequent raids on our camps. Our KPVs were linked in a quadruple mount, and they were very effective."

Carl winced. "I'll bet the fuck they were."

"But we also had missiles, Strela 3 man-portable systems. I brought down three aircraft with those."

"Yeah, I'll remember to stay on your good side," Carl grimaced. "Hold tight, I'm going to run up the engines and just try running her around the courtyard. We don't want to wait until they need us to find it doesn't steer properly."

He sat in the cramped driver's position and fired up both the V8 engines. Gracia wormed inside the turret. There was a small seat that she could perch on and peer through the gunsights that surrounded the firing position. Nolan took the commander's seat next to the driver. The deafening roar of the V8s quieted as they warmed up, and Carl reduced them to idling. Then he used the complicated gearing and clutch mechanisms to get the vehicle rolling. They maneuvered around the courtyard until Carl pronounced himself satisfied.

"She'll get us to Copacabana and back, but Jesus this is one helluva pig to drive."

"It's a pig to ride in," Nolan agreed. "I'd imagine the troops would be permanently sick riding in this thing over a battlefield." He looked around as Gracia descended from the turret. "How did you get on with the firing position? Any problems?"

She shook her head. "Nothing I can't handle. I was able to check the night vision devices. It is just about dark enough. They all work as they should. If we get into a battle, I will need you to help me with loading the belts onto the machine guns."

"Yeah, I can do that. You'd better show me how it all works."

"Here, climb up next to the breach of the main gun."

He climbed up and was aware of the closeness of her, the earthy, raw scent of a fit, athletic young woman. A spicy tang, mixed with herbs, perspiration, and God alone knew what else. The end result was he found himself becoming aroused, and he had to control his breathing and his emotions to concentrate. Gracia showed him the ammunition lockers, the way the belts fitted into both guns, and how to join them together and clear a jam if one occurred. Finally, he couldn't take any more.

"I think I've got it, but I need to go outside. The air is stuffy inside this thing."

"Sure, I'll come too," she said cheerily. He groaned inside. It was the very distraction he could have done without. Yet he was male enough that he couldn't argue.

"I'll get something cold to drink. That'll make you feel cooler," she grinned. There was a sparkle in her eyes, and he realized this incredible girl knew exactly what kind of powerful effect she was having on him. The last thing he needed.

"You want a beer, Chief Nolan?"

"That'd be fine."

She came back with three bottles of beer, and chill condensation had formed droplets on the glass. They called for Carl to come out, and the three of them sat enjoying the coolness of the beer and the night chill that was beginning to set in. They looked up as Talley came over to them.

"The men are all ready. Jorge found enough civilian kit for them to change into."

"What about us?" Nolan asked. "You want us to change?"

Talley grinned. "They see you coming in that thing, and it'll take more than a flowery shirt to convince them you're not military. No, you may as well keep your kit on. Besides, the flak vest may be useful if a firefight develops, and that's likely to happen. Stay inside of here until you hear us call on the commo net. Then come like a bat out of hell. You're designated Bravo Four. Vince is Bravo Two." The unit sniper, of course, and he'd be busy this night. "And we patched the Colombians through to the same net, designated Bravo Three."

"I've got it. We'll be there."

He nodded to Gracia and walked back to the men. The Colombians had already started slipping out in small groups through a narrow side gate.

They sat around waiting. Jorge joined them and fiddled with an adjustment on the idling of one of the V8 engines so that they were perfect, or so he said. Nolan couldn't hear any difference and supposed it was just nerves. From time to time, he heard his comrades on the commo, whispered orders, and reports.

"Bravo Two, this is Bravo One, watch that building on your right. We just saw a possible sniper looking out the window."

"Roger that, One, I'll take him out now." It was Vince Merano's voice.

"Copy that, Two. Keep it quiet. They don't know we're here yet."

A patch of silence, and they looked at each other and then around the courtyard. They were sat on top of the hull, ready to go into action at a moment's notice, but at least it was cooler. Inside the BTR it was like a furnace. Another burst of static.

"Bravo three, this is One. Is your perimeter ready? Make sure no one comes in or out, Raoul."

"This is Three. Perimeter is ready, and we have the place buttoned up tight."

"Copy that."

"All units, this is One. We're going in."

Then all they could do was wait. The Seals, with their night vision and sound suppressed weapons, had a chance of killing the guards and spiriting away Castro's family before the Salazar soldiers even knew they were there. Nolan fervently hoped it would go down that way. If not, well, a pitched battle with well-armed narco traffickers with nothing to lose could be very, very bloody, and there were a lot of civilians in this equation. It wasn't to be. Even at a distance of several miles, sound carries a long way at night. They heard the distinctive sound of an assault rifle puncturing the still night with its staccato sound. Someone had emptied a full clip, one of the Salazars. So the battle had started.

"Bravo Four, this is One."

Nolan keyed the mic. "This is Four."

"Come and get us, Chief. We're inside a factory compound in the street behind the market. Raoul's men are defending the gate. It's the only place of its type, and we have gunfire all around us, so you shouldn't have any problems finding us."

"Copy that, One. We're on our way."

He was about to shout, 'go!' to Carl Winters, but Carl had listened to the call, and the two big V8s were already revving hard. Then he slammed down on the gas and Nolan and Gracia had to stop themselves from being thrown against the steel hull. The APC arrowed straight for the gates, but Jorge was ready, and they were already opening. The armored behemoth surged out onto the streets of Bello, and Gracia started shouting directions, picking up her bearings from the sights inside the turret.

"Left, next left. No, not that one, I meant right."

The eight-wheeler heeled over hard and took out part of a storefront as it lifted up on the suspension, Carl grimly steering it in the new direction. He flicked a glance over at Nolan, who grinned.

Women! Did any of them know their right from their left?

"Keep along this road. It's about four miles, then take the right fork."

"You sure this time, Ma'am," Carl shouted up at her over the roaring of the motors.

"Yes I am fucking sure, soldier. I made a slight mistake back there, that's all."

"Yeah, let's hope that store owner sees it like that. Right fork it is."

They hammered along through the night. Twice they met oncoming vehicles in the road; big, old American trucks, with the local lowlifes high on Tequila and cocaine, returning with their dates for a fumble on the back seat. Both Colombian drivers saw their lights and tried to play chicken, until they saw what was bearing down on them. Both times, the trucks wound up pushed into the long ditch that ran along the side of the tarmac.

"It's a local game," Gracia explained. "They like to show how macho they are to their girlfriends."

"Not this time they didn't," Carl said happily.

Talley's voice came over the commo. "Bravo One for Four, how close are you, Chief?"

He shouted so the girl could hear. "What's our ETA, Gracia?"

"Five minutes, no more."

He relayed it on to Talley.

"We can hold out for that long, Chief, but we're in a heavy firefight here. We grabbed the woman and the boy, and then the Salazars' soldiers came pouring out of the woodwork. We're facing upwards of two hundred of them here, and they're heavily armed."

"What about a Reaper strike, Boss? That'd do the trick."

"It would, yes. But we're in the middle of a civilian area, lots of private housing and apartment blocks. The bastards are very clever, and they've set the place up to be almost impregnable, without killing a pile of civilians. The last thing they want back in Washington is an international incident. Besides, killing civilians is not on my agenda. You'll need to take them down strongpoint by strongpoint. When you get here, you can lead us out and we'll follow. I reckon that heavy machine gun will keep their heads down for a time."

"Copy that, we're making full speed."

"Acknowledged, they'll open the gates when they see you coming. And keep it buttoned up, the place is like a hornets' nest since they found out we were here, and they started shooting."

"Copy that."

They were driving into the main street of Copacabana now, and already shots were 'pinging' off the hull. Gracia's voice came down from the turret.

"I see snipers' positions, Chief Nolan. What do you want me to do?"

"Take 'em out, Gracia."

Scarcely had he shouted the reply than the inside of the BTR-70 echoed to the cacophony of the two machine guns, the 14.5 mm main gun and the co-axial 7.62. He peered through the commander's periscope and adjusted it to see the area they'd just past. Their gunfire was devastating, taking great chips and lumps of brick and rock out of the front of the houses that were sniper positions on the street. The fire on their steel hull slackened as they raced along. Gracia alternated between shouting orders and firing the turret mounted machine guns.

"Left, yes, here, Carl. It's a tight turn, yes. Oh, you just knocked down half the front of their house. The guy that lives there is a Salazar soldier, so I wouldn't worry."

"I won't," was Carl's laconic reply as he wrestled with the controls.

"The street you need is a third of a mile along this road. Wait!"

The din of the machine guns assaulted their eardrums as the hull became like the inside of a boiler being hammered by a score of blacksmiths. This time they heard screams as the hail of lead smashed into the defenders.

"As I was saying, about a third of a mile, take a right turn just before the used car lot. It's coming up now. That's it, yes, right here. Oh, Paco will be unhappy. You just took away the front of his special offer of the month."

"He'll find another."

Carl swerved to the right, and in front of them, they could plainly see the factory compound where Talley and the rest of the troops were holed up with Castro's family. The place was under siege, and gun flashes could be plainly seen coming from firing positions all around the high brick wall guarding the building.

"Take it slow," Nolan ordered. "We need to weaken their forces as much as possible, so the more we kill now, the easier it'll be to get out. Gracia, take out as many of the attackers as you see."

"Chief Nolan, I need you to load. The last belt just went through the gun."

"Okay, I'll be right there. Carl, stop here. We need to knock out a few of these gunners before we drive the last few yards."

He ripped of his night vision goggles and climbed out of his seat, conscious that the guns had ceased firing, and the incoming fire had intensified. Up in the turret, there was barely room for one, let alone two. They were close to each other, very close, and kept bumping heads as Nolan worked rapidly to change the belts, linking the new one to the empty belts so that the guns would fire again. Bullets kept clanging against the turret, only inches from his head, and he thanked his stars for the Soviet built armor, almost half an inch thick, that protected them. In the dim light of the turret, he could see the warlike gleam in her eyes, and the brilliant white of her teeth as she pulled her lips back in a half snarl. And the smell of her now, it was so overpowering. She'd been sweating in the enclosed heat of the BTR-70 and the fierce battle she'd been waging against the Salazar soldiers. The thick, deep scent of musk, combined with a spicy, floral odor, perhaps her perfume, to make a heady mixture. He was almost done when both their heads turned at the same time to face each other. It had never occurred to him that his male scent might be having the same effect on her, yet she was clearly as aroused as he was. They leaned slightly forward, their lips just about touched, the faintest brush.

"Later," she said hoarsely.

"Yes, later," he replied, just as hoarsely. Then she was firing again, and he squirmed out of the turret, donned his night vision goggles, and sat back in the commander's seat.

"Okay, Carl, take it slow, and ease her into the factory yard."

Carl nodded and engaged the gears. The huge V8 engines throbbed, and the ungainly vehicle lurched forward again. Nolan keyed the commo.

"Bravo One, this is Four, we're right outside."

"We see you, Bravo Four. Opening the gates now."

The double gates slowly swung open, and Carl drove through into a scene of indescribable carnage.

Nolan climbed up through the hatch and onto the hull. Talley ran across to him. Sniper fire was still coming into the compound, and both men ducked behind the hull. As they leaned forward to talk, they heard Gracia using the turret gun to take on the snipers.

"Thank Christ for the APC," Talley said. "We got in here without any of them knowing we'd arrived, but there were literally hundreds of them. The moment one stumbled into us, he shouted the alarm, and this firefight started."

"Are the hostages safe?"

"Yeah, as I said, we got them out okay, and they're inside the factory building. Raoul is with them."

Nolan looked around the factory yard. There were dozens of bodies lying on the ground.

"He should be out here, directing his men."

Talley just shrugged. "The ones on the ground are not ours. The whole platoon came through without a scratch.

Half of them are Salazar's people, and the rest are Castro's Colombians."

"Yeah, without him, the rest will be demoralized. Can you get him out here, Boss?"

Talley nodded. "Sure, I'll go get him, then form up the convoy to go out. You'll be leading us with the APC. The machine gun trucks can go at the back and in the center. The rest will be strung out in between."

Nolan nodded. "It's a plan. They'll be keeping their heads down after the hosing that Gracia's giving them. We can wrap this up and go to the next stage of the operation."

Talley looked back at him, his face grim. "There's another complication. Raoul interrogated a couple of Salazar's people. Jacks is running out of time."

"How long has he got? What're they planning?"

"We'll talk when we get back, but it's not looking good. I'll round 'em up, and we can get out of here. How's the ammunition in the BTR?"

"It's okay. We have enough to see us out of here. When we get back, we need to ask Jorge if he has any supplies stashed. That is, if we need this beast again."

"Okay, lock and load, and I'll get the rest of them moving."

Nolan climbed aboard the BTR-70, and immediately he started to sweat again as the clammy heat enfolded him. The interior stank of oil, gas, gunpowder residues and most of all, the strong, musky scent of woman, of Gracia. She was checking the alignment of the feed belts for the heavy machine gun. She looked out and smiled as he came near.

"How long before we leave?"

"A few minutes. How's that gun, any problems?"

She shook her head. "Not really, no. This Soviet equipment needs more maintenance than American weapons, so I was just running through the standard checks. It's all loaded and ready to go. We have over four hundred rounds of 14.5 millimeter and almost a thousand rounds of 7.62, so that's plenty to fight our way out of here."

"Is there anything I can do?" he asked her.

She gave him a searching gaze. "Not right now, no, Chief Nolan, but if the guns have problems, I'll shout for you to come up and help fix it. Otherwise, I'm ready."

They'd moved closer so that their faces were only six inches apart. They stared into each other's eyes, and Nolan felt her looking inside his soul. They rocked together slightly, and then they were kissing. Their arms went around each other, and they held their bodies close.

"If we get out of here," Nolan breathed when they pulled slightly apart. "I'll…"

"Ahem." They whirled as Carl Winters cleared his throat. "I thought I'd come aboard and start up. Or do you want me to…"

"We're fine, Carl. Get this beast rolling."

He gave her a last look and then climbed down and into the commander's seat.

"How's it all looking?" he asked Carl.

"All good, Chief. I dipped the fuel tank. The gage isn't working, but we've got more than enough to take us back to Bello. Engines are running well, so we're ready to move out. You okay, I mean, you know?"

Carl looked at him in a mischievous way. Nolan returned the stare. "I'm fine, Carl. But I'll feel better when this one is over and we can go home. This one is turning real messy."

"Don't they always?" he grinned. Nolan realized that Carl was actually enjoying himself. Maybe that was to be expected when you were driving an armored antique. Carl had always had an affinity for all things mechanical.

He'll soon change his tune if the Salazars bring out any missiles, he reflected soberly. I'd better warn Gracia.

He climbed back to the turret and mentioned the possibility of shoulder-launched rockets.

"I am well aware of the dangers of MANPADS, Chief Nolan. I shall keep alert."

"Yeah, that's good."

He climbed through the top hatch and onto the hull. The convoy had assembled and looked ready to go. Talley was in the center truck, standing next to the gunner manning the M60. He waved to Nolan, and the Chief heard his voice through his earpiece.

"We're ready to go. Raoul has two of his men on the gate. As soon as we start rolling, they'll open up, and jump on the nearest truck."

"Copy that. We're ready to pour it on as soon as we get out there."

"You'll need to. I downlinked a map just now from the UAV they have over our heads. Infrared shows trucks loaded with men still arriving. It's going to be a close run thing."

"Are the Colombians up to it, you think?"

"They're Special Forces, so they should be," Talley replied.

"We are ready," a new voice came on the net. Captain Raoul Castro. "We have fought our way in here to save my family, and I will not fail them now. These animals will be beaten, have no fear, Chief Nolan. My men will play their part."

"Yeah, I hear you, Captain. Boss, we're ready to roll."

Talley's voice came over loud and clear. "Head 'em up. Move 'em out!"

The net was alive with laughter. The trail boss' traditional shout from the old TV series 'Rawhide', that started Clint Eastwood on his movie career.

"I'm on it," Carl shouted across to him over the roar of the engines.

He slammed his foot down on the twin throttles, and the heavy APC lurched forward. Nolan watched through the open viewport to see the gates already beginning to open. A few rounds struck the more heavily armored front of the BTR, and then they nosed through into the open street. It was time to run the gauntlet of Copacabana.

They made a sharp turn and headed towards the main street that led out of town. The firing increased, and the steel hull echoed to the jackhammer sound of the heavy machine gun as Gracia went into action. She fired in short, controlled bursts, the mark of a trained machine gunner. Outside, Nolan could hear the cries of the besiegers as her bullets started to find their mark, but there were a lot of them, too many of them. He could hear the shouts over the net.

"One of the Colombian trucks got hit, and they must have got the driver. He's swerved out of position."

"Watch out, there's one up there, he's aarrhgh!"

"Vince, on your three o'clock, at a window twenty feet up. He's killing Castro's men."

Nolan was a sniper. It was his skill, his trade, and the specialty that set him apart from other men. Hearing

Vince's sniper skills being called into action jolted him into action. He leaned across so Carl could hear him.

"I'm going on the hull to take out some of these shooters. There're too many of them."

Carl nodded. "Stay low, Chief. You can shoot from out of the hatch, and it'll give you some protection."

Nolan nodded, grabbed his SWS sniper rifle, and unfastened the hatch. Gracia popped her head down from the turret to see what he was doing.

"Chief Nolan, no, the gunfire is too heavy!"

"That's why I'm going out there, Gracia. Besides, the trucks behind haven't got an armored hull. They have to take their chances. I'll shoot from behind the steel hatch."

Before she could answer, he clambered up through the hatch and wedged himself so that he could shoot over the top of the open lid.

The first target came into view, the window of a third floor apartment. Four Colombians were leaning out shooting; three with assault rifles and one with a large pistol. Nolan sighted on the man with the pistol who could be their leader, and fired, four shots, four hits, despite the movement of the APC. This was no time for double taps, and no time for making sure. Just shoot the enemy as fast as possible and move on. He sighted on another shooter crouched behind a car parked in the street. The car offered visual cover only, as it was not armor plated. The man ducked down. Nolan estimated his position and fired through the car doors. His 7.62-millimeter bullet smashed through the thin metal, and the man shrieked as he was thrown backward by the shot. Another man ran out of a nearby apartment block to pick up his rifle, and Nolan shot him even before he'd got back into cover. The noise was deafening, Gracia's 14.5 millimeter and 7.62 millimeter machine guns firing quick, short bursts. The two M60s, also firing disciplined bursts, interspersed by the HK416s of the Seals and the Heckler & Koch G36 5.56 millimeters of the Colombian Special Forces. Firing back was an assortment of weapons from the Salazars' soldiers. American M-16s, Soviet made AK-47s, and just about every rifle and pistol that had ever fallen into the hands of the traffickers. Nolan felt a tug on his jacket as a slug narrowly missed him, then a bullet hit him fully in the chest. Despite his flak jacket, he was thrown back to hit his head against a steel stanchion fitted to the deck of the APC.

"Chief Nolan! Are you okay?"

It was Gracia. She'd stopped firing when she saw him hit.

"I'm fine, don't stop firing. We have to get out of here."

"Driver, take the next lane on the left. It will lead us out to the main highway that will take us back to Bello," she shouted. Then she started firing again.

Carl swerved into the narrow lane, barely wide enough for the Soviet armor, and he accelerated down the street, squashing flowerpots and bicycles that were leaning against the sides of the apartment block. But there were no shooters, and they were almost clear. A man ran into the road ahead of them, and Nolan shouted a warning.

"Missile, dead ahead. Someone take him!"

The man had the missile pointed at the armored car, ready to shoot. He must have had his finger on the trigger when Gracia hit him with a long, concentrated burst from the two machine guns. The man was thrown back as if hit by a truck; his missile launched and soared harmlessly into the sky to land in the distant jungle. Nolan felt the bump as they rode over his bullet riddled body, then Carl swerved onto the main highway, and they were heading back to Bello.

Nolan watched the vehicles as they turned out onto the main highway. As far as he could tell, they'd all made it. No, one was missing. He'd heard an explosion and burst of heavy gunfire seconds before they made the turn, someone had been ambushed by the Salazars. He keyed his mic.

"Bravo One, this is Four. How are we doing, Boss?"

"Our platoon got out okay, but Castro's men lost a truck, about fifteen men aboard."

"Any chance of survivors?"

"None. There was another missile shooter. He was in that street just before we turned into the lane. It was a direct hit on the cab, and when the truck was brought to a stop, the rest of them set on it like a pack of wolves."

They were both silent for long minutes as the convoy raced away from Copacabana towards Bello. Then there was a series of enormous explosions back in the town.

"What the hell was that?" Carl asked on the net. "What are they doing back there?"

"It's what we're doing, PO. The downlinked images showed them forming up inside that factory compound we left. I guess they were checking to see that we'd all gone, and they were forming up a small force to come after us. I called in a Reaper strike, and what you just heard was the sound of a barrage of Hellfire missiles."

Nolan watched the flames leaping up from the place they had just left. The whole town seemed to be on fire; an illusion caused by the leaping flames of exploded and burning fuel tanks that backlit the town.

"That'll slow 'em down a piece," Carl grinned happily, as he relaxed on the smooth, tarmac road.

They drove straight to Jorge's yard and parked inside. He slammed the gates shut. On the way, they'd noticed the town of Bello was silent, dark and shuttered. The inhabitants had heard the shooting and explosions. They could hardly have missed them. But it was someone else's business, not theirs. These were survivors of a deadly conflict; the drug wars that held way over the lives of millions in the South American sub-continent. These people knew when to keep their heads down. Not a soul had stirred as they had made their way along deserted streets.

"What's the deal with the Admiral?" Nolan asked Talley when they'd dismounted.

"Call the men around, Chief. I want you all to hear this."

They gathered in a horseshoe in the center of the courtyard, the Navy Seals and the survivors of the Colombian Special Forces. Castro's men had lost a total of eighteen dead, with a few minor wounds to the rest. As for the Seals, they were almost unscathed, just a few scratches and flesh wounds. Talley stood with Castro at the head of the horseshoe so that each man could see and hear what they had to say.

"It's not over," Talley began. "We embarked on this rescue operation to free Captain Castro's family. That would enable him to ally his forces with us, and using his local knowledge, free Admiral Jacks and complete out mission. We're a long way from doing that. We've hit the Salazars hard, and they're hurting but not hard enough. But the problem is this. The two Salazar soldiers we interrogated both told the same story. Admiral Jacks is to be executed tonight. They're using a video camera to broadcast the execution and send it out on prime time television."

"We need to get in there and get him out," Nolan said quickly. "That just can't be allowed to happen."

"Yeah, agreed," Talley replied. "But after this ruckus, they'll be waiting for us to do just that. And the second they think we're getting near, the Admiral's dead. They'll slaughter him out of hand. It may be there's nothing we can do to save him."

CHAPTER EIGHT

Nolan sat drinking a cold beer in the shade of the APC, his back leaning against one of the huge, rubber tires. Gracia sat cross-legged on the ground, also drinking from an icy bottle of beer. Since Talley's announcement of the fate of Admiral Jacks, there'd been an atmosphere of gloom descended on the courtyard. After the shock and hopelessness had sunk in, they'd slept fitfully through the rest of the night, all except for Talley. He'd spent hours in communication with San Diego, attempting to make some sense of the situation they were in. So far, it looked hopeless. The only chance was an airborne attack by a large force, probably a brigade to make certain of overcoming the Salazars. But such attacks were not easily planned, and one thing stood in the way, the Colombian government. Talley had explained the politics to them, his face creased in lines of worry.

"Even if the Colombians did want to give our people the go ahead, and assuming we could get the Rapid Deployment Force in country in time enough to save

Jacks, it would be political suicide for them to agree. They'd be out of office within weeks of the people finding out they'd allowed a large scale invasion on Colombian soil by American forces. So my guess is, it's not gonna happen."

"We have to do something," Nolan insisted. "We can't let them execute Jacks on prime time TV."

Talley nodded. I agree with you, Chief. You tell me what we can do, and I'll give the go ahead."

But there was nothing he could suggest. For all of their military skills, and the immense power of the technology they could employ, through the use of drones and other aerial assets, they had to face simple facts. Navy Seals employed stealth to reach their targets. Their numbers and weaponry were too small for large-scale head-on confrontations. Yet the Salazars were fully alerted, so stealth was out of the window. The UAVs could punch holes in the Salazars' infrastructure, but they couldn't magically lift the Admiral out of the Salazar camp. So they'd broken up into small groups and tried to catch up with some sleep. If a plan to save Jacks did materialize, they wanted to be ready to put it into action.

"It will be bad for your country if they go ahead with this," Gracia murmured to Nolan.

He'd been lost in his thoughts. The idea that one of theirs, a Rear Admiral no less, could be executed on Primetime TV was astonishing, abhorrent. And for Navy Seals to sit around while it happened, well, that just didn't happen.

"It'll be very bad, yeah. It'll make gangsters like these Salazars, as well as terrorists, think that they can play games with our military while we're powerless to stop them."

Before she could say more, Roscoe Bremmer walked

up to them.

"Hey, that's gonna be something, those guys executing a real, live Admiral on the tube. Damn, that'll be something."

Up until then, Bremmer had kept his head down, and Nolan grudgingly admitted he'd done a good job. When the fighting was at its thickest, Bremmer was often there, handling his weapons and taking down enemies as if he'd been born to the trade of the Navy Seal. Yet here he was, back and undoing all of the admiration he'd earned from Nolan and the rest of the Platoon, by playing the 'chip on his shoulder' black man again.

"It won't be something, Bremmer. It'll be a disaster."

"For you, maybe, but a lot of folks will see another white boy get topped. Make a change from black boys being taken down by redneck cops in L.A."

Nolan could feel Gracia listening on with incredulity. He felt his anger rise until he could not stop himself.

"Bremmer, you bastard, this is one of our own people! He's a Seal, for Christ's sake. This isn't your stupid fucking black on white crusade. You're talking about your shipmate, and you're making yourself sound like a damned traitor!"

"A traitor! The fuck you say, Chief. I broke my back to get into this unit, and I've shed blood on operations in the Gulf before I even signed up for Seal training. I ain't no traitor. You should watch what you say, whitey. What are you accusing me of here? Are you the Navy version of the KKK? It ain't my fault that foolish old man came on this mission and got in everyone's way. He got caught, and it could have been all of our lives on the line to try and get him back. It's only fucking luck that we can't get in there and do that job. I know he's one of ours, but he's no business being here. No black boy would have been so stupid. What, are you going to do, hang me from a tree?"

"Cut it out!"

Talley's voice was like a pail of cold water tossed on the heated coals of their disagreement. Bremmer had finally exploded, and despite his incredible racist and ghoulish rant about the Admiral, there was some logic to what he'd said. Jacks had no business coming on the operation, and his capture had the potential to seriously embarrass America and put many lives at risk. But still, he was a Seal, and Seals had no business talking like that about their comrades.

"You don't know what you're talking about, Bremmer. There was a reason the Admiral came on this mission, and it's one that no one is supposed to know. Drew Jacks has spent his life fighting for the Navy Seals, both on foreign battlefields and home in the US, defending us against those who would do America harm. Black and white!" he snapped at Bremmer, leaving no doubt as to his meaning.

"You don't get it," Bremmer replied angrily.

"No, you don't get it. For once, shut up and listen!"

Bremmer closed his mouth, surprised by the Lieutenant's tone. Talley was known to be Mr. Cool, and nothing ever fazed him. Except now, Bremmer had managed it.

"Admiral Jacks is the single most knowledgeable officer in the whole of the US where South America is concerned, and trafficking in particular. The President asked him to do this," he looked significantly at Bremmer. "Yes, your Commander in Chief. He's angry at the increase in drug related violence, north and south of the Rio Grande. And he asked Jacks to look for permanent solutions to the problem, whilst we were engaged in taking down the Salazar empire. Normally you're right. A senior officer wouldn't come on this type of operation. This was a one off. And there's a second thing. The man had cancer, and he only has months to live. He wanted to do this, to sacrifice if necessary his last few days and weeks, to do something for his country. When the President found out, he wouldn't go along with it, but Jacks persuaded him. So you take your pick, Bremmer, for an officer in your service, for your Commander in Chief, and for your country. Which of those means anything to you? Remember which culture is worst affected by the drug problem. And it isn't Admiral Jacks' people."

Bremmer was already squirming. "Shit, I didn't know nothing about that, Boss."

"I couldn't give a damn what you did and didn't know, Bremmer. What I value is loyalty to this unit, to the Seals, and to America. And yes, if they go ahead with this execution, it'll hurt us badly. Other than a suicide mission or saturation bombing, I don't know how to stop it happening."

"Perhaps I can help," Gracia interjected.

The three Seals looked at her closely.

"How?" Talley asked.

"There is a wedding celebration tonight in the Salazar compound, south of Medellin. I have an invitation."

"You what? How the hell did you get that?"

She looked grim. "I was FARC, remember. They don't know that I left the movement, and I met with them on occasion to arrange the drug shipments. They sent me and my husband an invitation."

"You mean they're planning on this execution on the evening of a wedding party?" Nolan asked incredulously.

She nodded. "It is exactly the kind of thing that would

appeal to their cruel nature. They have a younger brother, Vincenzo, who is getting married. It will be his initiation into the management of the business."

"I don't understand," Talley interrupted. "What's so special about a wedding?"

"It is simple. They do not trust the highest ranks of the organization with men who are not married, even when they are close family. But when a man is married, he will have a wife and children. It means that there are hostages, should the man decide to betray them. They have demonstrated that they are ready to murder wives and children if anyone dares to cross them."

"Gracia," Nolan asked. "Your husband, where is he, still with the FARC?"

She laughed. "No, he is dead."

"I'm sorry."

"Do not be. He was the son of my FARC Commander. I was ordered to marry him, and it was made clear that if I failed to obey that order, I would be in extreme danger. Don't get me wrong. He wasn't such a bad person, not at first. I thought I could handle being married to him. But the Commander, his father, is something of a psychopath. I afterwards found out the son was starting to go down the same road. He had already started to beat me, and then he was killed."

"By the Colombian Army?"

She smiled. "No, by one of his squad leaders. He had been screwing with this man's wife. Colombian men have a possessive nature where their women are concerned, and this one put a knife in my husband Pepe's throat. It was a release, and believe me, I was not sorry he was dead."

They were silent for a few moments, contemplating the

brutal conditions that she must have lived under. Finally, Talley prompted her for a location.

"They have a ranch on the outskirts of El Santuario, about forty miles to the south east of here."

"Is there any chance we could make a direct assault on his ranch without being seen?"

She laughed. "After last night's battle, every Salazar supporter will be on full alert. The second we move out of Bello, they will track us, no matter how silently we travel. I can assure you, the whole countryside will be looking out for strangers. The second they see you moving towards El Santuario, it is likely they will kill the Admiral."

"It's what we're trained for, Ma'am. Silent assaults are our business," Talley said quietly.

"And protecting their interests is their business," she replied. "Believe me, if we try to head in the direction of El Santuario, we would not even get out of town without the Salazars being told. They have been hurt badly by your attacks on their facilities in Medellin and in Copacabana. They will have thousands of local people watching to make sure that they are not surprised again tonight. This will be their revenge on America for making them look such fools, and a way to demonstrate to the people that they are still powerful. If they were hit again tonight, all it would show is that they have lost their strength, and the other families would set on them like packs of wolves. They will not allow that to happen."

"I see. I'll need to think about what you've told us," Talley said. "I suspect we may need another platoon to make a HAHO drop on that ranch."

"What is HAHO?" she asked him.

Talley explained the fine art of high altitude, high

opening parachute entry. "Its benefit is to allow our men to jump a long way away from the target at a great height, so they'll be undetected. They just glide in, steering their parachutes and using GPS technology to navigate to the LZ."

She nodded. "I understand, but you should know that their ranch is protected by anti-aircraft missiles and machine guns. They also have constant communication with their people in Colombian air traffic control, and every aircraft that crosses the Colombian borders, and heading in the direction of Medellin, will be known to them. Even if your men do arrive undetected, they will find maybe five hundred fighters around the ranch, and all of them heavily armed. The second a shot is fired, they will execute your Admiral."

Talley was silenced by the enormity of the odds stacked against a new attack.

"What was your idea?" Talley prompted her.

"I thought to accept the invitation to the wedding and go with my husband. Once inside the ranch, it may be possible to find the Admiral and free him."

"But your husband is dead."

She grinned at Nolan. "But you are not dead, Chief Nolan. And you speak perfect Latin American Spanish."

"But I'm not Hispanic."

"I could make you look more Colombian than he was, if necessary."

"It may be the only way, Chief," Talley urged. "If you can get inside that place, you could secure the Admiral, and maybe give us time to launch a full scale rescue attempt from the outside. If you'll light up the targets, we can call up a lot of ordnance, so you wouldn't be on your own."

"What kind of ordnance?" Nolan asked suspiciously. "UAVs may not be enough for that kind of close in fighting."

"I was thinking along the lines of those AC-130 Spookys the Air Force is tanking off the coast. There are two of them keeping station. That's a powerful piece of ground support, once they know what they're supposed to shoot at."

Nolan thought of the awesome power of the mighty Lockheed gunships. Fitted with the General Dynamics GAU-12 Equalizer, a five-barrel twenty-five millimeter Gatling-type rotary cannon, they were able to bring immense firepower to distant battlefields. The Equalizer was operated by an electric motor, and with a fire rate limited to 1,800 rounds to reduce barrel wear and overheating problems. The one-inch caliber, six-inch long mm cannon rounds had a range of two miles.

"That could certainly swing it," Nolan said thoughtfully. "But it'll depend on me getting in there with a Laser Target Designator, the LTD."

"I promise you I will get you in there," Gracia said.

"With the laser targeting equipment, and my weapons?"

"How large is this laser equipment?"

"About the size of a VCR."

She was thoughtful for a few moments. "I have an idea for the LTD. But weapons, I think not. You can carry a weapon to the wedding, most men in this region do. But we will certainly be searched and any weapons locked away. They will not allow armed men to walk around, and that is certain. But the laser, yes, I can get that in. There will be many guards, all of them armed. I suggest you take what weapons you need from these people."

"Okay, we'll do it. How are we going to arrange this?"

An hour later, Nolan was regretting his decision. His hair had been dyed jet black and chopped into a conventional Latino style. Jorge had found him clothes more suitable for a wedding than his dark camo gear and body armor. Now he wore high waist pants, a tight jacket, and a white shirt unbuttoned almost to his navel.

"I feel like a Mariachi singer," he complained to Gracia. "Won't they be suspicious?"

"No, Chief Nolan, men around here vary widely. Some will wear New York fashions, others traditional Colombian clothes, and this is very suitable for a wedding, believe me. But you must take that shirt back off, I have something I need to do."

"What? Tell me, what gives?"

"Just take it off and stop arguing."

She proceeded to carefully apply make-up, a dark foundation to his skin. Finally, she styled his hair with oil, to make it slick straight back from the front. He checked himself in the mirror and couldn't make up his mind whether to laugh or choke. He looked like the kind of South American popularly seen in films. What North Americans would call a 'Spic', and with all of its negative connotations.

"It is good," Gracia commented. "But you must remember, you are Pepe Montez, my husband, and currently a Commander in the FARC. If you act macho, you'll be able to block any questions. FARC don't discuss themselves for security reasons."

"They don't?"

She laughed. "They're as much talkers as anyone else. But it sounds tough and mysterious. That's all you have to do if you're asked any awkward questions. You're the strong, silent type."

"Yeah, I've got that."

Talley was listening. "Hell, we could do with someone like Gracia in the unit. She sure knows how to get our Chief Petty Officer to play ball."

She gave him a grin. "It is a woman thing, Lieutenant. As long as Chief Nolan plays the part of my husband, he will be accepted as a Colombian." She turned to Nolan, with a fierce look. "That means you'll need to be all tough and protective of your woman. Lots of contact, kisses, you need to make it convincing."

"Hell, I'm not sure we should be paying you for this, Chief. It sounds more like pleasure than work."

Nolan flushed with embarrassment. The trouble was Talley wasn't far wide of the mark. He found himself looking forward to the closeness with this exotic and fascinating woman. Except that she could get hurt if things went badly, and that was something he vowed to work hard to avoid.

"How are we gonna get there?" he asked, to change the subject.

"Jorge has a vehicle he will lend us," Gracia explained. "It is a UAZ-469, an SUV vehicle manufactured by UAZ in Russia. The UAZ can drive in virtually any terrain and is very easy to fix, so they are popular with paramilitary groups like the FARC. Some fell into private hands, abandoned or sold off. Jorge told me he'd won his in a card game."

"As long as it gets us there," Nolan replied.

Just then they heard the sound of an engine running, and the UAZ nosed out of the workshop and into the courtyard. It was an ugly, angular vehicle, with little of the charm of the American equivalent, the Willys. The canvas top was split in places and repaired with duct tape, but the engine sounded smooth enough, and there was only a little white smoke from the exhaust. The door opened and Jorge climbed out.

"I've checked it all over, filled her with gas, and topped off the oil. Tires are all good, so you shouldn't have any problems."

"And even more important," Gracia added, "it's recognizable as a FARC vehicle. It'll suit out identities."

"And if someone is there who knows the real Pepe is dead?"

She lifted the hem of her skirt. Strapped to her leg was a slim stiletto. "Then I will kill him."

Talley handed them the Laser Target Designator. "How are you going to disguise something like this? It's obvious it's a piece of military hardware."

Gracia took it. "I need five minutes and you will see."

She went into Jorge's home and emerged a few minutes later carrying a beautifully wrapped wedding present, of the shape and size of a Laser Target Designator. Both men nodded approvingly.

"You're hooked up to the commo?" Talley asked anxiously.

"No can do," Nolan replied. "When they search me, it would be an immediate giveaway."

"I will carry your communications equipment," Gracia offered.

Nolan gave her a worried look. "How can you do that without them finding it?"

"Don't worry. They will not look where I will hide it."

He felt an erotic thrill at the thought of this beautiful creature carrying his equipment in some intimate part of her body. He didn't ask exactly where, but just speculating about it was enough to get him thinking thoughts that bore no relation to the mission.

"You'd better get moving," Talley brought him out of his reverie, probably deliberately. He could hardly have failed to notice how his Chief was enthralled with Gracia. Nolan nodded.

"Yeah, we'll get on the road. As soon as we arrive, and I can get the commo fitted up, I'll, er, shit, what was I saying? Oh yeah, I'll call in."

"You sure you don't need a cold shower, Chief? It's pretty hot out here," Talley smiled.

Nolan turned away so that his platoon leader couldn't see his face glowing red. They climbed into the jeep and drove out of the courtyard.

"Remember who you are," Gracia leaned over and shouted over the noise of the engine, which sounded like something ripped out of a tractor.

"What do you mean?"

"I mean that you're a Colombian, a FARC commander, and a real lady's man. So make sure you drive that way. No one gets past you, and keep your foot pressed down on the gas as much as possible. Anyone gets in your way, blast the horn, and make sure they jump."

Nolan pressed the horn button. "It doesn't work."

She sighed. "You'll need to improvise."

They roared on along the main highway that ran east from Medellin and Bello. Eventually, Gracia pointed out a right turn onto a narrow track that headed south. They hit the first checkpoint after five miles. A truck was parked across the track, and four men with AK-47 assault rifles stood nearby. They drew to a stop, and one of the men came to the window.

"What is your business?"

Nolan scowled at him. "My business is my business. Get that truck out of my way."

The man returned the scowl. "If you have business on this road, you must tell me. Otherwise, turn back."

"My business is FARC business, nothing to do with you."

The man paled slightly. "I'm sorry, Senor. We have no quarrel with the FARC. Are you going to the wedding?"

Nolan gestured at Gracia. "Show this imbecile the invitations."

"Hey, who the fuck are you calling an imbecile?"

Nolan climbed down, slowly, from the SUV and stood six inches from the man's face. "You, imbecile, check the invitations, and get that piece of shit truck out of my way!"

The man sized up Nolan and recognized a fighting man. He turned away and looked at the invitations proffered by Gracia. Finally, he nodded.

"You can go."

Nolan gave him a sneer as he put the UAZ into gear and drove on.

"That was excellent," Gracia said in an approving tone. "If I didn't know better, I'd say you were a one hundred percent macho bastard Colombian, one who beats his wife and whores on a Saturday night."

"Now there's a thought," Nolan grinned.

She playfully punched him on the arm. "Don't try it, Chief Nolan. I'm not some dumpy stay at home wife willing to take it for the sake of the family. I'd slit your throat."

He laughed. "Yeah, I think you would, girl. Except that we're not married, and I don't go whoring."

"Never?" she sounded astonished.

"No, never, if I'm in a relationship, I believe in loyalty to your partner."

"Isn't that the way your Navy Seals operates?"

"Yeah, exactly like that. When you're a Seal, you don't moonlight with the enemy."

She gave him a serious stare. "You are a good man, Chief Nolan. When this is over, I would like to know you better."

He thought of his dead wife, Grace. Then he thought of Detective Carol Summers back in San Diego. Did they have a relationship? No, not really, nothing permanent, and no commitments. And if he had to choose, what would he do? He looked at the beautiful, mysterious and exotic girl on the seat next to him and felt warmth he hadn't felt in a long, long time. Not since Grace. Real warmth, and a true meeting of souls. He nodded at Gracia.

"Yeah, I'd like that too."

They drove on for the next few miles in silence, both lost in their own thoughts. She jerked him out of his trance.

"The ranch is coming up. It's about half a mile ahead, so you'd better start slowing and remember you're my fiery, macho Colombian husband. Your name is Pepe Montez, Commander Pepe Montez."

"Yeah, I got it."

The ranch was a small estate, bearing little resemblance to a working farm. The central group of buildings was in a square piece of ground, surrounded by a continuous wall of about eight feet high and built of stone. It was topped by razor wire, laced in coils. At the corners were guard towers, all of them manned, and all of them equipped with what looked like a light machine gun. At the barrier, a man stood in the center of the road, holding up his hand for them to stop. Around him were a half dozen Salazar soldiers, armed with assault rifles. The man in the road had a pistol in a holster. He leaned in the window and held out his hand.

"I am Manuel Rivera, security chief. Your invitations?"

Nolan gave Gracia a casual nod.

"Show them to him."

He read them carefully. "Pepe Montez and Gracia Montez. You will need to step out of the car to be searched."

Wordlessly, Nolan got out and stood waiting, a careless look on his face, as if it was all too boring and completely beneath him. The man with the pistol approached him.

"Mr. Montez, I…"

"Commander Montez, of the FARC," Nolan corrected him.

"I am sorry, Commander Montez. Are you carrying any weapons?"

Nolan sneered. "What kind of a question is that? Did I not tell you I am a FARC commander? Do you think we fight our wars with fountain pens? Of course I am armed."

He reached down to his waistband and slowly pulled out a Makarov nine-millimeter automatic pistol, another gift from the Soviets.

"Here, and make sure you look after it. I do not want one of your thieves stealing my weapon. "

"Assuredly, Commander. If you don't mind, the metal detector?"

Nolan nodded, and he ran the wand over his body.

"That's fine, Sir. I have to check your woman."

The Chief glared at him. "Anyone touches my wife, he's dead."

"But, Sir, I have my orders. I must do my job."

"Look at her, you fool. Do you think she is carrying a weapon? Where the fuck would she carry it, do you think she has a machine gun in her cunt? Or maybe jammed between her tits?"

Gracia was wearing a very short, very tight shift dress. It clung to her curves and accentuated her beauty, as well as making it clear she couldn't be concealing a gun.

"Commander," the man flustered. "If I could just check the lady's purse, then that would be fine. Please, I must do this."

Nolan waved him forward. "But I warn you, keep your stinking hands off her. Any man touches her, and I'll cut his balls off!"

They checked the purse and came up empty. Two men were rummaging through the UAZ, and both shook their heads. Nothing. Another had an angled mirror on a pole to check underneath, and again, he came up with nothing. Then Rivera picked up the one thing they'd missed; it was too obvious.

"What is this?"

Nolan gave him a hard look. "Are you serious, hombre? What the fuck do you think it is? Or have I come to the wrong place, and there is to be no wedding here?"

Rivera weighed the package in his hand, clearly thoughtful. "What is in it?"

"It is a portable, 3D television system, the very latest. There is also a large collection of 3D DVDS, and they are not Disney cartoons either."

He looked at Nolan and weighed the package again. He looked thoughtful, and already Nolan was deciding which of the guards to take first to get his hands on an assault rifle. Then Rivera nodded.

"That's fine. Enjoy the celebrations, Commander. Senora Montez," he nodded to Gracia and looked around as another vehicle approached.

"That was close," Gracia breathed. "I was about to grab one of the assault rifles."

"The short guy standing just behind you."

"How did you know?"

He smiled. "Because that's the guy I would have gone for."

They drove further inside the ranch compound and parked at the side of the huge, central dwelling. It was much more than a house, more than a ranch house. It was astonishing to find such a building on the outskirts of a Colombian village.

"It looks like…

"Yes, they had it built as a joke. It's a copy of the White House in Washington."

The climbed out of the UAZ, almost bumping into a man quickly walking past, and he stared at them with suspicious eyes.

"Who are you?"

They gave him their names and he relaxed.

"You are very welcome to my brother's wedding. My name is Victor Salazar."

CHAPTER NINE

For several long seconds, the two men stared at each other.

"How does your campaign progress, Commandante Montez?"

Salazar watched him carefully, and Nolan felt tense. For some reason, a lot rode on his answer. He was about to when Gracia came around his side of the UAZ and almost fell into his arms, draping herself over him. The Colombian's eyes narrowed.

"Who's your friend, my husband? Oh, it's Mr. Salazar. We met once before, at a conference between the cartels and our regional leaders in Medellin, at the Hotel Drago."

He relaxed and nodded. "Of course, I remember, yes, we cemented our new agreement to supply you with sufficient cocaine to buy weapons, in return for FARC protection from the Colombian Army."

"An agreement that I do not believe you have entirely kept to, Senor Salazar."

The man's eyes flashed with anger. "What do you mean? Every ounce of cocaine we promised has been given, not a single shipment has failed to reach you."

"Yes, I know that. But when the Hondurans continually increase the price of their weapons, it means we must pay much more to get what we need. In the spirit of the agreement, you should increase your shipments. Guns do not come cheap."

Salazar looked even angrier. "I do not like your attitude, Commandante Montez. If the weapons cost more, that is nothing to do with me."

Nolan shrugged. "If you wish to leave your security to the clowns I saw at the gate, that's up to you. But believe me, they wouldn't last five minutes if the Army attacks."

"They are good men! Every single one I recruited and trained them myself."

"But they are not professional soldiers, Mr. Salazar. The FARC is the only barrier to the Narcotics police and the Army trampling all over your operation. If you want to do it yourself, that's fine. We shall finance our weapons elsewhere."

Salazar sneered. "Who would give your army money to buy weapons, Commandante?"

Nolan shrugged again. "There are many countries who would be prepared to help us."

"Name one!"

"The United States, for one. Of course, the price would be to destroy the traffickers, people like yourself."

"You dare to threaten me in my home?"

"You asked me a question, Mr. Salazar. Did you want a dishonest answer, and an answer that may lead to the destruction of your business?"

Nolan could feel Gracia holding her breath. He'd gone as far as he could with the pissing contest. Had he gone too far? It was a risk he had to take. They stood glaring at each other in silence, and Nolan could almost feel Gracia's hand inching towards the knife under her skirt. Then Salazar smiled and laughed.

"Bueno, Commandante Montez. What you say is true. It would be stupid to deny it. Yes, the United States would pay very well to have my business interests destroyed. You make your point well, and I shall contact the regional headquarters tomorrow and offer to match the shipments to the price of the guns. It is as well you spoke, so there are no misunderstandings. I like a man who is honest. They are very scarce in my business."

He held out his hand, and Nolan shook it. Then he held out his hand to Gracia, but she looked at Nolan and waited. He gave her a curt nod, and she took Salazar's hand.

"Commandante, you and your beautiful wife will want to freshen up before the main event. Please, let me show you into the house, and I will have my servants take you to a guest room. It is the very least I can do for my FARC friends. Tonight will be a special night, a very special night."

"I'm please to hear it, Senor Salazar."

"Please, call me Victor."

"Then call me Pepe."

"Very good, Pepe. As I said, it will be a very special night."

"Weddings always are, Victor. A time to cement alliances."

Salazar nodded. "That is true, but tonight, we have some extra entertainment, something very special, and a chance to give the fucking Americans a bloody nose."

"Victor, my wife! Your language, I know she is a soldier, but still…"

Salazar spread his hands in apology. "Of course, I meant no insult. As I said, we have something special lined up."

"Yes, and what is that?"

"A surprise, my friend, but one you will appreciate. Come, I will find you a guest room."

He led them through the porticoed main entrance and into the huge house. Inside, it was also a faithful replica of the White House, except that everything was too gaudy, too flashy, the taste of a cheap thug rather than an educated statesman. Victor waved his hand at a passage that led off the main entrance vestibule.

"That is where I conduct my business. In the West Wing," he laughed heartily.

A servant approached and hovered nearby. He beckoned him to come forward.

"Angel, take these two people to the guest room, and make sure they have the best we are able to offer. Show them were everything is and leave them to rest." He looked back at Nolan and Gracia. "The celebrations start in three hours, at seven. I will send a servant to wake you in case you are sleeping. Give your gift to Angel. He will carry it for you."

"Thank you, Victor. Your kindness is a sign of your valued friendship."

Salazar beamed his thanks and went off to continue supervising the approaching celebrations. Nolan and Gracia followed Angel up the wide, sweeping marble staircase and along a passage to a spacious bedroom. The servant showed them into the room and put the wedding present on the dressing table. The windows were wide and decorated with heavy damask drapes. The furnishings were of the very finest and most expensive, including the mock antique four-poster bed. Sadly, the taste of the person who had put the furnishings together was singularly lacking, and both Nolan and Gracia pulled faces at the garish ensemble.

"The bathroom is over there," he pointed. "There is a mini-bar and, of course, if you require any food, just pick up the phone and call."

They thanked him and he left.

"Hey, don't you think Salazar was…"

Nolan stopped her, putting his finger to his lips. He pointed to the ceiling, to the huge light fitting in the center, and she got the message.

"Charming," she finished. "A nice man, and someone that can help us in the FARC a great deal."

"That is so," he agreed. "Now go and prepare the shower for me. I need to freshen up."

Her eyes widened at his brusque order, but she grinned.

"Yes, my husband, whatever you say."

As she passed him, she put her lips close to his ear. "You played that a bit close to the mark. I thought that pissing contest was going to end in tears."

"You told me to play the macho Colombian."

She laughed out loud and whispered a reply. "Not that well, my husband."

He ran the cold shower long enough to get the dust and dirt of the past couple of days off his skin. Gracia had brought along her makeup, and when he was finished, she started to re-apply the foundation cream to his skin to darken him sufficiently to pass as Pepe Montez. They made desultory conversation, knowing how dangerous it was to make any kind of a remark that was out of character to the people they were supposed to be. As her hands worked over his face, Nolan felt himself becoming uncomfortably warm.

"Hey, you want to ease off on that, Gracia."

"Why is that, my husband?"

She was a woman, and she looked down at his groin and grinned. "I see. That looks very interesting," she whispered in his ear. "Do you find me very attractive, my husband?"

"You know I do," he whispered back.

"And you want to do something about it?"

"We're supposed to be working," he objected. But it wasn't the only reason.

The decision was taken out of his hands. She held him gently and pushed him down on the sumptuous bed, all the while kissing and fondling him. It was too much, and he kissed her back, and his hands started exploring her body. The sex was urgent, almost rough in its intensity. They were two people in a situation of maximum danger, and both knew that there was every chance they wouldn't get out of the place alive. The human urge to procreate when facing death overcame them, and their lovemaking was a chaotic act of despair, of arousal, and of raw human emotion.

"Mm, that was good, my husband. You are truly a sexual athlete," she murmured, loud enough for the microphones in the room to pick it up. She nudged him to make a suitable macho reply.

"Of course," he said, as offhandedly as he could. But he leaned down and whispered in her ear. "That was good,

Gracia. You truly are a wonderful girl."

"And lover?" she cocked an eyebrow at him.

"Not bad, for a wife," he quipped. She playfully cuffed him on the shoulder, and he gripped her to him. For long minutes they held each other, luxuriating in the warmth of their closeness. Then he released her.

"It's time to make a start."

"Yes, I know."

She'd removed the commo system unnoticed, and it was now hidden inside her purse. She handed it to him, and he went back into the bathroom and ran both taps on the bath, then flushed the lavatory. There was enough noise to drown out any eavesdropping. He pushed the earpiece into place and made contact.

"Bravo One, this is Four."

They'd agreed, as normal, to keep the same designations all through the mission.

"This is One, reading you strength three, good enough." It was Talley's voice, and he'd answered immediately.

"Copy that. We're in. I'll call you in two hours."

"Any problems, Four?"

He thought of Gracia. That could be a complication, sure.

"None. Out."

He turned off the taps and left the bathroom. Gracia had touched in her makeup, and she looked glorious, smoldering with sex appeal.

Christ, she's some woman.

He nodded at the door and mouthed, "Let's go. We need to find the Admiral. We'll leave the wedding present where it is."

The party was already in full swing. Drunken

Colombians mingled with stern faced wives and giggling whores, shipped in for the occasion. At the side of the huge house were several warehouses and workshops, and further along a helipad with a Rolls Royce engine Bell 407 executive helo sat on the tarmac; nothing but the best for these cocaine traffickers. There was so much noise from shouting, drunken people and a band enthusiastically playing Latin American music from a stage that had been erected at the end of a formal garden, there was no need to whisper.

"What are we looking for?" Gracia asked.

"Somewhere secure. Somewhere they could hold him out of sight of the wedding guests."

"That could be anywhere," she protested.

"Maybe, but I guess they'll keep him close enough to keep an eye on him. He won't be far from here."

"In the White House?"

"No, that's not very likely. They'd need somewhere like a secure basement to hold him." A sudden thought seared into his brain.

Something secure like the White House Situation Room. Is it built that close to the original in Washington? It could be. He explained his idea to Gracia.

"So we need to go back inside and look around?"

"Yeah, that's right. But we'll need to make it look good. We'd better have a drink, a good few drinks. It's the perfect excuse if we both look pretty far gone."

They walked around the area that had been cordoned off for the party, taking drinks from waiters that flocked around like seagulls in a public square; except that every one of the white jacketed men looked much more hard and tough than the average waiter. The only exception was the girls who served drinks, and they had obviously been hired more for their bust sizes than any fighting abilities.

They made their way around, talking and laughing at the drunken jokes, sipping out of each drink, then pouring the rest on the ground when no one was looking. The area was packed with laughing, chattering people in various stages of intoxication. Overhead, strips of bunting were tied between the trees, and there were dozens of lanterns ready to switch on when night fell. The music was loud, and it wasn't difficult to blend into the cheerful party atmosphere. Near the stage was a huge gazebo decorated with white silk hangings and garlanded with thousands of flowers. The spot for the ceremony to take place, of course. But they weren't here for a ceremony. They were here to bring life to the Admiral and death to the Salazars.

"We need to get inside and find the Admiral," Gracia murmured. "They won't miss us in the middle of all this noise and partying."

Nolan nodded. "You're right, it's a good time. Let's head back inside."

They crossed the area of noise, laughter and music, and walked up the steps underneath the massive white portico.

"Commandante Montez, how can we help you?"

Manuel Rivera, the Salazars' security chief, stood just inside the door. To one side of him was one of the guards, carrying a modern M4-A1 military carbine. Rivera's pistol was still in the shoulder holster, and his eyes were hidden behind his mirrored sunglasses. Did he suspect anything? But why should he? This was an obvious point for him to be able to monitor the wedding guests so that anyone who entered or left the house would be noted, and he had a good view across the ground to the stage where the band was now playing a slow lament.

"We're returning to our room, Senor Rivera. My wife is ill."

"I am sorry about that, Sir. I'm afraid at this late stage the house is closed to guests. We are making certain arrangements. It is the order of Mr. Salazar."

"It's not way to treat a guest, Rivera. My wife needs to lie down for an hour, and besides, our wedding present is in the room. Just give us an hour, hombre."

"I cannot, please will you leave the house."

"Fuck you, my friend. You will not treat me like an enemy. Either you trust the FARC or you do not. If you will not allow us up to our room, we're leaving, and I shall make sure our headquarters knows of the way you treat our people. You're not the only family that we can deal with. There are two others in Medellin. What's it going to be?"

Nolan had planted his feet square onto Rivera, and the two men faced each other like prizefighters. Nolan recalled that he'd handled this badly; macho Colombian pride would not allow Rivera to back down.

"What's going on, Manuel?"

Rivera looked at the new arrival. At first, Nolan thought it was Victor Salazar, but this man was a couple of years younger, and slightly paunchier. So it had to be Alberto Salazar.

"These people, Alberto, Commandante and Senora Montez, they wish to return to their room. But as you know, Victor said that no one is to enter the house right now. You know what is going on, and we cannot risk any problems."

Alberto waved a hand airily. "Let them through,

Manuel. Victor's orders were not for honored members of the FARC." He clapped his hand on Nolan's shoulder. "We need each other, is that not so, Commandante?"

Nolan nodded, keeping his face grim. "It is so, and we do not treat each other like traitors or spies."

"Exactamente. Manuel, let them through."

"But, Alberto, I..."

"I said let them through, Manuel. Now!"

Rivera nodded. "Yes, Sir." He stared at Nolan. "You can go inside to your room." He turned to the guard with the assault rifle. "Francisco, go with them in case they get lost. Wait with them until they come back down to the party."

He looked back at Nolan. "I am sure you understand. I have to take security seriously."

Nolan nodded. "Come, Gracia, you can lie down for an hour, and we'll come back down for the wedding."

"You'll be in plenty of time, Commandante. It doesn't start for another two hours. But we do have another event taking place just before then, you might..."

"Alberto!" Rivera's voice cracked like a whip. "Victor was clear that no one is to know the details until it takes place. He was very firm on that."

Alberto nodded. "Yeah, maybe you're right. I'll see you all later. It's going to be a great evening."

They made their way up the grand staircase, closely followed by Francisco, carrying his assault rifle. When they entered their room, he gave them a sneer and lounged against the wall opposite their door. Nolan gave him a neutral glance and closed the door.

"What do we do now?" Gracia whispered.

"Unwrap the LTD. The show is about to start."

"The guard, will he be a problem?"

"No, but he will be the source of an assault rifle. When the time comes, we'll get him in here, and I'll take it off him."

He got out the commo and pushed the earpiece in, then keyed the mic.

"Bravo One, this is Four."

"This is one, you're strength Four."

"We believe the Admiral is in the basement of a copycat White House, probably in the situation room."

There was a silence. Then, "Say again, Four."

Nolan explained the situation. We estimate he has an hour and a half max."

"Copy that. What's the plan?"

"We're about to search the house and find a way down to where we believe they're holding him. The shit will hit the fan in about an hour or so. Will you be ready?"

"We're on the way. I'll alert the AC-130, and we'll keep the Reaper on standby too in case we need extra firepower. But you know they'll be alerted the second we move out."

"Understood, we'll deal with it. The plan is to locate the Admiral, and then light up some targets for them to clear an exit for us. Are you bringing the BTR?"

"That's affirmative, Four."

"We may need it, Bravo One."

"Yeah, about time we had something useful from the Soviets. Good luck with finding Jacks."

"Copy that. Four out."

Nolan looked at Gracia. "You're very ill. In fact, I think you're dying. It would be even better if you were naked. Make it happen."

She nodded, stripped off her clothes and lay down on

the bed. Then she started moaning, louder and louder, and soon she was screaming in agony. Nolan flung open the door, and the guard looked up, alert.

"Francisco, my wife, she is gravely ill. Is there a doctor here?"

"A doctor, is she that bad?"

Nolan was waving his hands, the agitated, worried husband. "See for yourself, man. I think she may be dying."

The man rushed into the bedroom, and his eyes nearly popped out of his skull when he saw Gracia's naked body on the bed. When Nolan hit him, he went down as if poleaxed, and the Chief had to hastily grab for the rifle to stop it clattering to the floor. He checked the man was unconscious and pushed on his carotid artery for a few seconds.

"You'll kill him," Gracia admonished him.

Nolan shook his head. "Not this time, it'll just hold him under for a while longer. But when the attack comes in, he may wish he were dead. Get your clothes on, let's go."

While she was dressing, he unwrapped the LTD. There was no need for subterfuge, carrying a stolen assault rifle in this house was as much a declaration of hostile intent as in the real White House. Gracia finished tidying her clothes and rapidly checked the body of Francisco.

"We haven't got time for that," Nolan said in irritation. "Every second counts now. We have to find him. Bring the LTD. I guess we're going to need it."

She stood up nodded. "Let's go."

They hurtled down the back stairs to avoid the security checkpoint at the front. On the lower floor, they started searching for a way down to the basement areas. After fifteen minutes, they'd checked every possible doorway and corridor, with not a sign of a basement entrance. Even more ominous, Manuel Rivera was still on station in the foyer, surrounded by four guards who regularly patrolled the house, so they had to hide in an empty room whenever footsteps came near.

"This is crazy," Gracia exploded as they waited in a cleaner's closet for a guard to pass by. "We haven't a clue where they're holding the Admiral. There may not be a basement in this house."

"No, he's spent millions getting it right, and he won't have missed one of the most famous features. Everyone has heard of the Situation Room, so you can be he'll have one somewhere."

"Where is the entrance in the real White House?"

"I haven't a clue. I've never been there."

"Then why not call up your Lieutenant and ask him?"

Nolan stared at her. "Christ, yes, why didn't I think of that?"

He called up Talley.

"Bravo One, this is Four."

"Go ahead, Four."

"I need to know the location of the White House Situation Room."

There was a brief silence. "Are you serious?"

Nolan explained what he was after, and Talley acknowledged.

"I haven't been there, Four, but I'll use the satcom to ask someone. Back in two."

They waited, and Gracia peered out of the door. "It's all clear. We can go when we're ready."

Nolan nodded as his earpiece came to life.

"Four, this is One."

"Reading you, One."

"The Situation Room is below the West Wing, in the basement."

The West Wing, the entrance was off the foyer guarded by Rivera and his men.

"Copy that, One. What's your ETA?"

"Twenty minutes. We've already taken down a roadblock, so they'll be on full alert. Be careful."

"Copy that, out."

He explained the situation to Gracia.

"All hell is about to be let loose. Our people are on the way, and Rivera will be checking out the defenses. It could be our chance. Let's go see the situation at the front of the house."

They left the closet and quietly walked back to the foyer. It was empty, and the wide, heavy oak door that led to the West Wing was partly open, just across the floor and less than forty feet from where they stood. Outside, they could hear shouting, men running to prepare for the coming action. So now it had started.

"Let's get into the West Wing. It's now or never, I guess."

They ran lightly across the wide expanse of the foyer, conscious that they were still making too much noise on the marble floor. But it couldn't be helped. They reached the door to the West Wing and pushed through. They ran down the corridor, past the Cabinet Room and stopped just after the door to the Oval Office.

"I guess we need to head for the lobby. The elevator and stairs for the Situation Room will be in there."

"And exactly why would you wish to go the Situation Room, Commandante? Put down that rifle."

Nolan looked around slowly. Manuel Rivera stood a few feet away, and this time his pistol was not holstered. He was flanked by several of his men, all carried M4-A1 carbines, and identical to the one he'd taken off Francisco. He tried to bluff his way out and held onto the carbine.

"Victor Salazar told me there was a show going on and we were welcome to watch. Why are you threatening us with those guns?"

Rivera sighed. "Because you are carrying a weapon stolen from one of my men, and because Mr. Salazar has given orders to shoot anyone who tries to enter the Situation Room. Put down the rifle, and I will give you the opportunity to talk to Mr. Salazar later. Otherwise, I will have to shoot you both. It's up to you, Commandante. I suggest you put it down and put up your hands. And you, Senora Montez! What is that you are carrying? Vincenzo, take it from her. We will examine it later, but it is certainly not a wedding gift." He sneered at Nolan. "Is it, Commandante? I assume that is your name, but we will know for sure very soon."

Nolan put down the rifle and raised his hands. Rivera gave rapid orders to his men.

"Take them, tie their hands and put them in the Press Office."

He smiled at Nolan and Gracia. "You will find it most comfortable, Commandante. We had it especially fitted out for guests. I must go now, but I will speak to Mr. Salazar, and you will see me later. Believe me, I think you will tell me the truth about what you are really doing here." He turned to the man holding the LTD. "Vincenzo, put that on the desk in the foyer. I will inspect it later."

They were hustled along the corridors to the Press

Room by two of the guards. But no press had ever entered this place. It had been converted into something with quite a different use. The walls were hung with iron loops, and in the center of the room was a heavy wooden table. It was splashed with a dark red substance, blood. Close to the table was a steel post, about five feet high and cemented into the floor. The ground around it was also covered with dried blood.

"Over there, and face the wall, hands behind your backs," one of the men gestured with his rifle. He stood well back with his finger on the trigger. The other man had Gracia similarly covered, and Nolan had no chance to take both of them.

One maybe. But not two!

They both did as they were ordered, and he felt the pressure of plastic cable ties being fastened together. Then they were pulled over to the post and fastened to it, back to back.

"Enjoy your stay, my friends," one of the guards sneered. "The post you are tied to is a whipping post, a specialty of Mr. Salazar. He will enjoy introducing you to its delights. I have little doubt he will start with your woman. Have you ever seen a woman's bloodied bones, Commandante? It is an unusual sight."

"Yeah, not as unusual as seeing your bleeding body on the floor of this room, hombre. Take off these cuffs, and I'll show you who's a real man."

The man hammered his fist into the side of Nolan's head, and he saw stars for a few seconds.

"I'd save your insults, my friend. You'll need all your energy for later."

He laughed again and nodded to the other guard. They

walked out of the room, and they heard the heavy oak door being locked.

"I didn't see any windows when they brought us in here, Gracia. Can you see any your side of the room?"

"None, but even if we could get out of these cuffs, we're locked in, Chief Nolan."

"Yeah, and they're about to murder Admiral Jacks."

"Do you think Lieutenant Talley will get here with his men in time to save him?"

"Not without air support, and the only way they'll get that is if we identify and light up the targets for them."

"So what are you going to do?"

He was thinking the same question, with no answers. "I honestly don't know, Gracia. I think this may be the end of the line."

CHAPTER TEN

He could feel Gracia pulling against the plastic ties.

"Can you crouch down a little, Chief Nolan? I need to fix my skirt."

"You're not serious? They're about to torture and murder us after they've killed the Admiral. This is not time to worry about your skirt. I'd be saying your prayers if I were you."

"So you're not interested in the knife I have strapped to my inner thigh?"

He nearly choked with relief. "You're serious?"

"Of course. It was quite a problem finding room for Francisco's gun as well, in my underwear, but I managed."

He laughed out loud. "Gracia, you are an absolute wonder woman. What the hell would I do without you?"

She didn't reply. They'd both bent their legs slightly, sliding their plastic ties down the post.

"That's it! I think I can reach it now. Hold it there."

He waited while she wriggled around to extract the knife, then she started sawing through the plastic.

"Tell me something, Chief Nolan. What are you planning to do when you get home to America?"

"Do? I'll take a long, hot shower, a few cold beers out of the icebox, and catch up on the baseball. Why?"

"I didn't mean that. Are you in any relationships, with women?"

He understood but didn't reply at first; he was thinking hard.

"Or men?" she prompted him.

"Hey, you've got me wrong, Gracia. I thought I showed you what my preferences are."

She grunted as she cut through the last of her cuffs.

"That's true. You know, I like you tied like that. It's very sexy."

"Dammit, stop playing around. Our people are in trouble."

She grinned. "And I'm freeing us so we can help them. Stand still."

He felt his bonds slacken, and he pulled his hands free.

"We need to get out of here, and fast."

He examined the door; in the absence of any windows, they had to get it open.

"Gracia, hand me the pistol."

She passed him a small automatic, a small frame .380 ACP semi-auto Beretta PPK.

"That guard had it in a small holster strapped to his belt. I thought it might come in useful."

He nodded.

"When you were shouting at me to stop wasting time."

He grinned. "I'm sorry, Gracia. You were right. Now I need to get this door open. The lock is solid and built into the woodwork that's heavy oak. It'll have to be the hinges.

Get back, and I'll attempt to shoot them off."

He pointed the gun and fired. The bullet ricocheted around the room, and they both dived to the floor. Nolan got to his feet and checked the hinge. The bullet had just dented the iron. Clearly, the door fittings were made from high quality iron. After all, this was the White House, or as near as was possible in Victor Salazar's crazed mind.

"It didn't do any good. It's more likely to kill us than break open the hinges."

"We'll have to wait until a guard comes back. We have a gun, so we can break out then."

He stared at her. "My platoon is fighting its way through to us. They need those targets lit, and the Admiral could be killed at any moment."

As he finished speaking, they both looked at the screen, but so far there was no sign of the execution. Nolan slumped to the floor in despair. He wanted to blast away at the door, to get out of the room and help his comrades, but it was as heavily built as the door of a bank. Gracia sat beside him.

"You can't do everything, Chief Nolan. Sometimes you have to take a back seat and allow people their fate."

"There's no such thing as fate. We have to get out of here. Nolan prowled around the huge chamber, searching for inspiration, anything that would give them hope. Waiting for a guard to open the door could be too late; too late for Bravo Platoon, and too late for Admiral Jacks. Gracia was leaning against the wall behind the door with her slim knife in her hand, ready to strike if anyone came in.

"You didn't answer my question."

He looked at her. "What was that?"

"I asked you about relationships."

"Jesus Christ, this is hardly the time."

"It may be all the time we have left, Chief Nolan. Surely it is better to enjoy it rather than end our lives in misery."

"We're not going to end our lives."

"So you say. But it may not be your choice to make."

He was appalled at her fatalism. And yet, maybe she had a point. When the door opened, if there were four or more armed men outside, they'd find it impossible to overcome four automatic rifles with a tiny pistol and a knife. Except that the door hadn't opened yet, and there were no armed men about to torture and kill them. He looked again at Gracia and saw how desperately she needed some warmth from him; some sign of their humanity, and of what they'd shared, both in and out of bed.

"Gracia, if we get out of this, there's no one I'd want to be with more than you."

She brightened. "You mean that?"

He thought briefly of Carol Summers, the detective in San Diego with whom he had an on off relationship. But she wasn't here, facing death in a Colombian torture chamber. And besides, Gracia was, well, fabulous. A girl he was growing to like more and more with each hour he spent with her. And these bastards wanted to kill her. He raged inside.

I can't let it happen. Even if I have to rip that door off with my bare hands, like they used the rack in here to rip peoples limbs off. Wait, the rack!

He looked at the mechanism, pulleys, ropes, and gears. He thought back to his physics lessons, was it possible? It was sure worth a try.

"Gracia, your knife, cut these ropes on one side of the

rack."

"Why? They will only be angry and make us suffer even more if they beat us."

"Just do it. We're going to rack the door off."

She looked up with dawning comprehension. And doubt.

"Are you sure?"

"Would you sooner stand here and wait to die?"

She rushed to cut the rope fixed to one side of the contraption. He was encouraged to see how strong it was. She had to use the serrated side of the blade to saw through it.

Human limbs are sure strong, he mused.

The rope would have to be pretty tough to withstand the strain, tough enough to pull the door off its hinges? That remained to be seen. The heavy oak door had iron fittings, so perhaps they were used for some kind of torture. They appeared to be bolted all the way through it, so he tied the rope to four of the rings. Then he walked to the rack and started to turn the spoked wheel that tightened the ropes. They creaked as they took up the strain, and he turned it further, feeling the pressure mount. Gracia threw her strength against the spokes, and the ropes tightened even more. Nolan felt the muscles in his arms bulging as he gave every ounce of his strength to turning the spokes. There was a slight 'crack' from one of the hinges as the metal fractured internally, but still the door held fast. He knew his strength was at its limits. He was giving it all he'd got, and it still wasn't enough.

"Gracia, we need to give it one last push, everything we have. Think of something that makes you angry. These bastards are kidnapping babies for their organs, stabbing pregnant women, hacking the limbs off old people, now one, two three, heave!"

They both threw the last reserves of their draining strength against the spokes and held it. Nolan thought his arms were about to fall off. He'd never known such exquisite agony, not even during the Seals training course, the infamous Basic Underwater Demolition School, BUDS, at the Naval Special Warfare Center in Coronado. His brain fogged with a multi-hued series of images that spilled through it, almost like a psychedelic illusion. And then the door moved.

"Keep the pressure on. We're nearly there!"

He heard Gracia grunt, and he pushed with the very last dregs of his strength, and suddenly it gave. With a huge crash, the door popped off its hinges, ripped out the lock, and hurtled inside the room. They were free.

They both had to stop for precious minutes to regain the feeling in their aching muscles. The sound of gunfire was loud, automatic fire, pistol shots, and the occasional thunder as a grenade exploded. The attack had begun. They rushed out of the door and along the passageway. There was a window overlooking the rear of the grounds. Nolan tried the commo again.

"Bravo One, this is Four."

The reply came straight back. "Where the hell are you, Four?"

He explained they'd been locked in.

"You're clear now?"

"That's affirmative, One."

"We need some of those targets taken out, Chief. We're still outside the main gate, and they're pouring down fire from the four machine gun towers."

"Copy that. Are we patched through to the AC-130?"

"Yeah, they can hear everything."

"Good. Give me a few minutes. We'll recover the LTD and get up on the roof. Out."

They ran out to the foyer. There were two men standing inside the main door, both carried M4s. Nolan shot them both on the run, hitting them with the small Beretta bullets with shots that took both men in the heart. There wasn't time to aim for a more definite killing spot, but he got lucky, and they both went down. He picked up their M4s, removed the spare clips from their pockets, stuffing them into his own, and looked around for the LTD. But Gracia had found it behind the reception desk. She gave him a questioning glance.

"Do we go straight to the roof, Chief Nolan? The Admiral is still in a lot of danger."

He hesitated only for a fraction of a second.

"We have to take those guard towers down, or none of us will escape. We'll come looking for the Admiral when the job's done."

He handed her one of the M4s. "I'll lead off. Just don't let anything happen to that LTD."

She nodded, and he rushed for the stairs. They raced out onto the roof, straight into a group of four Colombians who were grouped together, preparing to pour fire down on the Seals and Castro's men assaulting the gate. Nolan fired a short, accurate burst and cut down all four.

"Gracia, the laser, quick!"

She handed him the device, and he switched it on immediately.

"This is Bravo Four. I have a fire mission. I'm about to light up four successive targets."

A voice broke in and answered in a calm, Alabama drawl. "Bravo Four, this is Hammer One, we're waiting on your call. How much longer before you can activate that laser?"

"I'd guess one minute, Hammer One. Wait one."

He checked the optical sight and pinpointed the first tower, nearest the gate and the most dangerous. He keyed the mic.

"Hammer One, this is Four. Target is illuminated."

"Roger that, Four. Firing now."

Nolan turned to Gracia. "Get your head down low. There's gunfire coming in."

It was as if God was shouting his rage, sending down his displeasure on those on earth who had displeased him. The heavy cannon fire hit the tower, and it disappeared in a thunderous barrage of heavy caliber shells. Nolan immediately shifted the optical sight to the second tower.

"Hammer One, second target is illuminated."

"Copy that."

For the second time, the thunderous roll of gunfire rained down from the heavens. The AC-130 was barely visible in the sky, sliding in and out of low cloud, but it was doubtful if any of the targets even glimpsed the instrument of their deaths before it ripped them into small pieces. Nolan shifted again. It was more difficult. Someone more knowledgeable than the others had put two and two together and made four. Nolan could see a man pointing up at the rooftop, directing his men to fire on them. Manuel Rivera, of course. Other than Victor Salazar, he would be the most dangerous opponent. A stream of automatic fire slammed into the masonry just below the parapet where they crouched. He threw himself at Gracia, forcing her to take cover low on the rooftop. He ran fifty feet to the other end of the roof and sheltered behind a chimneystack. He could see the next tower, but he was almost invisible from the ground.

"Bravo Four, this is Hammer One. Where are you, boy? We're waiting on our next target."

"This is Four, lighting up now, Hammer One."

"We're ready for you."

He sighted the LTD on the third tower and radioed the fire order. Like the previous towers, it erupted in a hail of cannon fire. Already, the defensive fire was beginning to slacken as Salazar's men began to suspect that there might be a power more awesome than their employer's at play today. Some of them were already melting away. They were backlit by the eruption as the fourth tower, painted by Nolan's LTD, erupted in a hail of heavy caliber rounds. Then he ducked as a long burst of automatic fire chipped stonework from the low parapet next to his head. He crawled back to where Gracia had stationed herself. There was a small hole in the stone parapet, probably to drain rainwater off the roof when the storms lashed the surrounding countryside. Gracia was using the M4 to take single, well aimed shots at Salazar's men. While he watched, he saw Rivera leap aside as a bullet chewed up the ground between his legs.

"Damn, I thought I'd aced that bastard."

"Men like him, they don't go down easily," he told her. "Where the hell is the Platoon?"

As if in answer to his question, he saw the heavy gate burst inwards, and a BTR-70 come racing into the yard. They saw Rivera point to it and watched him urging his men on to make an attack on the armored vehicle, but equipped only with assault rifles, they drifted behind cover. Then Rivera saw the danger of his exposed position and joined them. Bravo Platoon had arrived, together with Castro's men in a half dozen trucks that followed the APC in.

"We need to get downstairs, Gracia. It isn't over. We have to free Admiral Jacks."

She nodded. They scooped up the M4s from the fallen Colombians and hurtled down the stairs. The foyer was empty of guards, but a man with an MP5 ran right into them from inside the West Wing. His eyes flared in astonishment, and he raised the machine pistol, but Nolan and Gracia both took him down with short bursts. Nolan glanced at the open front portal to the outside where the battle was raging.

"If they come through that door, we'll be trapped down in the basement. Sooner or later, Rivera is sure to organize a retreat into this building. It's an obvious strong point."

"I'll stay here and cover you, if you can make it to the stairway."

He didn't like it. She would be on her own until Bravo arrived to reinforce the position. But he had no choice.

"Make sure you stay under solid cover. Rivera could come in here at any moment."

"I will. Good luck, make sure you kill Salazar."

He grinned at her. "I will."

Nolan raced into the West Wing and found the stairs that led down to the basement, to the Situation Room. It was unguarded, and it occurred to him that with most of Salazar's people tied up in the battle outside, he was probably running short of men. Then he arrived at the entrance he sought. It was even emblazoned with the seal of the President of the United States, another of Salazar's poor attempts at humor. He opened the heavy, armored door and walked in.

Jacks is still alive. Thank God!

The Admiral was tied to a chair at the end of the room, his mouth covered with a gag. The chair was positioned underneath a huge flat screen TV. He looked up when he saw Nolan. He looked around the room cautiously, but there didn't seem to be anyone else around. It seemed crazy to leave an important hostage unguarded, but there was no one. He ran forward and reached the Admiral.

"Sir, you're okay. This is Chief Nolan, Bravo Platoon."

One eye opened. The Chief was shocked to see that he'd been beaten badly. The other eye was closed and covered in a huge bruise. There were cuts on his face that had been left untreated. He cut away the gag, and the Admiral sucked in air greedily. Then he managed a faint smile.

"What took you so long, Son? I thought you'd be here hours ago."

"I'm here now, Sir. We'll get you out of here."

"Yeah. How did you get past Salazar?"

"Salazar? I didn't see him. There's no one here. They're all outside trying to defend the ranch from our people."

"But, he has to be here. His security center…"

He stopped at the sound of a man's hands clapping together. Nolan whirled around to see a man had come through an unnoticed door at the side of the main entrance. He stood there watching them. Victor Salazar, flanked by bodyguards on either side. He carried no weapon, but each of the four guards carried an A4-M1, the four barrels pointed directly at Nolan and Jacks.

He didn't raise his own weapon. It was obvious the four

men were waiting for an excuse to fire, and even if he could dive under cover, Jacks was unable to move. For several seconds they stared at each other. The bodyguards' gaze was hard and feral, like panting dogs about to fall on a wounded prey, and Victor Salazar seemed quite relaxed for a man whose ranch was systematically being destroyed by an invading force of well-equipped soldiers. Then he spoke.

"Put down your weapon, American, you are clearly no Commandante of the FARC. Unless, of course, you and your Admiral wish to die here."

Nolan hesitated. Would Gracia come looking for them? No, she would stay at her post, covering their back against being cut off by Salazar forces coming into the house. Could he take these men, before they cut him and Jacks down? No, they had that special alertness that was common to elite troops the world over. They were alert and watchful, ready to open fire in a split second. He weighed his options. It would be better to try and beat them with guile rather than guns. He laid down his M4. Salazar smiled coldly.

"You are very sensible, American. Tell me your real name."

Nolan stood silent until Salazar nodded at one of his men. "Shoot the Admiral in the knee if he hasn't answered me in five seconds."

The bodyguard started walking towards them. The Chief knew he was beaten.

"Nolan."

His eyes widened. "Nolan? So you are the man who was responsible for destroying my operation in Ciudad Juarez. That is incredible, that you should take the trouble to come to me. I am so pleased to make your acquaintance at last." He turned to his bodyguards and snapped out an order. "Two of you, go and search this Mr. Nolan, then tie him to a chair. He is in time to watch the show. If I wanted anyone to join us for the execution, it would be him."

Nolan noticed the video camera erected on a tripod in the corner of the room. Salazar saw the direction of his gaze.

"Yes, the camera. It will broadcast my little entertainment for the whole world to see. How do you think your American compatriots will react, Mr. Nolan? A full Admiral executed on prime time television. I'm sending it over the Internet too, so that no one can miss it. And when that is over, I have some further entertainment for you, Mr. Nolan."

"You're wrong, Salazar," Jacks croaked. "I'm not a full Admiral."

"No? What then, a Rear Admiral? Yes, of course, that is it. But you will do, my friend. You will be quite sufficient to teach your countrymen a lesson they will never forget."

The bodyguards took hold of Nolan in an iron grip and searched him. It was a thorough search, and they missed almost nothing. The men piled the contents of his pockets on the table and then tied him to a chair close to Jacks. He tested the knots. The guards knew their business, and there was no way he was going to escape without help. Salazar walked towards them.

"Do you know who will pay for all of this damage to my property, Mr. Nolan? The Americans. Yes, they can create havoc with their bombs and machine guns, and I shall meet with my associates and merely put up the price of my cocaine to pay for the place to be rebuilt. You may wonder how long it will take me to recover the money. No more than a month at the increased prices. So you see, what you have achieved is, nothing."

"You're wrong, Salazar. There are a lot of troops out there, and when they've finished off your men, they'll come down here and start looking for you."

Salazar yawned. "Is that right? Do you take me for a fool, Mr. Nolan? Do you think I haven't prepared for something like this? After the execution of the Admiral, I have prepared a tunnel that leads from the basement to a helicopter pad in the jungle. It is a secret known only to me and my bodyguards, and a comfortable way to leave all this nonsense behind. And when I have gone, I have a surprise for your men."

He took a small, black box out of his pants pocket, like a cellphone.

"This is my doomsday device. The house and grounds have been prepared with explosive charges. As soon as I leave, I shall use this device to start the timer. Twenty minutes after I send the signal, the explosives detonate, and the house and everything around it will be destroyed. After all," he smiled coldly, "if I am to rebuild, I do not want the expense of demolition. I may decide to build something better than this American monstrosity, something modest, of course, like the Palace of Versailles, in France. The Sun King, Louis the Fourteenth built it, I believe."

"I guess he had some help, Salazar. You know you're as crazy as a coot, don't you?"

"You think I'm crazy? Let me show you something, Mr. Nolan."

There was a security cabinet set into the wall. He opened the door and took out an envelope. He took out the contents only inches from Nolan's eyes. They were photographs, photographs of his children, walking into school, and playing on the front lawn outside the house. Nolan strained at his bonds. At that moment, he wanted nothing more than to take the Colombian apart piece by piece.

"You leave my fucking children alone, Salazar! This is nothing to do with them. It's between you and me. You're dead, and whatever it takes, I'll make sure that you're hunted down and killed!"

The Colombian sighed. "In Colombia, we always take care of the children. If they grow up, there is always the chance they may take revenge for their parents' death. It is much safer if they never have the chance." He grinned. "Either to grow up or to take revenge. So I spit on your stupid threats. They are worthless, as is your own life." His face lost the cruel smile, and he reddened with anger. "You think you can insult me and play stupid games, Mr. Nolan? You are nothing to me, nothing!" He nodded at the two bodyguards. "Break one of his arms. He needs to learn some manners."

One of the men took out his pistol, a heavy old American Colt .45, and smashed it repeatedly against the wrist bones of Nolan's left arm. He felt the bones breaking, and waves of pain welled through him, but he steeled his mind to ignore them, as much as he could. He knew the arm would be useless until he could get it treated, even if he ever got out of there. But for the time being, he had to stay alert and watch for any opportunity to stop Salazar. And save his children. He had one chance, and one only, the blade. They hadn't found it in his collar when they searched him. The bodyguards made one last check of his ropes, and

Salazar tossed the photos on the table. He walked to the end of the room and began fussing with the video camera, making it ready for his show. The bodyguards left Nolan and Jacks to join their master.

"Can you use the arm at all?" Jacks murmured to him when they were out of earshot.

Nolan shook his head.

Jacks grimaced. "You'll need to get it treated as soon as our people get here, otherwise you could use the use of it altogether."

"If we're still alive."

"It's not looking great, Chief, but we'll come out of it," Jacks said tersely. "I'm sorry about your children. Are they anywhere he can get near them? I assume the photos are recent."

"Yeah, they're staying with their grandparents upstate. Somehow, Salazar found them."

"Money talks. If you pay enough, you can find out anything."

Nolan heard despair in his voice, and he looked across at the old man. He looked tired and beaten, and there were the signs of near-exhaustion in his eyes. But there was no fear. He knew that Jacks would be ready to go down fighting, if that was possible. They had to try, and Nolan had one last throw of the dice.

"We're not finished yet, Admiral. How are your hands, do you have any movement in them?"

"Not a bit, sorry, Son. You got a plan?" The Admiral had become alert as he scented a chance to cheat death.

"I'm working on it, Sir. We're not done for yet."

"If you get us out of this, you deserve a commissioned rank, Chief. I'll make sure you get one, too."

"If you want to thank me, make sure I don't receive a commission."

"You don't want to be an officer?"

"No, Sir. We Chiefs are too busy running the Service. Besides, I have the best job in the world, why would I want to change it?"

Jacks smiled. "I can't argue with that. What can I do to help?"

Before he could reply, they both looked up. Salazar and his men were still at the other end of the Situation Room, and one of them shouted at his boss.

"Sir, the fighting has spread into the house. There's a gun battle going on in the lobby. We haven't much time."

Salazar pondered. "We need to make sure they hold out for a little longer. I'll go up there and give them some encouragement. They're not in the West Wing yet?"

"No."

"Very well, come with me. Are those two secure?"

"As the American Fort Knox, Mr. Salazar."

"Yes, I'd like to mount a raid on that place one day and relieve them of their gold, and another lesson for the Americans. Come, we need to check on our men. They need some help."

Nolan and Jacks watched them run out of the room to go up the stairs to encourage the defenders.

"He's leaving his people to die," Nolan muttered in disbelief. "Either our people will kill them, or his explosives will."

Jacks nodded. "He's a drug trafficker. Death is his business. By the way, we were talking about a way out of here. Any ideas?"

"You mean like the blade hidden in my shirt collar,

Admiral."

His eyes gleamed. "Yeah, something like that. If you shuffle your chair with its back to mine, I reckon I might be able to reach it."

They moved their chairs around, and Jacks felt for Nolan's shirt collar, but his hands were tied to firmly to the arms of the chair.

"I can't reach it, damn. Can you get closer?"

"I'll have to tip back against you. Ready?"

"As I ever will be, Chief."

Nolan rocked his chair backwards and forwards, and it tipped at an increasing angle until his head literally fell into Jacks' lap. The Admiral struggled to reach his collar.

"I've got it, Chief. Just give me a minute, and I'll twist it around and cut the line holding my right hand."

Nolan heard him grunting with effort as he tried to cut through the first bond. It took three minutes by his calculation, but he saw Jacks' hand lift into the air.

"Got it. A few seconds, and I'll be able to free you."

Less than a minute later, both men stood at the foot of the stairs that led up into the Oval Office and out into the foyer where the fighting was at its heaviest. The sounds of gunfire were loud, and there was the occasional 'crump' of an explosion as someone used a grenade.

"Salazar, he'll be back down here shortly," Jacks reminded him. "He'll want to attend my execution and make his escape. We could so with a couple of weapons."

Nolan looked around the room, but there was nothing.

"I'll go to the top of the staircase. There's any number of weapons up there from the men who've been shot. I'll be back in a few seconds."

"If you meet him coming down, he'll kill you."

Nolan nodded. "I'll just have to hope he's otherwise engaged."

He sprinted to the top of the stairs and into the West Wing. The fighting had spread into the interior of the building, and bullets zipped past his head as he looked out of the door. There was no way out, not until the battle had ended. In front of him a body lay on the floor, clutching an A4-M1. An identical rifle lay at their side. He rushed over to pick up the rifles one handed, wincing as raw pain lanced through his left arm. Then he looked down at the casualty. It was Gracia, her stomach drenched in blood.

CHAPTER ELEVEN

"Gracia, what happened, how bad is it?"

Her eyes opened. "Chief Nolan. I knew you would come. Did you find the Admiral?"

"Yes, he's fine. We need to get you a medic."

Her eyes looked into his, and he saw the pain. "It hurts bad. I think I'm going to die, Chief Nolan."

"No, you're not going to die."

He looked around, but the hallway was empty of any fighting. It had swept past Gracia and past the doorway to the Situation Room. Of course, Salazar! He'd rallied his men and was ordering them to clear the West Wing of the enemy so that he could make his escape.

Where can I take Gracia?

There was only one place. He slung both M4s on his shoulder, picked her up under his good arm, and carried her back down the stairs. Jacks stared at her as he staggered into the room.

"Who is she?"

"One of ours, Admiral. She's been shot."

"Put her on the table, and we'll take a look at her. I've handled a few gunshot wounds in my time. I'll do my best."

"She means a lot to me, Sir."

He glanced up. "Like that, is it?"

"Yes, it is. She was guarding the entrance so I could get down here. We can't let her die."

"As I said, I'll do what I can. Watch the door, and leave the other M4 near the girl. If the fighting comes down here, I'll be ready to use it."

Nolan unslung one of the assault rifles for Jacks and went to guard the doorway, ready to kill any enemy who came down the stairs. He hoped Salazar would come into his sights. The thought of that man ordering the death of his children had seared through him.

No matter how long it takes, Salazar has to die!

Since Grace's death, the children were all he had left to remind him of her. He would give everything to protect them, his life if necessary. He looked over at Jacks. The man had found some water in the bathroom, cleaned her stomach, and cut away her dress. The gunshot wound was clearly visible, still leaking blood.

"How is she?"

"Not good. I'll do my best to stop the bleeding, but she needs the bullet removed and a course of antibiotics to prevent any blood poisoning. She needs blood, too, and some morphine if we can find any."

"When our Seals fight their way through to us, they'll have a medical kit."

Jacks looked up. "It's a start, but she needs an ER room, and quick. And you're forgetting something. Even if they do fight there way through, Salazar will blow the place once he's made his escape."

"Do your best with her, Admiral. We'll deal with the problems one at a time."

He listened to the sounds of gunfire. They were getting nearer and nearer. Bravo Platoon and Castro's Special Forces were pushing Salazar's men back, and it wouldn't be long before they were all over the West Wing. And then Salazar would come back down to execute the Admiral and make his escape. Unless the fighting got too hot, in which case he would almost certainly make his escape and blow the building. The Admiral would still be dead, and he'd only miss out on his plans to broadcast an execution.

Where is the tunnel?

That was the big question. He'd said it was in the basement, but did he mean the Situation Room, or somewhere else in this rambling building? He heard a shout of pain and looked back at the table. Jacks had gone for more fresh water from the bathroom, and Gracia had picked up one of the photos and stared at it. She recognized them as obviously surveillance photos of potential targets for murder or kidnap, and she sat up to look at the others. The pain had caused her to cry out. He shouted for Jacks, but the Admiral was already running to help her.

"Your kids, Chief Nolan?" she asked him, her voice a hoarse murmur.

He couldn't lie to her. "Yeah, they're mine, Daniel and Mary."

"So they're the targets for Salazar?"

"Yes."

"Then you must kill him. You cannot fail."

"I won't, Gracia. But first we must get your wound treated. Try and hang in there. Our people will be here soon."

"Yes."

She lay back on the table, and her eyes closed briefly, then opened wide and stared at him. He understood the question in them. There was no need for words.

"We're doing everything we can. You should be fine. We don't believe the wound is fatal."

She nodded and closed her eyes again.

Jacks had come out of the bathroom, seen him with Gracia, and picked up his M4 to guard the entrance. He shouted over to Nolan from his position just inside the doorway.

"We've got company."

He grabbed his own M4 and rushed to join the Admiral. He could hear Spanish voices at the top of the stairway, Salazar with his bodyguards. They both started down the stairs. Nolan leaned close to Gracia.

"I have to go. They're coming."

She nodded slightly, but her eyes were tight shut as she did her utmost to cope with the pain. He picked up his M4-A1 one-handed and rushed to join Jacks. The footsteps were loud on the stairs, no more than twenty feet away. He raised his eyebrows at Jacks, who nodded. Both men stepped through the opening, stood at the foot of the stairwell, and loosed a long burst at Salazar and his men. They were both lucky and unlucky. Three of the bodyguards went down, killed or seriously wounded, yet Salazar survived. He shouted at his remaining man to shoot back, but it was unnecessary, the man had lifted his assault rifle and was firing as the two Seals jumped back behind cover. Bullets spattered all around them, and they waited for the fire to end. There was a loud 'click'. The two men needed no explanation; the gun jammed. They leapt back through the doorway and fired again. The sole surviving bodyguard screamed as several bullets ripped into him, but Salazar had ducked out of sight. They heard his voice, loud and mocking.

"You think you have upset my plans, Mr. Nolan, but it will be the last time. Goodbye. Manuel, do it!"

They looked up and saw Rivera's head appear over the top of the staircase. Then he started throwing grenades down the stairwell. They heard Salazar laughing insanely as bomb after bomb rolled around their feet. Both men shouted at the same moment.

"Grenade!"

Nolan dived one side of the door, grunting in pain as his injured arm made contact with hard concrete, and Jacks went the other way. The grenades went off, one after the other. There were six in all, and they produced a rolling thunder of explosions and hot shards of metal that slashed through the room. When the explosions ended, Nolan jumped up. He shouted to Jacks, but couldn't hear his voice. His eardrums had been savaged by the violent detonations, but there was only one priority uppermost in his mind. Salazar.

"Look after Gracia," he shouted at Jacks, hoping he could hear. Then he powered up the stairs, but there was no sign of the trafficker. He saw a movement in the corner of his eye and whipped up his rifle, but he recognized the figure of Will Bryce just in time.

"Will, have you seen Salazar?"

The big black PO1 shook his head. "No, we're still mopping up. There's no time to hunt him down until we've finished off the defenders."

"He's rigged the place to blow. There are explosives

everywhere. We don't have a lot of time."

"Jesus Christ! What about Jacks?"

"He's safe, downstairs. One of ours is wounded, Gracia. She needs a medic badly."

"I'll get Castro's medics onto it. He has a couple of good people."

"Is the Captain okay?"

"He is, just a couple of scratches, but he's lost over half his command."

Nolan looked around the destroyed and smoking West Wing, but there was no movement; everyone was either dead or had run. Then he heard the distinct sound of a door closing. He looked at Will.

"It could be Salazar. Can you cover me? We have to get this guy. He's trying to escape through some kind of secret tunnel."

"I'm with you, Chief."

They ran through the deserted building. When they came to the room where they thought they'd heard the noise, there was nothing to be seen. A dead body lay on the floor, one of Salazar's men, and the walls were pockmarked with bullet holes. The door to the room had been blasted off its hinges, but there was nothing to indicate a door that led to an escape route.

"Where are we?" Will asked.

Nolan shook his head. "I've no idea, but it must be something pretty important. It looks as if it's fitted for high level conferences." Then it he recognized it, the huge, dark mahogany table; he remembered seeing it in pictures. "It's the Roosevelt Room."

"It doesn't seem likely, Chief. If I was building a bolt hole, this is the last place I'd put it."

"Maybe that's what he wants people to think. Help me search this room, see if we can find anything. We both heard that click, and it sure sounded like a door or hatch closing."

"Yeah, maybe," Will nodded gloomily. But he took one side of the room while Nolan took the other. They tapped along the walls, then looked underneath the big conference table, nothing. "I don't think it's here," Will continued. "We've searched everywhere. All that's left is the fireplace, and I doubt he went up the chimney. Shouldn't we be clearing out of here and warning the others?"

Something rang a bell in Nolan's mind.

The chimney! Is it possible?

It sounded like something from an adventure film. And yet, Salazar had billions to spend in the most outrageous fantasies, of which the replica White House was one.

"Help me look around the fireplace. There could be some kind of a secret door."

They searched around the huge, marble structure, Nolan knew that time was running out if there was to be any chance of stopping Salazar.

"Chief, there's something here."

He joined Will on the other side of the big fireplace where the marble uprights should have been cemented flush to the wall, and there was a tiny gap.

"Look around for something to open it with, Will. If this is it, there'll be a hidden button or lever. There must be something."

They tapped all around the ill-fitting marble, without finding anything unusual, or anything that could be used to open a hidden door. Nolan feverishly searched around the ornate marble structure, but there was nothing."

"Maybe we're in the wrong place," Will murmured. "We could try out in the hallway."

"Maybe, but something tells me we're real close."

"You stay here and keep looking. I'll search outside."

"Okay," Nolan replied, his mind still searching for what they'd missed. He was sure it was there; it had to be. They heard a noise outside in the hallway, and both Seals turned quickly, their rifles raised, but it was Talley with Roscoe Bremmer. As they moved, Will caught his boot on the fire irons, the ornate, wrought iron implements that stood on the hearth. But they didn't fall across the floor. Instead, there was a 'click' as the base that held the tools tipped over, and the fireplace moved at one end, revealing an opening about two feet wide.

"I'm going in," Nolan said quietly.

"Going in where?" Talley asked.

"Salazar's escape route. He has a helo waiting in a jungle clearing, and if we don't get to him fast, he'll get away."

"Salazar? I thought you said you'd seen him making his escape into the jungle opposite the ranch?" He stared at Roscoe. The black man looked embarrassed. "Damn, Boss, several of us saw him, and we were sure it was him. I doubt Salazar is in here."

Talley looked at Nolan. "Well?"

"It was Salazar. He was here only minutes ago."

He nodded. "Maybe Bremmer was mistaken. You'd better go get him. Take Will with you, and call if you come across him. Don't forget the AC-130 is still overhead."

"Boss, Salazar had sewn this place with charges. It's likely to go up at any time, so you need to get everyone out of here. If he's pressed the remote detonator, the countdown has already started."

Talley didn't stop to question him. He barked orders at the men who'd come into the room.

"Get everyone out of here, and check every room. The building is rigged to blow!"

They didn't wait to acknowledge, the seconds were ticking by. Nolan squeezed through the narrow gap and into a tunnel that was surprisingly well constructed. The walls were lined with smooth cement, and lights were set into armored bulkhead fittings in the roof, which was high enough to allow them to walk upright. The tunnel ran straight for the first hundred yards and then twisted at a right angle. Water seeped onto the floor that was an inch deep.

Another sharp bend appeared after three hundred yards, and the tunnel ran as straight as a die. Ahead of them, perhaps another five hundred yards away, they could see the bright light of day streaming into the tunnel; the entrance that someone had left open. They ran on until they stood at the foot of a long ladder propped against the wall. Nolan went up first and poked his head cautiously out of the hatch. There was a thunderous noise, and his automatic reflexes made him duck back down. But it wasn't someone shooting at him. In front of him was a Bell 427 Twin Turboshaft helo. The noise had been the engines starting with a roar. He looked back out and could see Manuel Rivera reaching down to help pull Salazar into the fuselage.

He didn't hesitate. His M4-A1 had a full clip, but this was a shot that required accuracy, not wild, automatic fire. With his feet on the ladder, and his good elbow on the ground outside the hatch, he sighted carefully plum center on Salazar's body. Even so, it was a difficult shot.

Salazar was moving as Rivera pulled him upwards in to the cabin. The first bullet took him in the lower body, and the man twisted in pain as the hot metal hammered into him. Rivera looked across the clearing, saw Nolan, and turned to shout something to the pilot. Nolan fired again, and again. Both times he saw Salazar's body jump as the bullets hit him. The helo started to ascend, and he fired a fourth bullet; this one aimed at Rivera. The security chief flinched as the bullet hit his boss. He'd been pulling him upwards, and Salazar's body shielded him so that the drug lord took the hit intended for him. He looked down quickly at his boss and decided he'd done enough. He let go, and the body of Victor Salazar dropped back to the ground as the helo soared into the air. The Chief ran over to it and knelt down to check for any signs of life, but the Colombian was dead. Will Bryce ran up beside him.

"Is that it?"

"Yeah, that's it. I don't know about his brothers, but they won't be hard to kill, they weren't Victor Salazar."

"They're both dead." Will explained how the two had led the defense of the ranch compound. "They both went down fighting. At least at the end they were men, not running out like this one."

It's over. My family will be safe, and the Salazars have been destroyed.

"That's the best news I've heard in a long time, Will. Let's go back through the tunnel and see how things are in the compound."

Will shook his head. "No way I want to go back underground. That tunnel looked mighty near to collapse, and the spring was leaking through the walls something bad."

Nolan smiled and agreed to walk back. It would be an opportunity to check out the extent of the damage to the compound. When the Seals left, there would be nothing but a smoking pile of rubble in this patch of Colombia. They walked along a narrow jungle pathway for a couple of hundred yards, and then the trees gave way to the huge, open area hacked out for the Salazar ranch. Smoke hung in the air from the gunfire and explosions, and when they walked through the gate, the devastation was obvious. Everything had been damaged, either completely or in part. Only the White House still stood, but they'd evacuated, waiting for Salazar's own demolition charges to explode. Casualties lay everywhere, and Castro's men were going around administering to them as best they could. Nolan hunted for Gracia. He finally found Jacks running past and grabbed his arm to stop him.

"Admiral, Gracia. Where is she?"

The older man stopped and darted a glance to where a pair of medics administering morphine to some of the worst of the casualties. Nolan followed his look.

"What's going on? She can't be that bad. When I left her, she'd only taken a non-fatal hit."

"You're right, the wound wasn't fatal, but those grenades Rivera tossed down the stairwell did the damage. The shrapnel bounced around the Situation Room, and the walls are all concrete. She took a fragment of metal in the side of the head."

"So she's…"

Jacks nodded. "I'm sorry. She was killed instantly."

Rivera! He nearly blacked out. He saw Gracia's beautiful face, the face that reminded him so much of Grace. Both dead, both killed by drug traffickers. A red mist obscured his vision, and he had to prop himself with his assault rifle as his knees buckled. His emotions were a tortuous turmoil of hate and despair, of grief, and loss, and anger.

Rivera!

"He's getting away, Admiral. Rivera! We need to contact the AC-130 and make sure they shoot him down."

"It's already been done, Chief. The helo disappeared in the ground clutter around Medellin. Even if they'd located it, they couldn't open fire above a civilian area."

Talley came up to them. "I'm sorry about Gracia, Chief. She sure was something."

"Yeah, thanks, Boss. Listen, Rivera got away."

"I know that. They tried to shoot down his helo, but his pilot was either too clever or too lucky."

"You don't understand. He'll want revenge, and that means he'll target my family, my kids. Now that he's escaped, he'll make it his number one priority to kill them, in return for us busting Salazar's operation."

"Where are they now? Are they safe?"

"They're with their grandparents. No, they're not safe, not now Manual Rivera is after them."

"You need to contact the local cops, and get them to increase protection on them. Do you know anyone who can make things happen?"

He thought about Carol Summers. The detective was in San Diego, and the kids were outside San Francisco. But she knew the system, and knew him and his family. He nodded.

"Yes, I do, the detective in San Diego PD."

"Okay, I'll get a patch through to them, and you can speak to her personally. Anything you want, I'll get NCIS onto it."

It took a few minutes, but soon he recognized Carol Summers' familiar voice.

"Carol, this is Kyle. We're out of the country on a mission."

Talley was standing within earshot, so he had to be careful. Her voice sounded puzzled and slightly cool.

"Is everything okay? Are you hurt?"

"I'm fine, yeah. It's the kids. One of the kingpins has escaped, and he may try to take revenge on the kids."

"Shouldn't you ask SFPD to handle it?"

"I'm asking you, Carol. Dammit, you know how these things go. They need to hear it from one of their own, not me. I'm just a member of the public."

She was quiet for a few moments. Then he heard her say, "I'll get right onto it, Kyle. Are they still in the same house, with the grandparents?"

"Yeah, that's right, same place."

"Leave it with me. I'll talk to someone up there, and see if we can get them to increase surveillance."

"Christ, they're in danger, Carol. See what you can do won't cut it!" he shouted at her.

He felt himself going dizzy with anxiety. It was good just talking to Carol Summers, even though he was certain she couldn't fully understand the severity of the threat. There was so much he wanted to say to her, and so much agony he wanted to share with someone. Except that maybe he was wrong about her, about her caring. The red mist started to creep in front of his eyes, and he found himself struck dumb, unable to speak. Finally, her voice penetrated the thick mist. She sounded cold.

"Is anything wrong, Kyle? Are you sure you're okay? I said I'd do my best."

"No, it's, I dunno."

He thrust the commo handset at Talley and walked quickly away. Sure, he was trained for everything, to fight, to kill, to survive for long periods in extreme terrain. But how could they train you for grief? She'd been a fine girl, Gracia, with a whole lifetime in front of her.

Just like Grace.

And she'd met a similar end. Were they doomed, these women he came into contact with, doomed to be shot down like dogs by these narco-scum? And was he doomed to live his life always checking the shadows in case there was someone waiting to get in a lucky shot at his kids. It only took one round each, two bullets, and his family would be lost forever to him. They couldn't train you for that. It was a burden you had to bear.

But Christ, it's hard, so hard.

He felt his eyes begin to moisten. It was ludicrous, a tough, hard-bitten Chief Petty Officer of the US Navy Seals, almost crying while on a mission in enemy territory. Except that he was human. And he was alive. Yes, as long as he lived, he'd finish Salazar's chief murderer, Manuel Rivera. He'd find him. No matter where on the earth he tried to hide, he'd find him. And he'd kill him. Abruptly, he felt better. He was no longer the hunted. He was the hunter. And he was hungry for blood.

"Chief, are you okay?"

Talley had come up behind him. He turned and saw the Lieutenant almost flinch when he saw the expression in his eyes.

"I'm okay. Let's get this mission squared away and go home. I've got some things to take care of."

CHAPTER TWELVE

His mind must have wandered elsewhere, as one moment he'd avoided continuing the conversation with Carol Summers, the next he heard the roar of rotor blades approaching from the north.

"Chief? How's the arm?"

He looked up at Vince Merano, the other unit sniper.

"Yeah, the medic put it in a temporary splint. Where're we at?"

Vince looked at him with a puzzled expression. "For the last fifteen minutes, we've been preparing for exfiltration, Chief. The Blackhawks are coming in now, and they're taking us off, together with Castro's wounded. The Colombian Air Force is on the way to collect the rest of them, and they've got a whole heap of regular army shipping in on a convoy of trucks to secure the area. For some reason, they don't trust the local law to take care of this mess."

"I wonder why not."

Vince gave him his old, familiar smile. "We're going

home. I gather you're worried about Rivera."

"I am, but not as much as Rivera should be worried about me."

"So you're gonna take him down?"

Nolan nodded. "This mission was always personal, Vince. It wasn't just about denting the Colombian drugs trade. The Salazars declared war on my family, some complicated macho Colombian thing. The last of them is Rivera, and he's the only one who matters. Until he dies, Daniel and Mary will always be in danger. I owe it to them to see this through, and that means Rivera goes down."

Vince nodded. "You know we're always around. You want anything, and we'll come a-running."

"Yeah, thanks. But something tells me this is going to go to the wire. It'll be man to man. It'll be either me or him."

* * *

Nolan watched the landscape of Colombia fall away as the Blackhawk gained height and headed at maximum knots for the USS Ronald Reagan, the Nimitz class nuclear-powered aircraft carrier that would carry them part way home. He felt flat, and a taste in his mouth that was metallic. Maybe he was getting too old for this type of work; the sudden violence and death they brought to this kind of a mission, and then a helo to take them out for the journey home, ready for the next one.

Perhaps I'm just tired. I'll be fine after some rest. And after I've killed Rivera.

It was the last thought before he blacked out.

He awoke in a bed in the carrier's well-equipped

hospital. A nurse was changing the dressing on his arm. Sadly, the rating was a young man with a pimply face, stiff, carroty hair, and a bad case of halitosis.

"How are you feeling, Chief?" the man asked him as he finished the dressing. At least he was good at his job. The dressing was neat and comfortable, although his arm throbbed.

"I'm okay, yeah, thanks. What happened to my arm?"

"The surgeon reset the bones. He says you'll be out of commission for a few weeks, but if you're careful, the arm will recover as good as new. He'll be here to talk to you later."

Nolan nodded his thanks. "We're headed for San Diego?"

"That we are, Chief, ETA tomorrow at midday. I can't wait to get shore leave and get back to see my kids."

He didn't look old enough to have a family. "How many do you have, Seaman?"

"Two, Chief, a boy and a girl."

He took out his wallet and showed Nolan a photo of two children. Both had stiff, carroty hair, and Nolan had to work hard to suppress a smile. "They're great, nice looking kids."

"Yep, I think so too. You got any kids?"

"Boy and a girl, they're older than yours."

"I'll bet you can't wait to get back to them, either."

"That's right."

The nurse sensed that the conversation had made his patient uncomfortable, and he finished off filling in a chart, and left the tiny ward. Which left Nolan able to think ahead and plan how to deal with his next problem. Rivera. Of all of Salazar's people, Rivera was without doubt the most formidable. He'd have to use every ounce of his strength and resources to take the man down before he could attack Daniel and Mary. He could feel the numbness in his arm, tried to move it, and felt a sharp pain lance through his body. He let out just a tiny cry of pain, but the surgeon chose that moment to walk in.

"You shouldn't be trying to use that arm. It's only just been set. Are you trying to undo all of my good work?"

The carrier's surgeon was a full commander, and with a strong, confident manner on his pudgy face, the result of too much good food in the carrier's mess and too little exercise.

"Sorry, Sir. Thanks for patching me up. There's no pain, so I reckon it'll soon be time to remove the dressings," Nolan lied.

"Do you, indeed? You must be using some miracle drug that makes bones heal in hours rather than weeks and months," the surgeon smiled. "You need at least a month in those splints, otherwise you'll never get back the use of your arm. A full recovery will take you three months, so you'd better get used to the idea."

"I can't."

Nolan told him the whole story about his kids, about Manual Rivera, and about the threat to their lives.

"Surely you can't be the only person in the world who can protect them? Can't the cops help out?"

"They're doing their best, and there's one in particular, Carol Summers, an SDPD detective who's trying real hard, but they don't know what they're up against."

"She any good, this Detective Summers?"

Nolan told him about her, and the efforts she'd made to help him. Then he told him about Grace and the kids;

he told him everything. Even about Manuel Rivera coming after his family to pursue his vendetta. Afterwards, he was surprised, and he could only think it was the morphine that loosened his tongue. The surgeon was a good listener; a doctor who'd acquired an expert bedside manner, during his long years repairing broken sailors in one of the largest ships afloat. When his patient finally ran out of words, he didn't speak for a few moments, just mulled over what he'd been told. Finally, he nodded.

"She sounds like quite a girl, the detective."

"She is, yes."

"And you like her a lot."

Nolan had to think about that, and he realized that yes, he did like her a lot. But after that last outburst, when he'd all but accused her of not caring enough, she wouldn't be so keen to talk to him. Not when all the gratitude she got for her efforts, was him shouting at her. He explained it all to the surgeon.

Damn, why am I saying these things?

Normally, he didn't trust anyone with his personal thoughts and affairs.

"Yes, I believe I do," he replied, after a few moments thought. It was another surprise that he'd admitted it, but it was true. Yes, he did like her a lot. He had a twinge of guilt about Gracia, but realized it was something else, in another life. He'd met the fiery young Colombian. She was wonderful, and now she was dead. He was alive, and he had to move on, for the kid's sake, and perhaps for Grace too. She wouldn't want him to dwell on the dead, but on the living; the people the kids would need if they were to grow up with any kind of a normal life.

"But I doubt she'll be interested in me, not after I

chewed her out about not doing enough to protect my family."

"Was it a fair chewing out, Chief? Sometimes we all need some plain talking."

"No, it wasn't. She was doing her best."

"Good. So everything is straightforward, and you know what to do."

"What the hell is that? It's not clear to me, and as I said, she won't even be interested in talking to me."

"Not if you carry on with that line of bullshit she won't, no."

"Sir?"

The surgeon sighed. "Okay, I'll lay it all out for you. You never had a row with someone you love, said something you didn't mean?"

"Of course, yes, but…"

"And that was it, was it? The end of the relationship."

"No, but…"

"So you go to her, Chief, and admit you behave like a horse's ass. Thank her for everything she's done."

"Yes, but…"

"And when that arm I spent so much of my time and expertise fixing is fully recovered, get out and find that bastard who's causing you so much grief, and finish him for good. Deep six the bastard! I think that covers everything, was there anything else?"

"No, Sir."

"Good. Now take care of that arm until it's fully recovered."

"Yes, Sir."

The following day they docked in San Diego. Talley had taken notes of everything that related to Nolan's part in the mission so that he could be spared attending the mission debrief and take care of both his arm and his personal affairs. Nolan tried to call Carol Summers that first afternoon, but the SFPD told him she'd taken some leave. It rocked him to think that she'd taken off at a time like this, so maybe the surgeon had been wrong. But he put the thought out of his mind and called the grandparents. John Robson answered his call.

"Kyle, how are things with you? When did you get back?"

"A couple of hours ago. I'm good. I've got some leave, so I'll come up and see you and the kids."

"What happened?"

"What do you mean, what happened?"

"You only get leave when you're hurt, Kyle. Grace always told us that, and it worried her sick."

"Oh, it's nothing, just a broken arm."

"If you say so. Don't come up now, you've only just got back. Make it sometime tomorrow."

In the end, he agreed. His head was still woozy after the morphine, and provided he stayed off it, he'd be okay to drive after a night's sleep. He unpacked his bag and looked out the window at his Camaro.

How will it be driving one-handed? Well, I'll have to manage.

He felt lonely in the echoing, empty house. The kids were away, and even Carol Summers had gone off somewhere on vacation.

Great!

He needed company, so he picked up his keys, left the house, and started the Camaro. As he backed out of the drive, he clipped a small bush that marked the end of his neighbor's garden. He knew he'd have to give it a miss tonight. Besides, if he'd gone to Popeye's that would have meant a couple of beers, minimum, and the doc had warned him to stay off the sauce until he was clear of any morphine in his system. He carefully drove the car back to its space, went into the house, grabbed a soda from the icebox, and watched a repeat of one of last season's baseball games. He never saw the end, just woke up cold and in pain at two in the morning. But he resisted the urge to down a couple of morphine tablets. He needed his head clear to drive to San Francisco, and to do what needed to be done. He slept little after that, and by nine he was on the road. The journey of more than five hundred miles took him seven hours. Thankfully, the Smokey Bears were taking a break that day.

He knocked on the door of the Robson's vacation bungalow outside of San Francisco. Violet came to the door and invited him in.

"We're so glad to see you, Kyle. How did you manage to drive with your arm in a plaster cast?"

"No problems, Violet. Where are the kids?"

"They're out back, playing. Have you had anything to eat?"

"Yes, I'm fine," he lied. He'd lashed up a breakfast that morning and left in a hurry, only stopping to buy gas.

"I'll make sure I do something you'll enjoy for dinner. I'm sure you'll be hungry again. I'll make it a little earlier than usual, traveling can be so tiring, especially when you're hurt."

He smiled at her. She didn't fool easy and knew damn well he hadn't eaten in some time. Some women had that kind of built-in radar.

"That'd be nice, Violet. I'll go out back and see the kids."

He walked through the hallway, into the kitchen and out the back door, straight into Carol Summers. They stared at each other for a few moments. He was struck dumb, utterly astonished, for one of the few times in his life. Right there and then, his feelings for her were powerful, intense. And he felt so damned stupid.

"Carol, I, er...I've been, er," he struggled to remember what the surgeon had said. "I've been a horse's ass. I'm sorry."

She grinned broadly. "Nothing to apologize for, Kyle. You've just been you, and I wouldn't expect anything else."

She stood waiting, and slowly, hesitantly, he stepped forward and reached for her. Then they were in each other's arms. He tasted her lips, smelled the fragrance of her, touched her skin, and knew that somehow Grace was smiling down on him.

"You want to say hi to the kids?" she said as she pulled her lips away from his.

"What? Oh, yeah, what am I thinking? Of course I do."

The afternoon and evening passed in a blur. The kids were wonderful, excited to see him, yet happy with their surprise vacation at their grandparents' house. They were used to him being away, he could see that, and took his return quite naturally, just as they understood he'd be going off again.

"When are you going back to work, Daddy?" Mary asked him. Albeit a little sadly.

"Not for a long time, darling, several weeks. I'll be staying with you for some time."

"That's wonderful. Are you going to kill those nasty

men?"

He looked around the table, at Carol, and John and Violet, at Daniel, then tried to formulate a reply for a young girl.

"We're going to deal with that, Mary. You won't have to worry about it."

He tried to think of something to add, but Carol answered for him.

"You bet your bottom dollar your Dad's going to kill them, pumpkin. He just doesn't want to upset you."

"It doesn't upset me, Carol, or Daniel. We want them to be dead."

"People like that don't deserve to live," Daniel said angrily. "I'd kill them if I had a gun," he went on, looking at his father.

"You're right, Son. People like that don't deserve to live. But no more talk of killing. I'll deal with it, don't worry."

That night he shared a bed with Carol. It worried him slightly. After all, they were in the home of Grace's parents. She understood at once why he was quiet.

"It's okay, Kyle. Everything's fine. They don't want you and the kids grieving for all time."

"Yeah, they're good people. I have to get Rivera, though, or there'll be more to grieve about."

"We'll get Rivera, don't worry. For now, let's just enjoy each other."

The following morning, he wanted to call up the surgeon and thank him for showing him the way. They'd made love, gently and tenderly, so as not to injure his arm. And they'd talked until late into the night, until almost the lighter tendrils of dawn began to lace their bedroom with patterns of shadow.

"I thought you hated me," he whispered.

"I did," she replied in a joking tone. "But you were on a mission, and I understand how difficult it must have been for you."

She was silent for a few moments. And then she continued.

"There was someone, wherever you were. I felt as if," she paused to gather her thoughts, "as if your mind was on someone else."

He told her about Gracia, wanting to hold back nothing from this extraordinary girl who'd given so much to look after his family.

"Did you love her?"

He knew what she was asking, and why.

"I don't know. We were up against an army of fighters who wanted to kill us, and she did her utmost to help us. I just don't know. But what I do know is that I'm here, right now, with you. And the kids are safe. I feel happier than I've felt in a long time."

She pulled him to her. "If that's the best I can get, it'll have to do. I'm not complaining. But next time you go off to some foreign battlefield, keep your mind on the job, and stay away from any dusky maidens you may come across."

"Copy that, Ma'am. It's a promise."

Over breakfast Nolan felt a warm glow, looking at his kids happy and relaxed, Carol glowing with a natural beauty and contentment, and the grandparents looking on with satisfied smiles on their faces. He knew he'd have to start working on the thorny problem of Manuel Rivera before too long, but at least for a small amount of time, he could relax in the company of those he loved, and who loved him.

"What about a picnic today?" Carol asked, interrupting his thoughts. "We could pack a hamper and take off into the hills."

The kids jumped up and down with excitement. Violet shook her head.

"You guys go off and enjoy yourselves. You don't need us."

"Sure we do," she replied.

But they wouldn't be persuaded, and after breakfast, Carol took herself off to the market to pick up supplies while Kyle played in the garden with the kids. She returned with a box full of food and started to prepare their packed lunch. Then they set off and enjoyed one of the best days out Kyle had experience in a long, long time. The sun shone, the kids played, and he felt like a lovesick teenager walking hand in hand with Carol. Finally, they had to return to the Robson's for dinner. When they walked into the house, Nolan asked to use the phone.

"I just need to call in to Coronado."

Carol overheard him and gave him a sharp glance. "You're not working at present. You're supposed to be sick," she objected. "They can take care of themselves."

He shrugged. "It's something I always do, and I need to find out if there's any news."

It took an unusually long time for him to be patched through to the Platoon office, and the Navy telephone operator went through a long checklist of identification checks. Some sort of flap on, the brass called them from time to time, to make sure everyone was on their toes. Usually, the operator recognized his voice and put him straight through, but not this time.

"Talley."

"Hey, Boss, this is Chief Nolan checking in. Are you in the middle of some kind of drill?"

"It's not a drill, Chief. We've got trouble down here."

"In Coronado? Inside the base?"

"More to do with our personnel. Carl Winters got hit."

"Jesus Christ, how did it happen?"

"He finished a drink in Popeye's, came out, and started his car. Two guys came along on a motorcycle, and the passenger poked a MAC-10 through the driver's window and gave him a full clip."

So there was no need to ask if he was dead, it was forgone.

"Do you know who did it?"

"The local gas station attendant sold them gas for their vehicle. He was originally from Honduras, and he recognized their accent. They were Colombians."

So it had started, the revenge for the raid on Salazar's operation.

"They were quick."

"Yeah, our intel people reckon they were already planning to hit us for the previous operation, so they were in place and waiting for us as soon as we got back. But it wasn't just Carl. One of our people is missing. Roscoe Bremmer. They snatched him, poor bastard."

"I'll come back," Nolan said at once.

"No, there's no need. We've got a lead. Intel decrypted some of the stuff we brought back from Colombia. Apparently, Salazar bought a few thousand acres of woodland up near San Francisco, somewhere south of Lake Tahoe. It's a pretty good bet that's where they've taken Roscoe. The link to their place was well hidden under more layers of encryption, so we still don't have the exact location. We've sent the files to the NSA at Fort Meade, and hopefully, they'll be able to cut through the crap and give us an address. In the meantime, stay right where you are. You were closer to the action than we were, and it's likely they'll come after your family next."

"You'll let me know if anything changes?"

"Of course. Just take care of them."

He put the receiver down and went in to speak to Carol and the Robsons.

"I'll stay here for as long as necessary," Carol said immediately. "No way are these bastards going to win."

He smiled his thanks and looked at Violet and John. "I'm sorry for bringing this trouble on you. We can always move out and look for somewhere where they won't find us so easily."

"Nonsense!" Violet said, and her husband nodded. "Those children need us to care for them, now that Grace is gone. You stay here until it's all over."

"Thanks, I can't say how much I appreciate that."

"We're family, Kyle, and that's all you need to know. Listen, after dinner, why not take Carol and the kids to the local mall? There's a multiplex cinema, and you'll be able to take your minds off this dreadful business for a short time at least."

"Yeah, that sounds good. Carol?"

"I love a good movie. Shall I tell the kids?"

He nodded, and she walked off to find them. Dinner was a mix between the adults' somber realization that they were now the number one target of an active revenge operation, and the kids' excitement about going to the movies.

They enjoyed it, buckets of popcorn and enough soda to water a horse, despite the movie being below par. But the kids liked it. Nolan drove them home in his Camaro. He'd refused point blank to let Carol take the wheel. When they got back, the house was blazing with lights, and the television was on loud in the living room.

"John, Violet, we're back."

There was no answering shout, and Kyle went through to find them. There was no sign of either of them, just the TV on loud, and an upturned chair. Carol came into the room.

"Where are they?"

He shook his head. "I've no idea. They may have been taken."

She picked up the phone.

"Who are you calling?"

"The local SFPD. Whatever you think about the local cops, they need to be informed. They may have some leads, you never know, and I'll talk to them about the possible location of Rivera's hideout near Lake Tahoe."

She talked at length, and then minutes later the local sheriff knocked on the door with four deputies and a scene of crime technician. He shook hands and introduced himself.

"I'm Sheriff J T Pollen, and I run the local law enforcement in these parts." He was obese with a large gut hanging over his wide leather belt, which hung at a steep angle from the weight of the Colt .45 in his holster. He also had the rounded, red face and veined nose of a habitual heavy drinker. "I gather you think these good people were kidnapped?"

They showed him the scene that had greeted them

when they returned from the movies. Kyle went on to explain about the Colombian vendetta. The Sheriff looked dubious.

"So this is the reason so many of my people have been doing extra time, this, Colombian thing? Surely, it could be something simple. They could have just gone out."

"And the upturned chair, the television turned up?" Carol reminded him.

Pollen shrugged. "Maybe an accident, or they had a row, something like that. It happens."

He nodded at his crime scene tech. "Chuck, take a look around. See if you come up with anything. You guys," he signaled to his deputies hovering in the background. "Talk to the neighbors. See what you can come up with."

He looked at Kyle and Carol again. "I'm due back for a meeting with the Mayor, so I have to go. If they've been taken, we'll do our best to find them. But I think it's likely there's a more innocent explanation."

Nolan was about to argue with him and try and make the man see sense, but Carol smoothly intercepted. "Thank you, Sheriff, we really appreciate what you're doing."

Nolan stood transfixed with amazement.

After everything they've gone through, the fool is writing it off to something simple!

"Kyle, there's no need to antagonize him," Carol said when he'd gone. "We may need him. You never know."

"What the hell could we possible need from that idiot?" Nolan almost shouted in exasperation.

"We could need the help of his deputies. We just don't know. He may have access to a helicopter. It could be anything. Why alienate him?"

Nolan muttered a reluctant agreement. "So what're we

doing next? I guess I'd better call Coronado. They need to know about this."

Before she could answer, the phone rang. He picked it up, hoping for news about John and Violet.

"Hello?"

"Mr. Nolan?"

He was instantly alert. The voice was unmistakably South American.

"Yes. Who is this?"

"Never mind who it is. Do you want your children's grandparents returned unharmed?"

"Of course I do. What do you want?"

"We want you, Mr. Nolan. Write this down. I will not repeat it."

He recited a list of map coordinates, and Nolan jotted them down.

"It is a forest track twenty miles south of Lake Tahoe. Very isolated. We will make the exchange there. You may bring one person to drive these people home. You will stay with us. Our boss wishes to speak with you. When you arrive, flash your lights three times. When you see the answering flash, get out of the car, and walk towards the lights. When you have reached us, we will release the grandparents."

"What time will this take place?"

"At two hours after midnight, Senor Nolan. And if we see any cops, we kill the prisoners. I warn you. We have night vision equipment, and we are well armed, so do not try any tricks."

The line went dead, and Nolan hung up.

"Who was it?" Carol asked.

"The kids?"

"Don't worry, when I knew what was wrong, I sent them to bed. They didn't like it, moaned like hell, said their grandparents didn't send them that early." She grinned, but the smile was forced.

"It was the guys who took John and Violet. Colombians, no question."

"What did they want?"

"A swap. Me for the Robsons." He showed her the coordinates. "I have to get going. They said you could come with me to bring them back."

"Are you crazy? Not in a million years. And you'd leave the kids unguarded? Don't even think about it!"

"What choice do I have?

"To say no."

He sighed. "I can't, Carol. I'll call a cab. You're right about the kids. They shouldn't be left. I'll be fine. I'll be well armed and prepared. I reckon I can get the drop on them."

"You're a fool," she said in abject exasperation. "They'll kill you. And you haven't even got the use of both arms. You don't stand a chance."

"I reckon I do. Anyway, I'll call a cab. I'm going. John and Violet will come back in the cab."

A half hour later, the cab arrived. He'd said goodbye to the kids, picked up his holdall, and left. Carol refused to even acknowledge him going. As they drove away, he saw her white face looking at him from the open front door. She was frozen, didn't wave, and didn't smile. Just stood watching. Watching him drive to his death.

CHAPTER THIRTEEN

As the cab drove through the Californian night, he
reflected on his chances. He was no fool, and the veteran
of countless engagements. His chances were not good.
But he could still pull it off, simply because he was so
skilled and experienced in this kind of undercover combat.
And he had a few tricks up his sleeve. He'd hung on to the
blade in his collar, just in case. He hardly noticed it was
there, even if it did mean ruining otherwise perfectly good
shirts by cutting a narrow slot in the collar. In the holdall,
he had a selection of weapons he'd taken from a concealed
compartment in the trunk of his Camaro. He'd have liked
to have brought the Camaro and not relied on a taxi, but
John and Violet were old and may not be in a fit state to
drive the heavy muscle car home. And the Colombians
had said for him to bring someone else for that purpose,
so he needed to do exactly as they said to make it seem as
if he'd given in. They'd be intensely suspicious, of course.
But as long as he gave them no reason to start shooting,
there was a chance. It was a long drive, and the time was

one thirty when they reached the map coordinates he'd been given. They were on an isolated track with thick forest on either side. In the dark of the back seat of the cab, he checked his weapons. He needed no lights; part of his training was stripping and re-assembling pistols and rifles by feel alone. But the driver still heard the metallic clicks.

"What're you up to, Buddy? I don't want nothing illegal doing down in my cab."

"Just checking my tools, driver. Nothing illegal, don't worry."

The man grunted and let it go. Nolan finished his checks, put on a pair of night vision goggles, and stepped out of the cab. As he did so, he leaned into the open driver's windows and pulled out the keys.

"Hey, what gives?" the driver shouted angrily. Then he caught sight of Nolan, wearing his NVS goggles and cocking the lever on a MP5K, the Heckler and Koch submachine gun that was small enough to fit under a coat. "Look, no offence meant, Buddy. I'd like my keys back. I ain't going anywhere."

"You'll have them back when your return fare is here. Until then, I need to make sure of their ride."

He scouted up ahead until he'd found the most likely place where the Colombians would stop their vehicle. He planted the MP5K under a bush and walked back to the cab. He'd checked carefully with the NVS goggles, conscious that the enemy was similarly equipped, but all he'd seen was scores of trees, shaded ghostly green in the goggles. He tucked a knife in his left sock, and a small pistol, a Beretta 950 Jetfire, into his undershorts. The Beretta was a miracle of engineering; tiny, yet packing a nine shot clip.

It was his best hope that it might survive a rough search undetected. Then he picked up an M4-A1. They'd expect him to come armed, and it was the kind of weapon he'd bring. No surprises. Do exactly what they thought he'd do, and he stood a chance. Then he waited. And waited. He checked his wristwatch. It was a quarter after two and no sign of them. The minutes ticked by slowly, and then he heard a noise in the distance. Just after two-thirty, and a car stopped. Through his NVS goggles he could see it was a large Chevy Suburban. The lights flashed three times. And Nolan didn't move. The driver looked at him nervously.

"What's going on?"

"Wait. It won't be long."

Five minutes drifted by. The Chevy door opened, and he saw a heavy-set man climb out. He walked a few yards towards the cab.

"We can see you, Senor Nolan. We have night vision, too," he shouted. "You need to start walking towards us. Otherwise we will kill them."

Nolan edged towards the thick woods at the side of the track.

"I need to know that they're still alive. Show them to me," he shouted back.

There was a brief pause, and he saw the green shape of the man talking to someone in the Suburban. Then he shouted a reply.

"They are not here. We left them nearby. You will never find the place. You must come to us first. Then we will take you to see them."

Nolan cursed to himself. So it was a setup. He'd prayed the Robsons would be there so that he'd have a chance of releasing them. As they weren't, it meant they never intended keeping up their part of the bargain. He weighed distances, looked at the features of the track that lay between him and the Suburban, and tried to work out how good their night vision gear was; certainly not as good as his Naval issue equipment. And how many men were in the vehicle? Probably another three, as the Robsons weren't along. He was about to start forward and maneuver into a position from which he could take them, when all hell broke loose.

The first indication that something strange was happening was a dark shadow that flew overhead, like a giant bird of prey. He knew what it was instantly, a T10 free fall parachute, and standard equipment for the Navy Seals. Beneath it, a man was guiding it expertly to a gentle landing. Above it, another 'chute floated down, and above that, another.

"Chief, keep your head down," someone shouted.

He recognized the deep, bass tones of Will Bryce. Another voice, Talley, ordering the Platoon to lay down covering fire. Bravo Platoon had arrived. The action was fast and furious, and almost surreal as gunfire from more than a dozen Heckler and Koch 416s spat out their message of death. Nolan threw himself to the ground to stay out of the crossfire. The Colombians were returning fire, and he was in danger of getting hit by the withering fire that crisscrossed the forest track. Pieces of foliage fell onto his head, cut from the trees by the intense gunfire, and a scream came from the Colombians' position as one of them was hit. And then the impossible happened, the Colombians fought back hard. They brought up an M60, positioning it behind their Suburban, and unseen by the Seals. A hail of 7.62mm bullets hammered out, forcing the more lightly armed parachutists to desperately dive under cover. The machine gunner had no notions of using short bursts to conserve ammunition. He fired and held his finger on the trigger, only stopping to lace on new ammunition belts. Nolan crept deeper into the trees and ran towards the Suburban. It had stopped right where he'd expected it, and more importantly, next to where he'd stashed the MP5K. There was still time to retrieve the situation before the Platoon was forced to bring to bear heavier weapons. That would mean the death of the Colombians, and the death of the only lead to the whereabouts of the Robsons. As he ran, he wondered how the hell the Seals had found out where he was. There was only one answer, Carol Summers. She'd had the coordinates and times of the rendezvous. It would have been simple and straightforward to contact Talley. Somehow they'd managed to acquire an aircraft. Probably, Rear Admiral Drew Jacks had facilitated it and authorized the operation. He'd sure be keen to put an end to the antics of the Salazar clan. Yes, a short flight in a C-130 from San Diego, and a HALO drop would put them right on the button. Except that the unexpected M60 had endangered everything. He reached the spot and picked up the MP5K. The weapon was loaded, cocked, and ready. Only having the use of one arm meant that there was no time to play around when the bullets were firing. It was pick it up and go. Ahead of him, the machine gun had stopped firing, but only for a few seconds while they attached yet another belt of ammunition. The firing started again, the bright gun flashes lighting up the dark forest track, and in the intense stroboscopic effect, Nolan saw the enemy clearly.

One of them was on the ground, dead. Two men

manned the machine gun, one firing and the other loading. And the fourth man was kneeling down, and firing short, disciplined bursts with an M-16. He had to do something before Bravo Platoon rolled over them. There were only seconds before the grenades started to fall around their position. It couldn't happen. He had to take one of them alive. What he needed was a sniper rifle with night vision sights, not this short-barreled German built 9mm submachine gun; and a commo system so that he could liaise with the Platoon. But it was all he had. The Colombians stopped firing for a few seconds to load yet another belt. They were shouting at each other, exhilarated and obviously expecting to beat back whoever was shooting at them. So far they had no idea, and perhaps they assumed it was just Nolan and a couple of friends. Probably, they were hyped up on coke, using their own product to give them false courage. It meant they would be lax and utterly confident in their superior abilities.

They have a lesson to learn, he reflected grimly.

For most of them, the last one they'd ever need. He waited until they changed belts, and the track went dark. But he was in position. He ran out and shot the man with the M-16 from close range with a three shot burst, no more than ten feet away from him. The shooter was knocked to the ground, and Nolan ran into the center of the Colombians and the cover of the Suburban. The last thing he needed was to get hit by his own people. Both Colombians turned, their eyes wide with surprise and murderous intent.

Coke for sure.

He shot the man behind the M60 and gestured for the last man to put up his hands. That was when the grenade sailed over the Suburban and landed between them.

"Granada!"

Nolan recognized the word for 'grenade' in Spanish. But he was already moving. He ran forward, dragged the man down, and started rolling to the ground at the side of the vehicle. When the grenade exploded, it was as if the ground lifted, and the heavy Chevrolet bucked up and down on its springs as the rear of the vehicle was torn off in the blast. He felt a shard of steel slice into his leg, and the man he'd thrown down jumped as he was hit by more shards of hot metal. And then everything was silent, except for the ringing in his ears.

"You okay, Chief?"

He looked up at the man wearing night vision goggles. He recognized the voice, Will Bryce.

"I'm okay, but I'm not sure about this guy. Something hit him when that grenade exploded. I need him. He's the only link to where the Robsons are being held."

"I'll look at him now." He looked down, seeing Nolan's leg with his NVS goggles.

"Jesus, Chief, you've been hit. Your pants' leg is shredded, and you're bleeding badly."

"Forget that for now, Will. Just see to this guy. He has to tell us where the Robsons are being held."

Bryce knelt down and inspected the casualty.

"He's pretty bad, Chief. I don't think he's got long. Look, he was hit in the chest with a grenade fragment."

"Is he conscious?"

Bryce shook his head. "Not now, and I doubt he'll ever recover. He's going, and there's nothing we can do about it."

Nolan looked up as a group of Seals came up to the

Chevy.

"You okay?" Talley asked him.

"Yeah, I'm fine, just a scratch." Nolan couldn't help himself. He was angry, and there was a chance he could have handled this himself. "You severely wounded the one guy I was trying to keep alive to find out where the kids' grandparents are being held. I had this in hand, Boss, before you brought the Platoon in to help."

Talley looked sheepish and sounded defensive. "I'm sorry about that. When we got the word, Admiral Jacks insisted we go in and take the characters out. But just because they're all dead, doesn't mean there aren't a whole heap of leads to where they're holding your folks. Why don't we check everything out before the recriminations start? Don't forget, you're alive, and these characters are dead. For your information, I doubt you could have taken them. Not four heavily armed men, even though I'm sure you had a few tricks up your sleeve. The odds weren't in your favor, Chief."

Nolan realized he'd been on an adrenaline high, and Talley was right. Without the Platoon, he would likely have been killed. He mumbled an apology.

"I came over too hard, Boss. Thanks for what you did. You're right. I would probably have been killed."

"That's okay." He looked up as more of the men arrived. "Zeke, would you take a look at the SUV? See if there's anything that points us towards the hostages."

Murray glanced at the damaged Suburban. "You mean like the satnav?"

"The what?"

"Satnav. This is a top of the range model fitted with satnav as standard. We can interrogate it and find out everywhere it's been."

Talley grinned. "What are you waiting for, PO1? Chief, get someone to bind that wound on your leg. It looks as if we'll have some ground to cover if Zeke gets this satnav gadget working."

"Sure. How did you know where I was? Carol Summers?"

"The cop, yeah. She thought you'd be a goner without help. She sure put pressure on the Admiral to get an operation moving. Some lady, that cop."

"Yep, she is all off that."

Will began bandaging his leg.

"How's that casualty, any chance he'll pull through?" Nolan asked while he was bending down to fix the dressing.

"Not now, not ever. He went a few minutes ago, I'm afraid. Don't worry, Zeke will work some magic on that Suburban."

"Yeah."

But a few minutes later, Zeke Murray reported in. The news wasn't good. "The satnav was faulty, and the useless bastards hadn't even bothered to get it fixed. It doesn't help us at all."

"Anything else in the car or on the bodies, any kind of clue?"

"Nothing."

When the leg was bandaged, he went to chat to the Platoon members who'd come to save him. They were all there, except for two, Carl Winters and Roscoe Bremmer.

"What happened to Carl?"

Will answered. The black man paused, his face sad. "I guess our guard was down, I dunno. We'd left the base and were on our way home. A shooter on a motorcycle got him."

Nolan grimaced. "And Roscoe?"

"They were waiting for him when he got home. When he didn't report the next morning, a couple of the boys went around to his place. There were signs of a struggle, some of the furniture was smashed, and no sign of Bremmer. We've no idea what happens next. Maybe they'll make some kind of ransom demand, or maybe his body will appear on the side of some freeway, thrown out of a passing car. Who knows? But one thing I can tell you, Chief. They've bitten off more than they can chew. The brass is going crazy, and Admiral Jacks is having kittens. He wants these bastards taken care of, and fast."

"That's exactly what I was trying to do here," Nolan replied. "I just need a lead to get back on their trail."

"Not any more you don't," a voice interrupted. Talley.

"What gives, Boss?"

"Jacks contacted me, and they've decrypted the messages we sent to NSA. We have the location of the Salazar place."

"That's great. Where is it?"

Talley shook his head. "Oh, no you don't, not on your own. Things have moved on. This is not a simple domestic crime any more. These people present a clear and present danger to the US military. As such, an operation has been sanctioned that will finish these people for good. A full scale attack is in the planning stage."

"What about the Governor of California?"

"No, this had become domestic terrorism, and it's covered by the Patriot Act. It's Federal, Chief, out of the Governor's jurisdiction. Besides, these Colombians are protected by heavy defenses, and any local unit going in would get chewed badly."

"When are we going in?"

Talley stared at him. "We aren't going anywhere. You've been badly wounded, and you know you're on sick leave. We'll take care of this one."

"I have to go in with the Platoon, Boss. My kids' grandparents are in there. I have to get them out."

"It's too dangerous." He looked at him for a few moments. "Look, maybe you could go in on a support basis. You'd be an advisor, nothing more. You've had more run-ins with these people, so you'd be useful. But that's it. Don't even think about being part of the initial assault."

Nolan nodded. "Thanks, Boss." He was in.

The helos came in shortly after and ferried them back to Coronado. The NCIS sent in a tow truck to take away the Chevrolet and remove the bodies of the Colombians. It hadn't happened, any of it. Except that there was one loose end. Nolan was about to board the Blackhawk when he suddenly remembered the cab driver.

"Wait up, give me a couple of minutes."

He ran along the track, limping as the pain from his injured leg tore through him. The cab driver was still where he'd left him, unable to drive away without his keys. He shivered as Nolan tapped on his window. Slowly, he wound it down.

"I brought your keys, and I need to settle the fare. How much do I owe you? There won't be a return fare, by the way."

The driver stared at him. "What the fuck happened here?"

"Here? Nothing."

"Nothing! It was like a fucking war. I thought I was

back in Vietnam."

So he's a vet. That's useful.

"What unit were you in?"

"Seventh Cavalry, Master Sergeant. And I flew in enough Hueys to know what a helicopter looks like."

"So you were at Ia Drang?"

The man nodded. "Yeah, that was a wild one."

"Okay, Master Sergeant. I'm Navy, not Army, but we all answer to the same rules. Nothing happened here, you here? Nothing."

The man looked skeptical. But he recognized Nolan and Bravo Platoon as kindred spirits.

"Did you win?"

Nolan stared at him. "How could we win? Nothing happened." Then he grinned. "But if something had happened, which it didn't, yeah, we won."

The man nodded, satisfied. "Arabs?"

"Something like that?"

He grinned. "Good luck to you on your next mission that doesn't happen. Don't worry. I saw nothing. I must have fallen asleep."

Nolan watched him drive away, then ran back to the waiting Blackhawk and jumped aboard. They flew south into the night, heading for Coronado. And if they were as good as their word, the beginning of the end for these Colombians.

And maybe for John and Violet too, unless I can do something about that.

One thing he did know, these people were well resourced, and their compound would be heavily defended; which meant the Robsons could both get a bullet in the head as soon as an attack began.

I have to head that one off, but how?

When they touched down, Talley had forewarned the medics, and they rushed him off the helo and into the sickbay for emergency treatment on his wound. The duty physician grimaced when he pulled off the bandage.

"It's a bad one, Chief. It'll need a lot of stitches, I'm afraid. I'll give you an anesthetic."

"No anesthetic, I've got work to do."

"Hey, look, you need a few days rest. Otherwise, you could do yourself a lot of damage."

"No anesthetic," Nolan repeated. "Just stitch me up, Doc. I've got business to deal with."

The man shrugged. "It's your funeral."

But his work was as professional as any man could do, and he did feel better when his leg was cleaned and stitched, and the doc even tidied up his arm.

"I've put a new set of splints on you, some of the ones you had in there were displaced. You know you're supposed to stay away from strenuous activity with those things."

"I do, yeah."

He finally got away, entering the briefing room in time for the start of the main event. Rear Admiral Drew Jacks stood on the rostrum, pointing at an enlarged map projected onto the screen. He used a laser pointer to indicate an area below Lake Tahoe.

"Gentlemen, this is where the Salazar compound is situated. At least, that's what NSA tells us."

Talley shot up his hand. "How sure are they of this intel, Sir?"

Jacks looked uncharacteristically uncomfortable. "Pretty sure, Lieutenant. We've downloaded satellite imagery, and sure enough there's a large, unexplained compound in that exact area. Our people estimate there are upwards of fifty personnel coming and going. At the very least, it could be a storage and distribution center for their imports from Colombia."

"So why haven't the local law taken this place down?"

"That's a good question, Lieutenant. The answer is simple. These guys are pretty clever, and they've never given the Sheriff's Office any kind of probable cause to swear out a warrant. Even now, we can only legally go in under the Patriot Act. Our job is straightforward. Rescue the hostages being held there, if they're still alive. That's Roscoe Bremmer and the Robsons. After that, we're to destroy the place, and put it beyond use for anything other than growing trees. We leave tomorrow, timed to arrive two hours before dawn."

"RoEs, Sir?" Talley continued.

"Yeah, Rules of Engagement, that's an easy one. Do everything within your power to keep the hostages alive. And when they're secure, I'd prefer that these bastards don't leave that place alive."

"Is that an official order, Sir?"

Jacks looked at him sharply. "It's my order, Lieutenant. These people are our enemies, and they're fighting a war on the US in the guise of civilians. That means they have no rights under the rules of war." He looked around the assembled Seals. "If you want me to lay it out any clearer, I want them dead. Is that understood?"

"Hooyah!"

"Chief Nolan, I want a quiet word with you afterwards. That's all, dismissed."

Nolan waited patiently as the Admiral finished talking

to his men. Then he turned to Nolan.

"Chief, I'm sorry, but Lieutenant Talley tells me he asked you to go as an advisor. I have to say no. It's not on. I want you to stay here and recover."

"But, Sir, they're my family in there. I have to go in and do everything I can to protect them."

"We'll do everything necessary to protect them, and Roscoe Bremmer as well. He's our family too, you know."

"Yes, I know that Sir, but..."

"Forget the arguments. I've made my decision. You've been hit too hard, so you stay out of this one. Dismissed."

Nolan walked out of the briefing room and out into the cool, San Diego morning. He was tired, totally exhausted. Yet above all, he was in despair. How the hell could he tell Daniel and Mary that their grandparents had been killed, only months after their mother had been shot dead? The shock would do terrible damage to their young minds, to their emotions, still growing and developing in the violent world they lived in. He had to protect them, by protecting their grandparents. It was as necessary as protecting them from the Colombian vendetta. Yet how? He walked back into the briefing room. A young rating was clearing up the paperwork and photographs shot by the passing satellite. Nolan helped himself to a heap of stuff, and when the sailor approached, he merely brushed off the man's inquiry.

"Sorry, Sailor, I left these behind. I'll take them out of your way now."

"Yes, Chief. Thanks for that. I was about to bundle them with the other stuff."

"That's okay, it's all sorted now."

As he walked out of the door, with the documents

stuffed awkwardly under his one good arm, Will Bryce intercepted him.

"Chief, I'm sorry to hear you won't be with us in the morning."

"Yeah, me too, but those are the orders. I just have to live with it."

He glanced at the bundle of charts and photographs underneath Nolan's arm but made no comment.

"How're you getting home?"

Nolan shrugged. "I'll call a cab, I guess."

"Nah, let me give you a ride. I'm going your way."

They climbed into Will's big Dodge and drove the short distance. He thanked the big PO1, but as he climbed out, he got a surprise. Will leaned over and handed him a canvas holdall.

"It's a spare set off NVS goggles and personal commo equipment. I figured you might want to check them over, and make sure they're working okay. If you're on sick leave, you want to keep up with everything."

He took Nolan's sheaf of documents off him and tucked them into the bag, then handed it back to him with a grin. "That'll make it easier to carry your personal correspondence."

"I don't know what to say."

"That's okay. Just tell me you'll keep your head down. The boys need you, and even if you decide that you have to be there tomorrow," he looked sharply at Nolan, "which I know you won't, you're not so stupid as to disobey an order to remain on sick leave. Then make sure they don't blow your damn fool head off."

"Thanks, Will."

"Yeah. Take it easy."

CHAPTER FOURTEEN

He was back at Carol's. The house seemed lonely and deserted, and with that odd echo empty houses seem to possess. He longed for company, any company, to take the edge off the loss of first Grace, and then Gracia. But he had things to do. First off, he called Carol.

"How are the kids?"

"They're good, Kyle. You survived the exchange with Rivera."

"Yeah, I did. It was a setup. Good thing you got the Platoon involved."

"Kyle, I'm so glad. I thought I'd done the wrong thing. I was so worried."

"You did okay. How are the kids?"

"They don't know that anything was ever wrong. They're fine. Missing you and their grandparents. I'm so worried that something bad had happened to them. Kyle, do you think they could be...?

He knew what she wanted to ask him. And was terrified to hear a truthful answer. Yeah, they could be dead. The people that took them, they treated death as casually as a beer in the local bar. But if they'd killed them, they'd suffer. Christ, he'd make them suffer. In the meantime, Carol had the kids to protect, and she didn't need negatives to add to their burdens. And there was something more. He needed her, here.

"I'm sure they're fine. They're just being held against something these people want. You know how it works. But we've discovered their compound."

Her voice was shaky. "That's progress. I know how it works, yes. Sometimes it works. Sometimes, it doesn't, but I'm praying for the best. The kids' grandparents are so elderly, so vulnerable. They could be badly hurt. When does the operation begin?"

"They're going in tonight. It's an officially sanctioned operation to finish the Colombian operation, once and for all."

"And you're sure that John and Violet are being held in this compound?"

"We have to assume so, yes. They've got one of our people too, Roscoe Bremmer. Look, I'm worried about them too. In this kind of operation, things can sometimes go wrong. That's why I intend to make sure that nothing bad happens to John and Violet, but I need your help, Carol."

Her reply was instant. "Anything. What can I do?"

"Is there someone who can take care of the kids tonight? Someone reliable, someone from school maybe, a sleepover?"

"I can arrange that, yes."

"Okay, do it. I'm going to get some sleep. I need to be fresh for tonight."

"What are you planning to do?"

"If you'll help me, I intend to drive out there and get John and Violet out before the Platoon goes in. It'd be good to get Roscoe out too, if possible."

He didn't add 'If any of them are still alive'. He didn't have to, she was a cop, and she knew the score.

"Of course I'll help. You're in no condition with that arm to go up against these people. Christ, Kyle, if anything happened to you, I don't know what I'd do."

"Thanks, it's appreciated. Carol, you're some girl, you know that?"

"It's what I'm here for."

"I don't know what to say. Believe me, words are not enough. I…" He choked off what he was about to say and then went on with the briefing. "I'll hire a car to get back to you, then we can take the Camaro."

She'd heard the catch in his voice. "Kyle, it's okay, we'll pull this off. We'll need weapons. I have my Glock, but it won't be enough."

"The trunk of the Camaro, there's a hidden compartment at the base. There's plenty of stuff in there. We'll be fine. Thanks, Carol, I'll see you later."

He went to put down the receiver.

"Kyle!"

"Yeah?"

"You know."

"Yeah, I know. I feel the same way. See you later."

He lay on the couch, he felt too hyper to go up to bed and sleep properly. All he could do was doze and try to keep the turbulent thoughts out of his head.

Should I have involved Carol, a woman I'm falling in love with? No, that's not true. I've already fallen in love with her. Another person who got close to me and the kids, and now I'm putting her in harm's way. She could be killed. Yet I have to try, for the sake of John and Violet. Or should I? What do I do? I know I can't do it with one good arm. Damn! What the hell else can I do?

He finally fell into a fitful sleep and woke up feeling like little more than a corpse. He slowly took a cold shower, dressed and ate some breakfast, or was it lunch? He checked the time and discovered it was past midday. He had to hurry. Nolan called a local car hire office and booked a car to take him to San Francisco, then called for a cab to take him to the depot to collect it. The car was waiting for him, a big, dark red Dodge Charger, just the thing to eat up the miles between San Diego and San Francisco. The clerk eyed his broken arm doubtfully.

"You sure you're going to be able to control this vehicle with that arm, Sir?"

"No sweat, I've been doing it all my life."

"Oh, I see. Certainly, Sir, no problem."

The specter of dealing with a disabled client was enough to head off any argument. He handed Nolan the keys.

"Enjoy the drive, Sir. Any problems, give us a call. Have a nice day."

"Thanks, I intend to."

The Dodge was big, comfortable, powerful and fast. The journey up to San Francisco was fast and almost effortless. By 2000 that evening, he was pulling up outside the Robson house. Carol came out to greet him and flung her arms around him.

"I was so worried last night. I thought they were going to kill you."

"So did they, but they were wrong. This one is much

bigger, and if we can pull this off, the threat from Salazar's operation will be ended for good. But it won't be easy."

She put her finger to his lips. "Not now, Kyle. Let's share a few minutes before we get down to business."

He knew what she meant. A few minutes that could be their last. He relaxed and felt the soft warmth of her body close to him. For a few moments, the worries and agonies drifted away. He heard her murmur softly.

"When you called me, what I said…"

"Yeah, I remember."

"I think I'm falling in love with you, Chief Nolan. Is that wise?"

He pulled away and looked at her pretty, serious expression. "I reckon so." He softened his words with a grin. "After we free John and Violet, we should talk some more."

"At least you didn't say 'if' we free them."

"That's not a word in the Seals' vocabulary. If we go for a goal, we achieve it, always."

"Unless…"

"Yeah, okay, unless. But there's not gonna be any unless tonight. They're coming home. I can bring the kids home, and we can see about some kind of normality, without those Colombians running around pursuing come crazy vendetta. We'll be home free."

"It sounds great, Kyle. Wonderful."

"You'd better believe it. We have to make a start."

She disengaged herself from his arms. "I know."

He pulled out the maps and aerial photos from the holdall, and she helped him lay them out in the living room. Closer study of the photos showed the compound to be more formidable than the maps had suggested during the briefing. A low level shot, taken from about a mile away, showed a high wooden wall, constructed from logs, that surrounded the entire area.

"It looks like a Wild West cavalry fort," Carol smiled. "It must be about twenty feet high."

"Yeah, it does. They've used the local timber to construct it. That's very clever. And those logs will take a lot of punishment. They'll have to go in over the top. I'd guess a HALO drop straight into the center."

"Is that dangerous?"

"It is if they're waiting for us, yes. When a parachutist is in the air, he's at his most vulnerable."

"But why would they be waiting for them? They don't even know their compound has been discovered."

"They're not stupid. They'll anticipate the possibility. And so far, they've kept one step ahead of us. It would be best to hit the compound with a preemptive air strike, but with hostages inside that's impossible. The other way is to blast an entrance with explosives, but they don't know where the hostages are being held, so it's a tough call. But if things go well, we'll be able to get them out before they go in."

"How can the two of us manage that? It seems impossible. The moment they see us coming, they'll let loose with everything they have."

Nolan grinned. "Then we won't let them see us coming. By the time they realize we're around, we'll be on the way home."

* * *

They were quiet on the journey, and Nolan drove the

Camaro fast and hard. They skirted Sacramento and headed east on Route 50 into the Eldorado National Forest. By the time they parked the car two miles from the compound, it was past midnight. Nolan checked his wristwatch and set the countdown timer.

"We've got two hours before the action starts. If we move fast, we'll be at the compound by 0100. We have to be out of there by 0145 to us give enough time to get clear."

She grimaced. "Can we do it in forty-five minutes?"

"Provided nothing goes wrong. If we're not out of there in forty-five minutes, we'll be staying there."

"Do these things ever go wrong?"

She waited for him to answer, and Nolan cursed. He hadn't meant to alarm her, but in his business, they dealt in realities. He knew it was possible, and he had a plan for infiltration and exfiltration with the hostages. But plans could go wrong.

He remembered Operation Eagle Claw, ordered by President Carter to put an end to the Iran hostage crisis with the rescue of the Americans held captive at the US Embassy in Tehran. The plan called for six helicopters, and in the event, eight were sent in. Two helicopters could not navigate through a very fine sand cloud, and one was forced to crash land, the other returned to the USS Nimitz. Six helicopters reached the rendezvous point, but one of them had damaged its hydraulic systems. Sadly, the spare parts were on one of the two helicopters that had aborted. With insufficient helicopters to complete the mission, local commanders requested President Carter to abort the mission.

"Some. But this one'll be okay," he answered her.

She was quiet again, and he rapidly checked the gear they were taking with them. He strapped on the NVS goggles and inserted the earpiece in his ear. She looked at him.

"Where did that stuff come from?"

"Will gave it to me, so I'll be able to communicate with the Platoon when they come in. And the goggles will keep us out of trouble. Do you know how to use one of these?"

He handed her one of two M4-A1s from the trunk.

She nodded. "I'll manage. I'm a cop, remember?"

"How could I forget? Besides, you're out of your jurisdiction."

He felt a light punch to his good arm. "Watch it, buster. I'm not always in this good a mood."

Wisely, he made no reply. They put on camo jackets and armored vests, and she helped him fasten the straps. They both carried pistols. His was a standard Sig Sauer P226, and she carried her service Glock 9mm. He tucked four grenades into the pockets of his jacket, and when Carol insisted, gave in and allowed her to carry two grenades herself. Finally, he took out a further case from the trunk and opened it.

"A model airplane?" she uttered. "Are you sure?"

"Trust me, this is no model."

He assembled the aircraft, one of the RQ-11 Ravens. The small, remote-controlled UAV was launched by hand and powered by an electric motor. It could fly six miles at altitudes of five hundred feet above ground level, and over fifteen thousand feet above sea level at speeds of up to sixty miles an hour. Nolan explained it to her and showed her the electronic tablet they would use to view the compound.

"How did you get it? These things must cost the Pentagon a fortune?"

"This one crashed, and they threw it out. I took it home and fixed it up to fly again, with a couple of modifications."

"You're a man of many talents, Kyle Nolan," she gushed. "I'll have to remember that."

"Yeah. Can you work that tablet? I don't have a spare hand."

"It looks easy enough."

"It is." He worked the buttons, and the engine quietly started to spin the propeller. He set the desired course and altitude on the tablet, then picked up the Raven and threw it into the night sky.

"That's it? Won't it crash? We're not controlling it."

"It's flying itself using a built-in computer. It'll climb to altitude, and then circle on the course I programmed. That's right above the coordinates for the compound. Switch on the display, you'll see."

He leaned across and flicked a switch on the display, and her eyes widened in astonishment as the Raven's onboard night vision camera sent back a moving image of the forest two thousand feet below it. And then the compound came into view. The security lights were on, and they could clearly see guards patrolling the wooden walls.

"That's interesting. They have ramparts. That'll make it more complicated. Let's go, we've got ground to cover."

Carol watched the image for a few more seconds, noting a number of solid looking buildings, a warehouse and an unmistakable garage, with cars and trucks parked outside. And guards everywhere, even at this time of the night.

Could they know an attack was imminent? Surely not,

that could spell disaster for all of us.

She hurried after Nolan who was already striding away. She heard him say, "Keep behind me. I can see where I'm going with these goggles."

"Yes, Sir!" she snapped back.

He stifled a grin and walked rapidly through the dark forest. They made good time. The trail was well walked, and there were no obstacles to impede their progress, but even so, it was 0105 when they drew near to their target. The high wooden walls towered above them, and there was a wide-open strip around them, perhaps fifty yards wide. He wondered idly if it was mined, but it was unlikely. There were too many hikers and campers in these woods, as well as hunters. Mines would risk an incident that brought in the authorities. But there'd be sensors or some kind of warning system. He looked carefully at the ground and made out the faint reflection from the infrared of the NVS on a trip wire; very fine, and placed about a foot above the ground. It was almost exactly halfway across the open ground. He explained it to Carol.

"I'll stop when we reach it and show you where to step over it."

She nodded. "What about the guards? They'll be using night vision."

"They'll be looking the other way."

"Why would they do that?"

"Wait and see."

They started over the open ground. When they reached the trip wire, Nolan helped her over and called a halt.

"This is where my little box of tricks on the Raven will come in handy. I hope."

He activated a control sequence on the tablet, and they

both watched the display as the Raven headed away. Then it started back towards the compound, and lights appeared in the sky. Simultaneously, there was a low, humming noise.

"It looks just like a UFO," she breathed.

"It's supposed to. I thought I'd build something we could use as a diversion. The sixty-four dollar question is, whether they'll go for it?"

They waited in the middle of the open ground, watching the apparition in the sky. They were badly exposed to the defenders' night vision systems. Nolan knew the risk they ran. If they didn't go for it, the next thing they knew, they'd be diving for cover from incoming machine gun fire. They watched, and they waited.

"Look, it's working."

Nolan heard Carol's excited whisper and glanced at the display. They could clearly see the green figures running to the far side of the wall, pointing at the sky.

"Yeah, it's working."

He put the Raven in a continuous, tight orbit to the east of the wall at two thousand feet and programmed the light and sound for a further two minutes.

"Time to go."

He ran forward to the wooden wall, and she followed. Nolan crouched at the base and fired a tiny grapnel over the parapet, then started climbing, ignoring the pain. He reached the top, climbed over to the rampart, reaching down to help Carol over. As her feet touched down onto the wooden platform, the lights went out, and the sound ceased. They could hear shouting; Latin American voices.

"Dónde está? Dónde ha ido?" Where's it gone?

"Yeah, I wonder. Sort that one out, motherfuckers," he growled. "We need to get to the ground while they're still looking the other way, then we can start searching these buildings. Let's keep it good and quiet."

"Don't worry, I don't intend to make a sound."

He glanced across at her. She looked terrified. She was a cop, but this was way outside her normal duties. Nolan pulled the line over, dropping it down to the ground, and they quietly slid downwards to the beaten earth. Already, men were moving around, shouting to one another, dispersing and returning to their normal guard duties. It was time to go to work. They started with the nearest building, a locked storeroom, and an obvious choice for a prison cell.

"Keep an eye on the screen, and tuck it out of sight," he whispered to Carol. She nodded.

Nolan looked around. There was no one nearby. He took out his combat knife and struck the heavy hilt against the lock. It parted, and he cautiously opened the door and went in. There were wooden crates stacked in one corner, probably cocaine. He went back out, and Carol followed him to the next building, but it proved to be a workshop. As he closed the door, a guard came around the corner. They saw each other at the same instant. The man unslung his rifle, but Nolan double tapped him with the suppressed Sig Sauer, and he collapsed to the ground with a crash as his assault rifle skittered over the ground. It was impossible to lower someone quietly with one arm just after you'd shot him. He cursed silently, dropping into the shadows.

"Quién es?"

A guard came around the corner and saw Carol.

"Quién eres?"

He covered her with his rifle and walked closer, passing

Nolan who had pressed himself into the shadow of the doorway. He reached out one-handed and wiped the blade of his heavy combat knife across the man's throat. Blood gushed from his throat, and he dropped to the ground. This time Carol had time to hold him, lowering him carefully. He nodded his thanks.

"We're running out of time. We'd better go for broke and check the main house. Stay behind me."

He heard her mumble, "Yeah, and where the fuck would I get to?"

He smiled to himself and found a way through the shadows to the rear of the house. The guards were back on the ramparts, patrolling the area and watching for intruders. Watching the outside, not the inside. Still, there were other guards inside. It was only a matter of time before they discovered their dead comrades and sounded the alarm. To his surprise, the back door was open, and they slipped into a huge kitchen. They went past preparation tables, racks of pots and pans, and shelves laden with crockery and foodstuffs. The smell of spices was rich and exotic. Nolan opened the door, and they passed through into a hallway. They were in a large dining area, more of a dining hall, with a long table in the center, able to seat a score of diners. They kept on through the door and found they'd reached a wider hallway. Further along, an ornate staircase went to the upper floors, but of more interest was a doorway opposite marked, 'Sótano'.

"The door to the basement," he whispered. "It's an obvious place. I'd bet they're down there."

She nodded her understanding, and they walked across the hall, and he opened the door. Once again, it was unlocked.

"This is good and easy. They don't like locking their doors around here."

Nolan nodded, but he was unhappy. It was too easy, much too easy. He holstered his Sig Sauer and gripped his M4-A1 one-handed, ready to shoot. If they were walking into an ambush, he wanted to be ready to dish out the pain. The wooden stairway led down to a rough, concrete passageway. With the night vision goggles, everything was green, and more importantly, the space was empty. Until the light in the basement went on and blinded him, as a guard appeared suddenly from his station behind the stairs.

"Quién es?"

Through the flashes of searing light that had rendered him temporarily blind, Nolan could see movement below; then a loud gasp and a man's rough voice.

"Suelte el arma! Arriba las manos!"

The guard was holding a 9mm MAC-10, pointed straight at him.

He started to lower his rifle, desperately trying to recover his vision. Yet as long as the light was on, he was blinded, and he couldn't remove the goggles one-handed without dropping the rifle. His mind raced over the possibilities, and he realized he needed to remove the goggles before he could do anything. He put the rifle on the concrete floor and started to straighten, too late. Through his ruined vision, he saw a flash of movement and realized the guard was trigger happy, probably high on coke. He threw himself to one side, just as a half dozen shots blazed out of the gun barrel. He grabbed for his Sig Sauer, grunting as his shoulder crashed into the concrete with no second arm to stop the shock of impact. But he was too slow, too blind. He gathered himself to jump at the guard in the hopes of knocking him down physically, but from behind him there was the crash of a shot, and then another. He whirled around, and dimly made out the figure of Carol, holding her Glock 9mm. His sight became more focused, and he made out her face, white and stricken, as the echoes of the shots reverberated around the house.

"I'm sorry, I didn't think I had any choice. He was about to kill you."

"That's okay, you were probably right. You saved my life, but we need to get moving. I doubt we have more than a few seconds before they come down here to find out what's going on."

They ran down the last few steps of the basement and along a whitewashed corridor. A heavy door was bolted shut, top and bottom. He turned to Carol.

"Cover that stairway in case anyone comes down. Don't worry about shooting them. It's too late for that now."

She nodded. He slid open the bolts and found himself staring at John and Violet Robson. They goggled at him.

"Kyle! You came!"

He stared at them. Violet Robson had bruises on her bare arms and a black eye where someone had punched her.

Punched an old woman!

John Robson was in a worse state. One eye was shut completely, and one of his pants legs was covered in blood. His right arm hung down at an awkward angle.

Bastards!

They'd had some fun with these old people. They knew nothing to help their captors and could offer no resistance or try to escape. It was unadulterated sadism. He averted his eyes from their injuries. The time to dwell on them was later.

"Yeah, I did, and Carol's in the passage. We need to move fast, are you able to walk?"

He looked at John's leg.

"They roughed us up some, but yeah, if it means getting out of this shithole, I could walk all the way to Canada," John said.

"Right, let's get going before the shit really hits the fan."

John started forward but collapsed to the ground with a cry of pain. Kyle went to help him up, but Violet waved him off.

"You need to use that gun, young man, and with only one good arm, you can't spare one for John. You go ahead, and I'll help him. I'm quite capable, you know."

He smiled at her slightly ascerbic tone, but she was right. He watched her struggle to get John back to his feet, and then draped one of her husband's arms over her shoulder. She glared at him.

"We're fine, go on!"

They made their way up the stairs and out into the hallway. Nolan checked that Violet was still holding out with John, and led them through the dining room and into the door to the huge kitchen. And found himself staring face-to-face at a group of armed men coming through the kitchen towards him. They gaped but quickly recovered, swinging up their gun barrels. Bullets ratcheted into breeches ready to fire, and fingers tightened on triggers. There was no course of action he could take, save one. Any resistance he offered would get the hostages shot. He threw down his Sig Sauer and put up his good hand.

"Both of them, Gringo."

"It's broken, you stupid fuck! Can't you see it?"

The man came down to him and swung his rifle. Nolan felt a crushing pain to the side of his head. He collapsed to the floor, but it was enough to cover his movements as he tucked his combat knife underneath a wooden preparation table. He watched as the man stood over him, wondering if another blow was about to land on his head. But at the last moment, a voice shouted, "Stop!"

He looked up and felt an enormous relief wash over him. Behind Carol, a man stood holding an assault rifle. A black man, with a face he knew well. He'd obviously freed himself and appeared like a magic genie out of a bottle. Nolan stared at him.

"Roscoe!"

"Yeah, Chief Nolan. I wondered how long it'd take for you to get here. How you doin', Chief? And who's this with you? The cop?"

He realized that Carol no longer had her pistol. She had dropped it when they bumped into the Colombians. They'd have made it clear there was no alternative. He looked at the armed men. They'd lowered their rifles when Roscoe appeared.

"Yes, from San Diego. This is great, Roscoe. But we need to get out of here before the rest of them turn up. The Platoon will be here soon to finish off this place, so it'd be better if we were somewhere else."

"Is that so? What time are they set to arrive?"

And then he understood it all. The Colombians were relaxed, smiling, and holding their weapons loosely.

"You're with them."

Roscoe rolled his eyed upwards. "Well done, Chief, you got it right in one. It's a great gig, and more money than a man could spend in a lifetime. They're good people."

"You won't need much money, Bremmer. Your lifetime is going to be a lot shorter than you ever imagined," Nolan snarled.

"Is that so? What time does the action start, Chief?"

"Fuck you, Bremmer. The first you'll know is when they stick a gun barrel up your ass and blow your stupid brains out."

"Yeah?" He looked at Carol and nodded to one of his men. "The girl, put a bullet in her knees. One each side."

"0300, Bremmer."

Roscoe smiled. "That wasn't too difficult, now was it? Carlo, go and find Mr. Rivera, and tell him we're expecting company at 0300."

"Si, Senor."

The man ran off. Roscoe issued rapid orders in Spanish, and the Colombians gestured to Nolan to get up. He climbed to his feet. They gripped his one good arm and led him back to the basement.

"Just a moment," Roscoe shouted. "Search him, we don't know what he's carrying."

They stopped him and patted him down, found the grenades in his pockets, and Roscoe whistled appreciatively. "Wow, you could have done some damage with those." He glared at his men. "Make sure there's nothing else, then take them downstairs. When they're locked away, join me in the control room. We need to prepare for the arrival of his friends."

"Bremmer, you fucker, you can't do this to your own people," Nolan shouted desperately. "Don't you know the meaning of loyalty?"

"Sure, I know what it means," Roscoe grinned. Then

his grin faded to an angry glare. "It means poverty in a white man's world. It means being the token nigger wherever you go, and that includes your precious Seals. This organization has made me rich, man. It's given me promotion and everything I could want."

"Surely you know this place is know to the authorities? It's over, Bremmer. You're finished."

The black man smiled. "Over? You don't get it, do you? This business brings in billions. Sure, they'll take down this place, but do you think we haven't got others prepared?"

"So why don't you leave now? Why take the chance of tangling with the authorities?"

Roscoe shrugged. "That's the boss, the new boss, Manuel Rivera. He got pretty pissed over that business down in Colombia, so I guess he wants revenge. It means a lot to these people. Me, I couldn't give a flying fuck for any of it, but if he wants payback, then he get's it. Then we'll move our business to a new location, and we're back in business - us, and about fifty billion dollars. Maybe we'll buy ourselves a whole state."

He laughed. "Take 'em away, I've got work to do. I'll be seeing you, Chief."

"In hell, Roscoe."

He laughed. "Yeah, probably."

CHAPTER FIFTEEN

They were locked back in the room with John and Violet Robson. All of them were tied with thin rope, and even Nolan's useless arm had been tied tightly behind his back. They'd left a guard outside the room. Just before he'd slammed the door shut, he'd grinned at them and looked pointedly at his MAC-10 9 mm. The meaning was clear, come through that door and he'd be more than pleased to use it on them. Inside the room, Nolan was worried about John Robson. His face was chalky white, and his breathing came in short, uneven pants. Nolan was no medic, but he guessed the poor guy was on the verge of a heart attack. His wounds, and the trauma he'd suffered, had been too much for him. His face was perspiring with the obvious pain he was in. Time was not on their side.

If we don't get help soon, he'll likely die.

Violet had arrived at the same conclusion. "How are we going to get out of this?" she asked him. "We need to help John. He needs medical help urgently."

Her eyes met his with the unspoken message. 'My

husband is dying. You must help him.'

"We have to get ourselves out of here, somehow. We'll find a way," Nolan reassured her. But his arm was on fire, and he felt his vision going dizzy with the extreme agony.

They'd dragged his broken arm behind his back and tied the two wrists together.

Christ, not a blackout, not now!

Then he shook his head hard, to clear it.

Fuck the arm! I'm getting them out of this!

"But, we don't even possess any weapons, and we're tied up," Violet pointed out. "Perhaps there is no way out of this."

She murmured a few words to her husband as he groaned and doubled over. Nolan and Carol exchanged glances. He didn't have long.

"There's a way, Violet, so just keep him going a little longer. Carol, can you reach my broken arm, the sling around the cast?"

"I'm not sure, why?"

"Because I tucked my combat knife in there when Bremmer's goons jumped me."

Awkwardly, she maneuvered behind him. "I can feel the hilt of the knife, but I'm not sure if I can reach it."

Nolan remembered when he'd been held with Gracia. He felt a pang at the loss, the feeling of déjà vu.

I'm sick of these Colombian bastards constantly attacking the people I love, not to mention the attacks on me, and the guys in the Platoon. This time is the last time, no matter what. There's only one rule. End it!

"Let me try, dear. My hands are smaller, and I'm used to delicate things. I do a lot of knitting and sewing."

She made way for Violet Robson, who wriggled her

hands and managed to extract the knife.

"I've got it. What do I do with it?"

"I think cutting through the ropes that are holding us would be a good start," he replied.

"There's no need for sarcasm," she retorted. They all smiled, and she contorted her body into a position where she could cut through Carol's ties. The San Diego detective gratefully took the knife from her and sawed through Nolan's bonds. Within minutes, they were all free. He was about to try and get the guard to open the door on some pretext when a voice sounded in his earpiece.

"Bravo Two this is One, what is your status?"

They'd left his commo system on him. It was so tiny that they'd missed it when they searched him, the earpiece in his ear, and an almost invisible wire that led down to a collar mic. The Seals were coming in! He hit the transmit button.

"Bravo One, this is Nolan. Come in."

A pause, and then, "Chief Nolan? What the hell are you doing on this net?"

It was a voice he knew well. Talley.

"It's a long story, Boss. But I came to the compound to bring out the Robsons and Roscoe Bremmer before the attack hit. I didn't want them killed. We're being held prisoner in the basement of the main residence inside the compound. I found the Robsons, but they're badly injured, and they need medical attention right away. There's something else you need to know about. Roscoe threw in with the Colombians."

"You're kidding me!"

"No, it's true. He's second in command to Manuel Rivera. Right now, they're preparing for your attack, except that I told them you were coming in at 0300."

"Copy that. Can you extract yourselves from that basement?"

"I think so, yeah. We're working on it."

"Understood. We're here in strength. Jacks sent in Alpha and Charlie Platoons, and he wants these bastards terminated. When we leave this place, there's to be nothing other than rubble and dead bodies."

"It's about time. These people have played around with us for too long. I have a Raven circling the compound, you can lock into its downlink, and you'll have some good overhead recon."

He gave Talley the link to connect to the Raven.

"Yeah, thanks, Chief. I won't ask where it came from. We have a Spooky overhead, so they'll be keeping us up to date with the situation on the ground."

"I take it the assault begins as planned?"

"Yeah, no change. Vince dropped in a half hour ago and is positioned outside the compound. He climbed to the top of a tree, and he's looking down inside right now. I was just calling him. He's designated Bravo Two. I'll designate you Bravo Five, being as you've inserted yourself into the mission, and I'll let Alpha and Charlie Platoons know you're around. I'd suggest you keep your heads down until we've rolled over these people."

"Copy that, Boss."

Nolan explained to them what was going down.

"So we're to wait here? That sounds pretty risky if they decide to come and finish us off. What about the guard outside?" Carol asked. Her face was wreathed with concern.

"I don't intend to wait. It's time to get out of here and

join the fun." He banged hard on the door. "Guard, Senor, she's ill, she's dying, help us! Ayuda, esta emergencia, urgente. Ahora!"

He looked at the Carol and the Robsons. "We need to get back into position as if we're still tied. Violet, show us what you're made of. Pretend you're dying."

"I feel as if I am," she muttered. But she proceeded to put on a performance worthy of a Broadway show. She moaned and shouted in pretended pain, and they waited. After a few seconds, the bolts slid back, and the door opened cautiously. The guard peered in, and satisfied they were still secure, entered the room and walked over to the writhing body of Violet Robson.

"Lo que está mal?"

He lifted up her head to look at her face but recoiled as she drooled spittle on his shirt."

"Dios mío!"

He stepped back and went rigid, as Nolan's huge combat knife was pressed against his neck. Nolan waited while Carol rushed forward, relieving the man of a pistol tucked into his belt. She then stood back, cocked the action, and covered him.

"Step back slowly, and put up your hands, understand? Comprendas?"

"Si, si, Senor," the man replied shakily. He moved backwards toward Nolan, who reversed the knife and hit him hard on the head; a precise, aimed blow, and the man went straight down.

"Was that really necessary?" Violet asked him in a frosty voice. "He'd already surrendered to us."

"Only if we didn't want him getting free and attacking us from behind," Nolan said grimly. "Let's get moving. We

275

need to get to a secure position where they won't find us, and where we may be able to do some damage."

They struggled up the wooden staircase. Carol and Nolan helped Violet drag John up the stairs, each step causing him to groan in pain.

These fuckers are going to wish they'd never been born for doing this to an old man, Nolan vowed.

They pressed on upwards, higher and higher until they reached the third floor of the vast house. There, Nolan found a room with a single door and a window that looked down over the open compound. Carol locked the door behind them so that they wouldn't be surprised from behind. When they were secure, Nolan called in to notify Talley of the changed situation.

"That's good news, Chief. We'll look out for you, but keep your heads down. Vince has identified the armory. It's a small blockhouse with an iron door, about fifty yards in front of the house, slightly north. The Spooky is going to take it out in a few minutes, so I guess that should cramp their style a little. Then we're coming in."

"Copy that, good luck."

"Yeah, you too. See you soon."

He looked out of the window and noted the blockhouse. As Talley had said, it had an iron door. As he watched, a man walked up to it, unlocked it and went inside; presumably fetching supplies for the defenders. He turned to Carol and the Robsons.

"You need to keep your heads down, real low. Make sure you're well away from the windows."

"What's happening, Kyle?" John asked him.

"These people are about to get a taste of warfare, and it's likely to stick in their throats."

276

Just then he heard the machine-like buzzing noise of rounds pouring out of an electric Gatling gun.

"Hit the deck now, down, down, press your heads to the floor!"

He dived to the floor close to the window and raised his head just high enough to look out. It was as if nature's fury had unleashed a hurricane on the building. The heavy rounds smashed through concrete and steel, and the circling AC-130 held the point of aim long enough for the building to be reduced to a smoking ruin. Ammunition stores inside added to the destruction, as bursting rounds, shells, grenades and rockets exploded, causing the building to literally split apart.

"Carol, watch the door. Now they know I fooled them over the time of the attack, they'll be like a bunch of angry hornets."

"Don't worry, I've got it."

The storm outside ended as abruptly as it had begun, and then he saw Manuel Rivera for the first time. He ran out of the house with Roscoe Bremmer to the armory to check the damage. It only took them seconds, and he turned to Roscoe and shouted at him. It was impossible to hear what was said, but the meaning was obvious. Roscoe had told them to prepare for an attack at 0300, and it had started an hour early. The two men ran back into the house, and as they did, Nolan heard the sound of helos coming in. A swarm of MH-6 Little Birds swooped in over the wooden walls, and soldiers in dark camo began abseiling down as they hovered fifty or so feet above the earth. A man ran out with an assault rifle pointed up at the attackers, but he was cut down as Vince Merano went about his deadly business. The commo net was alive with chatter as the Seals mounted their attack.

"Bravo One, this is Charlie One, we've secured the rear of the storage building. We're setting charges now."

"Bravo One, this is Alpha Two, we've arrive at the main communications building. Four of our guys have the track covered, so they won't be going anywhere."

"Copy that, Alpha Two. Alpha One, what is your twenty?"

"Right outside the main gate, Bravo One. Charges set, ready to go on your order. It looks like it's hotting up in there."

"That it is, Alpha One. Go now, I say again, go now."

Immediately, there was a huge explosion as the main gates blew in, and even as smoke and debris lingered in the air, dark figures flitted through the night, surging into the compound and spreading out to search the buildings. Nolan saw John Robson watching, close to him.

"They're finished, Kyle. There's no way they can defend against this kind of power. I'd no idea this is what you did." His breathing was labored, but his color had improved.

"Yeah, it sure looks impressive, but they'll have a few tricks up their sleeves. What worries me is, how they plan to get out?"

"The Colombians?"

"The leaders, Manuel Rivera, Roscoe Bremmer, and maybe a couple of others. They never fight to the end. With these people, it's about profit, not ideology. They'll have a bolthole somewhere."

"But, they're all in the house. There's no way they'd get out. The place is surrounded by troops. They'd need, well, a helicopter to escape this place. And there's nowhere they could have a helicopter hidden away ready to take off.

They'd need a flat open area, and they're all under fire." He stopped, looking thoughtful, and upward. "Except for the roof, of course."

Nolan automatically looked up. "The roof, yeah, of course. If they had a way out, that'd be it. He keyed the mic.

"This is Bravo Five, for all units. It's possible they may attempt a helo evac from the roof. Could someone focus the overhead cameras there and keep an eye on it?"

"Bravo Five, this is Hammer One, we're running a slow circle overhead. We'll keep an eye on that roof for you."

"Copy that, Hammer One." He smiled to himself. The voice sounded like the same guy who'd helped them out over Colombia. He recalled the storm of gunfire that had reduced the armory to rubble, severely weakening Rivera's soldiers to resist the Seal onslaught. Whatever, they'd wreaked the same kind of devastation. He kept watch out of the window. The compound was alive with gun flashes as Seals ran around, gunning down the opposition. There was no mercy, and more than once a Colombian tried to throw up their hands and surrender, but they were shot down. Clearly, the orders from above were being obeyed to the letter. These men had defied the United States government, and even directly attacked the organization of the Navy Seals. They'd abandoned all rights, and torn up the rulebook. Now they were suffering the consequences. John and Violet looked on, horrified. They'd crawled over to the window and were watching the devastation below.

"It's a massacre," Violet uttered, in horrified tones.

"At least they won't be coming after us or the kids any more, after this little lot," John replied.

And then they heard footsteps outside on the landing.

The doorknob rattled, and there was a crash as a heavy body tried to shoulder the door open.

"Nolan, you in there?"

It was Roscoe Bremmer. Nolan gestured for them to keep silent.

After a pause, Roscoe shouted again. "It looks like your people have won this round. Nice move, deceiving us on the timing. But next time, we won't make any mistakes. You're dead, Nolan. You, your family, and everyone close to you. You'll be looking over your shoulder from now until doomsday. Maybe we will meet in hell, but you'll be there before us, I promise you."

"Don't think this is the end, Senor Nolan. You have caused me too much trouble, and this is the last time. As your friend Roscoe has said, you're going to hell, you and all of your people. Adios, Senor. And watch your back."

The footsteps retreated from outside the door, and they heard them on the staircase. Going up.

"We need to get after them. They're going to the roof. They must have a helo up there."

"But surely the gunship will take care of them," Carol murmured.

"Maybe, but they'll have some scheme to get away, so I wouldn't count on it. I'm going after them. Open the door!"

She flung open the door and stood aside as he went past her.

"I'm coming with you," she shouted as she ran after him.

"I don't need you. Look after the Robsons."

"You're wrong. You do need me."

"What for?"

"Because I have the pistol, and the use of both of my arms. Don't argue. I'm coming."

He grunted an acknowledgement and ran on to the stairway. There was a narrower set of stairs that led up to the roof. He started up and reached a door that unmistakably led out onto the roof. He opened it a fraction and stood back as a burst of fire from an assault rifle chipped fragments of woodwork next to his head.

"Shit, I should have expected that. They've mounted a rearguard to stop anyone coming after them."

He heard Carol calling him from an open doorway close to the roof door. "Kyle, this is some kind of an attic. There's a small window that overlooks the roof."

He ran in and was able to see the wide expanse of flat roof. A Colombian stood facing the roof door to make sure anyone who came through it would meet with a hail of gunfire. Further away, there was a heap of canvas on the roof. Four men were wrestling to throw off the canvas. As he watched, they succeeded. It was a Bell 429 passenger helicopter, the twin-engine model fitted with Pratt & Whitney Canada PW207D1 turboshafts. It was light, fast, and perfect for escape and evasion. Except when there was an AC-130 prowling overhead.

How the hell do they expect to get away without being shot full of holes by the Spooky's Gatling gun?

Then everything seemed to happen at once.

"Bravo One, this is Hammer One, we have movement on the roof. Looks like a helo they're planning to escape on. We'll take care of it for you."

"Copy that, Hammer One."

On the other side of the roof, Nolan could see a further group of four Colombians. They were uncovering another canvas-shrouded object.

Another helicopter, is that their plan?

And then it came into view, and the plan was laid bare before him. A large, steel object, shaped like a huge box was elevating upwards. Nolan recognized it instantly, a Gecko SA-8 twin surface to air missile system. It was the naval variant, mounted on a rotating launcher. The Gecko was a high-powered, short-range twin missile system. But the Spooky was only two thousand feet above the roof, much too low to defend itself from a missile launch. They'd be hit within seconds of the missile leaving its launch tube. He keyed his mic.

"Hammer One, missile launch. Get out of there fast!"

"Copy that, whoever you are."

But as Nolan watched, the first missile sped out of the tube, followed by another. Simultaneously, the rotor blades of the Bell 429 started to turn, and four men who'd been hiding out of sight ran out and climbed aboard; Rivera, Bremmer and two others. He held out his hand.

"Give me the gun, now!"

Carol gave him the pistol.

"Is it cocked?"

"Yeah, just pull the trigger."

He smashed the window by tapping it with the butt. The guard watching the door was alerted by the sound of breaking glass. Nolan fired once; a safe shot to the stomach, and watched him crumple to the base of the roof. He handed the gun back to Carol.

"Cover me, I'm going out to finish them."

"Kyle!"

He turned and looked at her.

"Don't die. Please, be careful."

He nodded and ran off, threw open the door, and rushed out onto the roof. The guard was groaning in agony, dying from the pistol shot to his abdomen, and his rifle lay on the ground nearby. Roscoe Bremmer had seen the man go down and was running to head off Nolan. They reached the weapon at the same time, but Roscoe was uninjured. While Nolan reached for the M-16, he shouldered him on his wounded arm. Kyle staggered as agonizing pain scorched through his body. Roscoe picked up the M-16 and stood facing him. He raised the barrel and smiled.

"You always were the fucking boy scout, Chief. You could have thrown in with us and had a good life. Get your hands over your head, and don't try anything funny."

"Living in the sewers isn't a good life, Bremmer. You're scum, just like your drug dealing friends."

Nolan put his hands over his head while he worked out the angles. The black man had positioned himself so that he was out of the line of fire from Carol's pistol. And then he remembered, as he felt something stiff and hard inside his collar.

Roscoe drew his lips back in a snarl. "Fuck you, asshole."

"No, fuck you, asshole!"

He snatched out the blade and using every ounce of his strength, threw it directly at Roscoe's face. The thin steel penetrated the edge of his right eye and the precision surgical steel went all the way through soft tissue to embed into the brain. The black man fell slowly to the ground, lifeless. But the sound of the Bell's turboshaft engines was loud on the roof as the pilot brought the throttles to take off power.

As he looked up, Rivera appeared in the open door. He smiled at Nolan and pointed an assault rifle at him.

Nolan rolled desperately to one side, and a trio of bullets chipped up the concrete where he'd been standing. But Rivera was bringing the rifle around to bear on him. He knew he couldn't avoid a burst of automatic fire, and his mind froze. He was a dead man. It was the end of the line. Rivera's eyes squinted, and he took on a serious expression as he raised the rifle to his shoulder to make certain of his aim. When he was satisfied, Nolan even saw his trigger finger move slightly as he took up first pressure. His smile broadened, but only for a fraction of a second. He seemed to freeze. His eyes flew open wide, and the smile was replaced with a look of astonishment. Then he slowly toppled forward, out of the cabin, and onto the concrete roof.

"Bravo Five, you need to keep that fool head of yours down. Next time, Chief, I may not be around to watch your back."

He felt the cold wash of relief rush over him. Vince Merano, covering the assault from a high position in a tree overlooking the compound, had seen it all happen.

"Thanks, Vince. I owe you one."

"And then some, buddy. What about the helo?"

"Can you see the pilot?"

"Is the Pope a Catholic?"

"Kill him."

The pilot's body bucked as Vince's double tap took him. There was no armor on the Bell 429, and the heavy, high velocity rounds penetrated the thin body and Perspex, taking the pilot in the chest and head. The machine tilted over, and the rotor blades screeched as they touched concrete, showering sparks over the roof. The massive kinetic power of the twin turboshafts kept the helo moving, causing it to turn like a children's toy, closer and closer to the edge of the roof. Finally, with a rending crash of tortured metal it went over. As it hit the ground, the tanks exploded when the sparks ignited the spilled high-octane fuel. The Bell disappeared in a roaring storm of smoke and flames. But it wasn't over.

"You motherfuckers! Think you can stitch us up with a couple of cheap commie missiles. We'll fry your asses!"

The shout came through his earpiece, and he looked up at the familiar voice of Hammer One. The Spooky had avoided the 'cheap commie missiles' and was returning to finish the job. The Gecko SA-8 was a radar-controlled launcher, and the operator had taken his eyes off the screen to watch the fight on the rooftop. The AC-130 had taken the opportunity when the threat receiver reported they were no longer a target and swooped in for the kill. For the aircrew, it was payback for a very nasty moment. The Gatling gun threatened to overheat as it poured enough metal into the missile position to destroy it utterly. When the gun barrel stopped turning, all that was left of the pride of Soviet technology was a pile of twisted broken parts, intermingled with the blood, bone and tissue of the operators.

Nolan sensed movement behind him and whirled. It was Carol.

"Is it over?"

He nodded. "Yeah, I guess it is. That's all of them."

"Until the next drug gang takes over the Salazar empire."

"There's always that. But they'll go down the same way."

"A lot of good people suffered badly, Kyle. They didn't go down easily."

"No. But we can't choose the way they behave. We can

only fight them when they threaten our way of life."

She smiled. "Is that Chief Nolan's philosophy?"

"It's the Seals' philosophy. When they threaten the security of the United States, they come up against us."

She pulled a face. "It's macho bullshit, Kyle. But I'll tell you this. I'm damned glad your outfit is there. Damned glad. Enough of that, can we go home now?"

He looked around at the smoking remains of the missile launcher, at the flames that leapt up from the burning helo, and at the corpses that lay on the roof, Rivera, Bremmer, and their Colombian henchmen. All dead. All gone.

"Yeah, I reckon we can. We're done here."

"So we can relax, the kids are safe?"

She's right. 'We' is right. We're a team, Carol and me. How could I ever have been so stupid? I could never have done any of it without her.

He nodded. "We can relax. It's time to put all this behind us."

"Us?"

She was waiting for him to say it, clearly and without equivocation. He grinned at her.

"Yeah, that's right, 'Us'. You, me, the kids. We're all going home."

CPSIA information can be obtained at www.ICGtesting.com
Printed in the USA
LVOW05s1421110813

347298LV00005B/779/P